SHATTERED

By

Sallie Baisley

NOTEBOOK|PUBLISHING

First published in the UK in 2014 by Notebook Publishing,
145–157 St John Street, London, EC1V 4PW.

www.notebookpublishing.co.uk

ISBN: 9780956553980

A CIP catalogue record for this book is available
from the British Library.

Typeset by Notebook Publishing.
Printed and bound in Great Britain.

PROLOGUE

Medway News: Saturday 19 May 2007. Chatham boy flees as police raid his house searching for links to Al-Qaida.

In the early hours of this morning several houses were raided including one on the White Road Estate in Chatham. Many residents in the surrounding area have been evacuated.

Police are saying very little at the moment, other than the evacuation is a precautionary measure, and they would like to question Ryan Arnold, who is more commonly known as Karim Malik.

The police have confirmed that there is a warrant out for his arrest and this is linked to the Terrorism Act.

White Road Estate, Chatham.

The police activity had naturally caused a lot of interest in White Road that morning, and Sharon knew she was in for a busy day. Sharon was the land lady for the local pub, more commonly known as The Bell Inn, which was situated just five houses down from the one that was receiving so much interest this morning. Fortunately the police had not cleared her out of the pub as they had done all the rest of the houses nearby – probably because they were planning on using the Bell for their lunch breaks and evening drinks before heading home. This suited Sharon just fine; the more business the better and she knew a drama or crisis always brought business to her doorstep.

The Bell Inn had been around for as long as the road itself. Nearly every resident of the White Road Estate had been in and indulged in the delights of the establishment at some time or another.

Dwayne Arnold, the father of the boy who the police were now frantically searching for, was one of Sharon's most regular customers. He couldn't be quite called a friend, but they got on. She sold him beer and cigarettes and ignored his obnoxious manner and flirtatious behaviour, and he enjoyed the fact that he didn't have to stagger too far to get home – not that he had been living at home for the past few months. His 'bit on the side' had decided to take him in after Betty – Dwayne's softly spoken angel of a woman – had finally seen sense and kicked him out.

Sharon had been in the business a long time and so was used to clients like Dwayne – big-mouthed, drunken twats who took great delight in 'dissing' their wives at every opportunity, but quick to put on the charm when a pretty bit of skirt walked in. These type of men sickened Sharon. She'd been a victim to someone of the same ilk and was now a single mum with four boys, so she knew the score and kept well away. But they did bring in regular money that kept her four kids at the smart independent school down the road, so she just kept her head down, mouth shut and got on with running a pub in probably the toughest area in Medway.

Sharon had just unlocked the door and was heading back to the bar when she heard the loud booming voice she had been expecting.

"Double Scotch followed by Tequila now," Dwayne demanded as he stormed into the bar. His face was bright red and Sharon could see the veins pulsating in his neck.

Now Sharon had seen Dwayne angry on more than one occasion, but never like this. His whole body seemed to be emitting an electric current that was so strong Sharon was afraid to go to near to him. He looked like he was about to explode; even his body odour reeked of anger.

Sharon slid the two glasses expertly over to his side of the bar. He grabbed them with his big hairy hands and downed each glass without even taking a breath. He then dragged his large right hand across his mouth in a wiping motion and demanded the same again. A cigarette was already in his left hand and his right hand was reaching for the lighter. Sharon was not about to remind him that smoking was prohibited in the bar, she was not going to get in this man's way —well man was too polite a word; rabid dog was a better description of Dwayne today.

Dwayne's only son was wanted by the police. Under normal circumstances this would actually be quite a "chuck up" for a father born and brought up on the White Road Estate and add to Dwayne's street "cred". It would show the rest of the borough that his boy was a

Chatham boy and ready to join the adult crew of drug dealing, motor theft, handling stolen goods, you name it; pretty much anything illegal was acceptable in the White Road Estate other than terrorism, and that was what Dwayne's boy was wanted for – the news was saying he had links to Al-Qaida.

White Road residents would not take quietly to a traitor living amongst them – a traitor whose kin and blood many of them drank with every night in the good old Bell Inn.

Oh yes, Dwayne's reputation was at stake. Sharon was well aware that Ryan – Dwayne's son – had not been in the area for some time, and that Dwayne was actually shacked up with his latest bird, and so wasn't actually completely in the know when it came to his son. But that wasn't going to make a blind bit of difference today. People were going to want answers, and they knew better than to expect the old Bill to provide the details they demanded. But Dwayne was one of them, and if he wanted to retain any 'street cred' whatsoever then he was going to have to talk, and talk he would, Sharon was certain about that.

Sure enough, the pub door was opening just as Dwayne finished his second shot of whiskey and so for the next eight hours Sharon worked her butt off as Dwayne gobbed his mouth off and drank and drank and drank.

And drunk he was - that is rather an understatement for he was royally slaughtered, but to give him his due he did manage to retain some form of credibility. This was mainly due to the fact that his natural racist nature had always been evident, and over the years his dislike for immigrants and those of a darker complexion had got steadily worse.

His distaste for his son was another thing that he had made clear many years ago. And God only, knew what would happen if Dwayne ever did manage to get his hands on that boy. Dwayne expressed his distaste for his son to his fellow drinkers; as far as he was concerned Ryan was dead in his eyes, and should he ever set eyes upon the boy again, he would take great delight in killing the boy in a slow and painful manner. In fact even the meanest of men in the Bell pub that night began to cringe when Dwayne described in graphic detail about how he would enjoy wrapping his arms around his son's throat and watching the life drain from his eyes as he squeezed the air out of his pathetic excuse for a body.

Once again Sharon just kept her head down and ensured that everyone got a refill as soon as they were nearing the end of their drinks. But as busy as she was she did let her mind wander to poor Betty – Dwayne's wife. Where was she today? She too had surely been kicked out of her house while the police searched it. How was she coping with the fact that not only was her only son wanted, but on terrorist charges?

With four boys herself Sharon couldn't even begin to comprehend how she would feel in such a situation. Yes she knew that Ryan had always been different, but he was still someone's little boy, and that someone was probably out there alone with no support whatsoever.

Betty was alone, and as for support she turned to the person she has always turned to in a time of crisis – God.

The police had come crashing through her door at six o'clock that morning. The sun hadn't even begun to rise and Betty was still curled up in bed fast asleep, dreaming pleasant dreams. What Betty wasn't to know was that would be her last decent night's sleep for many months to come, and her pleasant dreams were now a thing of the past. After today, sleep, when it came, would be fitful and haunted of images of her son and the path he had chosen. Never before had Betty dreamt of death, but after today all her dreams would be invaded by images of dead children, disfigured women and young men being dragged off to fight for something they didn't really understand. At the heart of all these dreams was her son – the cause of all this harm.

The loud bang on the door rapidly pulled Betty out of her slumber and she was instantly filled with fear, but the police were the last thing she had expected to see. She automatically presumed that Dwayne's latest 'bit on the side' had kicked him out and so he was returning home to vent his anger on her. This happened from time to time, and Betty had learnt to endure the beatings, and his unpredictable mood swings, however it still filled her with dread knowing that he was back in their home. At least Ryan no longer had to suffer at Dwayne's hands any longer, she was grateful for that much. Ryan had moved out eight months ago and although she missed his company she was glad that he was getting away from all the pain and sorrow that had been their lives for so long

– Dwayne being the main catalyst for all the heartache, bruising and unhappy memories.

But it wasn't Dwayne who came crashing through the door; it was the police demanding to search the house. They told her very little, but did ask her plenty of questions – all relating to the whereabouts of her son, who yes, had returned to the area in the last few days, but left last night. Betty tried to explain to the officers that he didn't tell her where he was going and she didn't expect to see him again for a while. She tried to make them realise that this was something Ryan had been doing for a while now; he would just up and leave one day without so much as a goodbye. Betty put it down to his disappointment in her and her failure to take charge of her life. She didn't for one minute believe that he was involved in anything illegal – not her Ryan. And why were they referring to him as Karim, and talking about links to Al-Qaida? Betty was certain that they had the wrong house.

At one point she wondered if this was something that Dwayne had set up just to upset her. She knew how it was done – she had lived in the White Road Estate long enough now to know that false information leaked to the police could result in a raid. However normally it was for drugs or stolen goods.

So Betty was under the illusion that Dwayne was behind the raid. Why the police were talking about terrorism she just couldn't understand.

And so on this occasion it was Betty's house that was raided. The police were polite as ever, but the bottom line was that she would need to find some other accommodation for the next few nights as they expected to be at the house for a while. WPC Martin did most of the talking; she clearly had been given the task of looking after the house's occupant. Betty was not a very worldly woman, but she could see straight away that this young WPC was not too keen on babysitting a middle-aged housewife and felt that her skills would have been better utilised if she had been given the opportunity to search the house. It was plain as day to Betty that this WPC Martin was sick of being given the boring jobs just because she was a woman.

On a different day Betty might have found it in her heart to explain to this youthful young lady that being a police officer or not, she was a woman, and men would always see that before noticing her uniform, so best she just crack on and get used to it – it was what Betty referred to as life, the life of a woman!

But on this particular day Betty did not have the energy or desire to assist this woman in the realisation that no matter what she did she would never be treated equal to a man. So Betty simply sat in the kitchen clutching her cup of tea which she hadn't even been allowed to make – poor WPC Martin had been given that chore as well. And after a few hours, when it became clear that the police would need to progress the search further than the cupboards, WPC Martin asked her where she would like to go. WPC Martin also made it quite clear to Betty that she was expected to provide the police with a statement. And as WPC Martin explained in no uncertain terms should Ryan make contact with Betty, it would most definitely be in Betty's best interests to inform the police straight away!

Betty was allowed the dignity of being able to throw a few essentials together, and then was escorted out of her own home. What was she to do now? Betty asked them to drop her off at the only place where she felt she would feel wanted and cared for – her local church. She was certain that the vicar would be able to find her a peaceful place to stay.

There was only one other place that she would have considered staying at and that was next door with the Khan family. However under the circumstances, with so much talk about Al-Qaida, terrorism and Ryan being referred to by a clearly Muslim name, Betty didn't quite think it would be appropriate to ask the only person who had been a true friend to Betty over the past seven years to take her in. And as Betty walked out of her front door she realised too that Nassir and her family had also been removed from their home – whether this was in order to search the property, or simply for a precautionary measure Betty did not know. Betty was also intelligent enough to know, that the comments she had overheard from the police would mean that Nassir and her family would not be welcome in the White Road Estate for the foreseeable future. What this had to do with Ryan and his close relationship with Nassir and her family Betty just didn't know, but she did have a bad feeling about it all. And it was for this reason she kept her head down low and her eyes downcast as she was ushered out of her home and into the police car. Unfortunately the flash of the camera caught her unaware, and as she lifted her head towards the flash another camera snapped away. Only then did Betty realise that this raid had alerted the media as well. Her face and home would now be plastered all over every newspaper in England within the next twenty-four hours. What in heaven's name was going on?

Betty had assumed correctly. Nassir had also received an early morning wake up call, however it was not from the police. She had gone to bed as usual shortly after the ten o'clock news on Friday 18 May 2007 and left Abdul (Nassir's husband) downstairs in the dining room. The room was more like a library and Abdul was as usual casting his eyes over literature. These days Nassir didn't even bother to disturb Abdul when he was caught up in the world of his books. This was one of the things that Nassir loved about Abdul – his unbelievable ability to shut off the rest of the world and become absorbed in whatever book or books managed to capture his imagination. And although these days Abdul spend hours on end in their dining room come library, Nassir could still see the love in Abdul's eyes as he raised them over his glasses and above his books to glance over at Nassir, either to respond to her latest question or simply to register her laughter whilst she was caught up in whatever TV show she chose to indulge in.

On reaching the top of the stairs, Nassir gently knocked on the door to her left, and then walked into Fareem's bedroom. Fareem was Nassir and Abdul's only child, and Nassir thanked Allah every day for the joy Fareem had provided her over the years.

He would be eighteen next month. Where the years had gone to she just didn't know. What Nassir did know was that soon Fareem would be leaving the family home to start a life of his own, but for the time being Nassir was content to have her family all under her roof. And so Nassir savoured that mother's right and lent down and kissed Fareem's forehead gently good night. Like his father Fareem raised his big round dark eyes away from the computer, glanced up at his mum, and whilst brushing his mop of thick dark hair out of his eyes he responded by saying good night.

It might have been the swish of the hair, or the look in Fareem's eyes, Nassir was not certain, but whatever it was it took her back six or seven years. In those days it was normally Fareem and Ryan that she would find glued in front of the computer. The boys were like brothers, and she had treated Ryan like her son. There was a time when the boys were inseparable, and Nassir thought it would always be that way, however in the past few months they had drifted apart. But on this particular evening she was reminded of their friendship and loyalty towards each other.

As Nassir closed Fareem's bedroom door and wandered into the bathroom to clean her teeth, she was surprised at how vivid her memory of Fareem and Ryan as young adolescents had been. Nassir hadn't seen Ryan in months, but on this particular evening something deep inside her soul had stirred and reminded her of times long gone.

However whatever it was that had brought this memory to the forefront of her mind didn't last long. Once in the bathroom she was unceremoniously drawn back into the real world with a washing basket overflowing with dirty clothes – Abdul had recently decided that he needed to work on his fitness and so had taken to running. Unfortunately for Nassir this meant more washing. And as Abdul was what you would call obsessive compulsive about everything he turned himself towards, running was no different. So Nassir now had dirty running clothes in the washing basket every evening. This mixed in with Fareem's rugby clothes made for plenty of work.

Nassir sighed deeply and began the tedious task of sorting the washing. Finally with all of her household chores completed she retreated to the sanctuary of her bedroom. As she snuggled up in bed her thoughts once again began to drift to Fareem.

Fareem was a good Muslim boy, who Nassir and Abdul both agreed had adapted to the Western way of life perfectly. He maintained his Muslim ways, but was able to easily enjoy life in the Western world. In other words he was a British Muslim. He did not have a problem with his identity as many Muslim youths of his era seemed to. Fareem, whether it be through good parenting, or simply being a sensible child was proud of being both a Muslim and British, but more than that, he was Fareem, and he would never use his religion, or ethnic origin to define his own being. And for this reason

Nassir knew that it was possible for the Muslim people to live in Britain in harmony. Fareem was living proof of this.

These were Nassir's thoughts as she drifted towards sleep. Little did she know that her sleep was going to be disrupted and a peaceful Britain full of harmony was a thought she wouldn't have for many months to come.

Nassir was woken in the early hours of the morning by the phone ringing. It took her a while to wake from her slumber, but finally fully awake she was aware of Abdul lying alongside her whispering into the phone. Late night calls such as this were not something that happened frequently and Nassir automatically presumed that her elderly mother had taken a turn for the worst.

As Abdul put the phone back in its place, Nassir turned to him expectantly, bracing herself for the worst. Not in her wildest dreams did she expect to hear the words uttered from Abdul's lips.

"It's time to move my dear. I don't have time to explain, you will just have to trust me on this one.'

'Abdul, what in Allah's name are you talking about? Is my mother alright?'

Abdul turned towards Nassir, gently put his hands onto her shoulder and looked deep into her eyes. 'Nassir, you need to listen closely to me now.'

Although his hands rested gently on Nassir, his voice and expression was far from gentle. There was a forcefulness in his tone that made Nassir's belly tighten nervously. So when Abdul asked once more for Nassir to gather her belongings and be ready to leave in twenty minutes, she knew better than to question him. As Nassir scrambled out of bed, Abdul headed towards Fareem's room.

Fareem had heard the phone, in fact he had been expecting it, and wasn't at all surprised when his father walked into the room and told him to be ready to leave in twenty minutes.

Although Fareem and Ryan hadn't been close for a while now, Fareem still saw Ryan as a brother. And so the night before when Ryan had contacted Fareem and asked to meet he had done so without question.

Ryan hadn't said much, and Fareem knew better than to ask. The truth be known Fareem didn't want to know what Ryan was involved in. He somehow knew that he wouldn't approve.

Ryan simply explained that he needed to go away for a while, that he had finally found his way in life and didn't expect to return anytime soon. Ryan's final statement was one that made Fareem realise that Ryan had inadvertently brought trouble to him and his family's door. He apologised to Fareem but assured him that his family would be looked after. Fareem was therefore not at all surprised by the early morning call.

Fareem simply nodded towards his father and did as he was told. Whilst gathering a few belongings together he happened to glance over at his computer. The screensaver was a photo of Ryan and Fareem as boys; it had been taken several years ago.

Abdul and Nassir had taken the boys camping for the weekend. It had been a great carefree few days with lots of sun and plenty of fun. In this particular photo the boys were standing on the beach holding crabs and grinning wildly. There was no chance that they would be mistaken for brothers – Fareem had pitch black hair, deep brown eyes and dark skin, while Ryan had bleached blonde hair, sky blue eyes and skin the colour of golden honey. What the photo did depict was a deep sense of friendship. It was because of this friendship that Fareem had given Ryan the hundred pounds he asked for. It was also because of this friendship that Fareem had made the decision to delete the hard drive on his computer. He didn't know what Ryan had gotten himself involved in, but he didn't have a good feeling about it.

Ryan had spent most of the previous day on Fareem's computer. He had been unusually quiet and preoccupied and clearly didn't want Fareem to see what he was researching. And then when they had met up later that night Ryan had been filled with a sense of excitement that Fareem had never seen him display. Ryan's eyes sparkled with anticipation and an electric current of pure adrenalin seemed to be pulsating through his body as he explained to Fareem that he had found his calling in life.

Even though it was a bitterly cold night in March, Ryan's body seemed to be on fire. He had only worn a short sleeved shirt, but was sweating slightly. His feet itched to be on their way and didn't stay still. Ryan's animated expressions left Fareem with no illusion that Ryan was on the verge of what he thought was a new and exciting adventure. However Fareem was not so sure of this. Fareem pulled his coat closer together and stuffed his hands further into his pockets; he could see his breath in the cold air. Ryan on the other hand didn't seem to even be aware of the environment around him.

Fareem prayed that Ryan's odd behaviour had nothing to do with the extreme group of Muslims that Ryan had been spending more and more time with recently. But deep down Fareem knew they were at the heart of Ryan's new self.

As Ryan turned away from Fareem that night and walked off towards the dark blue car in the distance, Fareem pulled his woollen hat even lower, stuck his hands deeper into his jacket, and wondered if the cold was the reason for the sudden chill that he could feel deep within his bones, or if it was the fact that he knew that his lifelong friend and companion was lost to a world that Fareem was deeply afraid of. The Ryan that he once knew and loved like a brother was as good as dead.

The young man walking away from him was a stranger who now went by the name of Karim Malik, who had chosen to join the most extremist Islamic group known to Fareem. And sadly Fareem hadn't seen it coming until it was far too late.

Fareem hoped that he would never see Ryan or Karim again. Fareem knew deep down in his heart that he shouldn't have given Ryan the money and he definitely shouldn't have deleted his computer hard drive. Fareem did not want to be put in this awkward position again. But what scared him most of all was that

Fareem loved Ryan like a brother. Their loyalty towards each other was unquestionable. And so, Fareem knew that by ending all contact with Ryan was the only way for Fareem not to be compromised again. Fareem despised the people that Karim had chosen to follow. They were not good Muslims. They were extremists who wanted nothing more than to cause pain and destruction to the Western world all in the name of Allah. They knew nothing about the true Islamic values; they distorted Islam for their own spiteful gains. But worst of all they preyed on young vulnerable Muslims like Karim. What was tearing away at Fareem's heart was that he hadn't seen it coming, and now it was too late. Ryan had always been there for Fareem, and now in Ryan's greatest time of need Fareem hadn't been there for him.

By 3:30 a.m. on Sunday 19 May 2007 the Khan family were driving down White Road towards the M20, with their few possessions thrown haphazardly into the back seat. They were leaving their home of seven years under the cover of darkness for reasons unknown to them all. As they turned left into Magpie Hall Road, they watched three police vans turn into White Road. When she saw them Nassir finally turned to the two men who meant the world to her and demanded some answers.

Abdul was the first to speak; he explained that the early morning phone call had come from Anwar – the mosque Imam or, for want of a better word, their community leader. Anwar had said very little other than that fact that the police would be crawling all over the estate within a matter of hours, and the locals would place the blame on all Muslims. Anwar stressed that he didn't know much more than that other than the fact that the Khan family would not be safe if they decided to remain in Medway. Anwar promised that he would call when he knew more.

Abdul turned sadly towards his wife and informed her that he wasn't willing to risk their safety and so had taken on-board the advice, and left their home, even though the details were minimal. Abdul then turned the attention towards Fareem and asked him to perhaps explain to his mother exactly what he knew about all of this.

Fareem had expected this. His dad came across as a softly spoken man who always had his head in the clouds, but this was not the case and Abdul was in fact an extremely shrewd and knowledgeable man. Abdul knew only too well how to keep his mouth shut and ears wide open. And that is why Abdul knew that Fareem had been in contact with Ryan/Karim and Ryan was behind the recent events. Fareem was far too sensible to plead ignorance and his respect for his parents was also too great. He also realised that in an odd sort of way he had assisted in causing his family great upset. He was also terribly afraid of the consequences of his actions, and for these reasons he didn't think twice about being completely honest with his mum and dad – well nearly honest.

And so as Abdul drove the family north, away from their home and towards a life they had said goodbye to many years ago, Fareem updated his parents on the events of the last few days. He breathed a sigh of relief as he finished. They said a problem shared was a problem halved and for the first time in days Fareem felt a sense of peace at being able to share his burden.

Abdul explained that he would call the police later on in the day and find out if they would be expected to provide statements. He wanted to be certain that the police knew his family had nothing to hide. He also wanted to make it clear that they had left town for their own safety. The police needed to understand that the residents of White Road would be looking for someone to hang out and dry, and in the absence of Ryan, Abdul knew that it would be his family who would take the hit. They were the only Muslim family on the estate, and everyone was well aware of the friendship between Ryan and Fareem.

The Khan family also all remembered the tension and bad feeling they felt in the estate after the 7 July 2005 bombings in London. For months afterwards Abdul had refused to let Nassir and Fareem leave the house alone.

And so as the sun began to rise above the White Road Estate on that Tuesday morning, life for many would never be the same. The Khan family hadn't considered this turn of events seven years ago when they headed to Medway for a better future.

Seven years ago Betty had had great dreams for Ryan; this was not what she would have predicted.

Where did it all go wrong?

PART 1

CHAPTER 1

April 2000. 24 White Road, Chatham, Kent – more commonly known as the White Road Estate.

It is Saturday afternoon and raining. Although April is meant to be the start of spring in the United Kingdom, the temperature hasn't bothered to reach over 10 degrees and when combined with the rain makes for a bleak day.

Ryan is bored. His dad is watching TV so that is not an option. He spent most of the morning engrossed in a book, but even that got boring, so he has chosen to do the next best thing and sit on the back of the sofa, gazing out of the front window. Although his eyes are fixed on the road outside, his thoughts are miles away. As usual he is day dreaming about a life away from White Road, away from his father, who is sitting in front of the TV drinking beer and watching the football.

Ryan's dad lets out a vulgar burp, raises his left bum cheek and farts.

Betty shouts from the kitchen, "Dwayne was that really necessary?"

The response is one that Ryan has come to expect from his dad.

"Oi bitch, this is my house, and when in my house I will do as I please."

Ryan's mum chooses wisely not to take the matter any further and simply ignores the remark and continues pottering around the kitchen.

All of this draws Ryan from his day dreaming and back into the real world, but his gaze remains on the road outside, and a car that is pulling into the driveway next door. The house next door has been empty for the past few months, so Ryan immediately looks closer, and it soon becomes clear that these are going to be his new neighbours.

"Hey Dad, look we have new neighbours."

Dwayne pulls himself away from the couch and the TV – this in itself is a chore as he doesn't want to miss the match, but his curiosity gets the better of him.

"Oh bloody hell, this is all we need, darkies moving in next door. You stay away from them Ryan, we don't need their sort in this street. You mark my words son, allowing foreigners, especially the dark ones into this country, is just asking for trouble." Dwayne seems to deliver this information in a form of fatherly advice, but it comes out as more of a drunken slur, and is concluded with another burp. As Dyane staggers over to the couch he shouts towards Ryan, "Now get your arse away from that window, stop staring at those wogs and get me another beer; do something useful for a change."

Ryan suspects his mum won't leave the conversation there, but wishes she would just shut up. He recognises the signs and his dad drinking in front of the football is a sure indication that trouble will follow. But every now and again Ryan's mum seems to take strength from an inner self, and it is at these times that he respects his mum for her pure strength of character, and moral conduct. She knows only too well that by standing up to Dwayne, and contradicting his views she will suffer, but she does it anyway. On these occasions Ryan is reminded of his mother's belief in herself and her desire to rise above his father's level, and as much as he admires this quality, he hates more than anything to see her hurt – and by God he knows his dad will hurt her.

Betty puts down her book and walks into the lounge towards the window to have a look as well. "Oh, Dwayne, don't be so judgemental, they seem alright to me, and I think it would do Ryan good to meet people from a different culture."

Ryan cringes as he knows that the volcano is about to explode, and sure enough it does. Dwayne suddenly spins around and glares at this wife. His eyes lose their drunken glazed look and take on a cold evil sharpness that seems to pour out of his pupils from deep within. Ryan's mum pre-empts his next move and steps back rapidly wishing now that she had kept her mouth shut. She throws a nervous glance towards Ryan just as the beast lets rip.

"Oi bitch, who the fuck do you think you are? Don't you dare talk to me like that. First you have a go about my habits in my own house, then you decide to encourage our son to mix with that scum. Just who the fuck do you think you are? A nigger lover? Is that it, you dirty white cow." Dwayne leaps off the couch and ploughs towards his wife. He is so angry that as he is shouting spittle sprays out of his mouth. He grabs hold of Betty's chin roughly in his big hand and squeezes. "I

31

asked you a question bitch – so are you a nigger lover, is that what you like, a big black cock? You disgust me whore, I've got a good mind to give you a bloody good beating just to remind you who the boss is."

Betty gasps as she attempts to respond, but his grip is so severe and no words can escape her mouth. She uses both her hands to try and prise his huge hand away from her jaw, but it is a fruitless gesture, as she knows that she does not have the strength to get away from him.

Dwayne in a sadistic sort of manner is using his other hand to stroke Betty's cheek, bit what others might deem a lovingly gesture, makes Betty's blood turn cold and her stomach clench in a tight knot. This is Dwayne at his worst.

He releases his grip enough to let Betty speak out, Dwayne, I am sorry, please, I didn't mean it like that." Betty then turns towards Ryan, and pleads, "Ryan why don't you go and play outside, go on, go outside."

Ryan recognises the look of fear in his mother's eyes. He knows that she is doing her best to keep the trembling out of her voice. He also knows that she is desperate for Ryan not to be a part of this punishment that Dwayne believes is his right.

Dwayne's voice booms in response, "Yeah, Ryan, go outside. Your mother and I need to have a little chat."

Ryan is not quite ready to leave his mum alone with this animal so tries his best to calm the situation. Deep down he knows it is pointless but he just wants his mum to know that he is there for her, and will do whatever he can to stop the pain. Ryan also knows that if he is not careful he will end up getting a beating too, and that is something that his mum can't bear. So in a strange sort of way, he stands up to his dad for his mum's benefit, but then knows that he will leave her on her own allowing her to receive a beating – for her own benefit too. This world is a strange one which Ryan can't quite seem to grasp.

"Dad, Dad, please calm down, I promise I won't have anything to do with them next door, please Dad, just stop shouting, Mum didn't mean it." Ryan grabs hold of his Dad's leg in a final attempt to get him to stop.

Dwayne just kicks his leg forward as though Ryan is just a slight irritation that needs swatting away. Ryan loses his grip as well as his nerve and starts heading for the door. Dwayne doesn't skip a beat and simply turns his anger towards his son.

"Don't you tell me what to do, you snotty nosed little shit, you have obviously been spending too much time with your nigger loving mother."

Dwayne raises his big right hand. Ryan realises it is time to go and makes a bee line for the front door, but he doesn't reach it in time. He tries to duck, but isn't quick enough and his dad's large palm connects with Ryan's left eye, causing a stinging sensation which is all too familiar. Ryan glances up at his mum, whose eyes are pleading desperately with him to go outside and leave her to fend off the raising temper.

Ryan powers out of the front door, only too glad to be out of the confining house. He takes two deep breaths and appreciates the freshness that has replaced the overbearing smell of his father – rank stale sweat mixed with cheap cigarette smoke.

Betty tries relentlessly to freshen and brighten the house with flowers and air fragrances and this generally works as long as Dwayne is out the house. His return to the bright and cherry home transforms it into a confining, dark, rank place where both Ryan and Betty do their best to keep their heads down and mouth shut. Both are terrified when the animal is unleashed for it brings pain and misery to all who touch him, smell him or are unfortunate enough to breathe in his air.

Ryan is tall for his age and takes after his father in that respect. Dwayne is 6 ft. 4 inches and built like a bull. The way Ryan is growing, it is almost a dead cert that he is going to have his father's physique. But that is where the similarities end. If it wasn't for Ryan's size he would be the splitting image of his mother. They both have that sun kissed hair and soft blue eyes, and skin that turns to golden honey when exposed to the sun. Betty's face is now lined with what seems a permanently frown, in fact these days it is only Ryan who is able to break through that frown. On days when Ryan can make Betty smile her face is transformed to that of someone far younger, with less concerns – someone carefree and happy. Betty is not carefree and happy today, and as Ryan runs out of the front gate, he is grateful for the long legs he gets from his dad that mean he can get away from the horror quicker. He turns left out of the gate and continues to run down the road, stretching his long legs to the maximum, the tears streaming down his cheeks, and his heart pounding with fear – fear for his mum, fear for their future. At the end of the road he turns right and heads towards the Coney banks.

It is cold for this time of the year – eight degrees – and Ryan has forgotten his coat, but that doesn't stop him, in fact as the cold air starts to burn his lungs he stretches his legs and runs faster, each stride and deep breath of icy air helps erase the recent scene at home.

He reaches the Coney banks and climbs down the steep slope to find his rock. This is where he comes to be alone. It's his place away from society where he can forget the world around him and live in his dreams. When he finally reaches his sanctuary, panting and gasping for breath, his legs ache with the recent excursion, but at least his mind is now clear of images of his father.

Ryan sits down and looks out towards the vastness in front of him. In the summer months the Coney banks are full of off road motorcycles roaring up and down, but at this time of the year it is only the odd dog walker who ventures this far into the undergrowth or kids smoking dope.

It is always at this stage that the guilt starts to engulf Ryan – if only he was strong enough to stand up to his father and protect his mother. He sits on his rock dreaming of the day when he will be able to take her away from this god forsaken place and that beast of a man. Ryan has already started saving. He has a money box hidden at the back of his cupboard in which he places any odd coins or notes. Every now and again Ryan's determined stare gives way to a dreamy expression. He might only be ten years old, but he has dreams and the determination of a child far older. He believes with all his heart that he will get away from this life and he will take his mother with him. If he gave up on this belief then he would have nothing, so already he has begun to plan for his future. Unfortunately though, even when he allows himself to dream and his expression takes on the dreamy look, his eyes remain hardened, and behind those eyes Ryan imagines causing pain to his father the way he does his mother. In his day dreams his is not a violent uncontrolled rage like his father's, but a calm, calculated one that will release both him and his mother from this tyrant who he calls Dad.

The cold air finally gets the better of Ryan and so he slowly heads back home. He arrives to see a young boy, probably the same age as him, only slightly smaller. The boy is carrying a box into the house next door; he glances up at Ryan and smiles a big toothy friendly smile. His jet black hair and coffee coloured skin accentuate the smile, making his teeth seem unnaturally white. Ryan quickly puts his head down, stuffs his hands into his jeans pockets and races inside – God help him if his father sees him talking to this dark boy with the toothy grin.

Ryan enters the house and realises straight away that his father is out – probably at the pub – and with any luck he will do his usual and stumble in drunk in the early hours.

36

The house seems serene again. A little light is on in the corner of the living room and mum has some incense burning – it's lavender, one of her favourites and he knows it helps her to relax. Mum is curled up on the couch reading a book and Ryan knows without even having to ask that it is the Bible. She glances up at Ryan as he walks in and opens her arms to him. Ryan can see her trying to hide the grimace as she stretches out to him – he has obviously given her a bloody good beating again. Thank heavens that this time her face seems pretty untouched.

Ryan responds to his mum's gesture and curls up into her arms; she strokes his hair and talks softly, soothingly. She forgives Dwayne's behaviour and promises Ryan that life will get better; she encourages him to be patient. She then reads Ryan one of his favourite passages from the Bible:

"Why do you complain, Jacob? Why do you say, Israel, "My way is hidden from the lord; my cause is disregarded by my god?" Do you not know? Have you not heard? The Lord is the everlasting God, the Creator of the ends of the earth. He will not grow tired or weary, and his understanding no one can fathom. He gives strength to the weary and increases the power of the weak. Even youth grow tired and weary, and young men stumble and fall; but those who hope in the Lord will renew their strength. They will soar on wings like eagles; they will run and not grow weary, they will walk and not faint" – Isaiah 40:27-31.

They then both say a private prayer, Ryan praying

for a release from this life and this man who causes such pain. Betty for patience and strength to help her endure the pain that her husband inflicts on her, but mostly she prays for the man she fell in love with to return to his happy carefree ways, although deep down in her heart she knows that this man never really existed and will never return.

It took Ryan another five years to realise that his mother would never leave the beast. When he finally realised that their prayers were different, and she was not asking her God to save her, but to help her endure, a change came over him. It was this new found knowledge that would direct his life towards a different set of beliefs.

The following day Ryan wanders into the kitchen to find his mum drinking a cup of tea whilst preparing the evening meal. She asks him to sit down; she wants to chat before the beast returns.

She explains to Ryan that she has met the new neighbours – the wife specifically. A lovely lady she says. She tells Ryan that Fareem is the son and the same age as Ryan and goes on to mention that Fareem will be attending the same school as him after the Easter break. She encourages Ryan to show Fareem around and to introduce him to the neighbourhood. Betty explains that even though his father will go mad, she wants him to grow up accepting all colours and cultures. She explains to Ryan that ignorance of others is what causes problems. Whilst talking Ryan notices a shine to her eyes, a radiance, a fire burning behind those eyes that he has not seen in years. This look in itself speaks alone to Ryan; this is clearly something that he can tell means a lot to his mum. He recalls the stories she used to tell him of her life prior to meeting his father. She took a year out of university to travel the world and her accounts of faraway places always brought that fiery vibrant look to her eyes. She says that she always planned to qualify as a teacher and then hoped to travel around the world teaching, returning to places and cultures that she fell in love with, but then she fell in love with Dwayne and travelling to distant places and people was put on hold for the man she loved. They were married within five months of meeting and Betty was pregnant within the first six months of their marriage.

CHAPTER 2

April 2000. The Khan Family.

Fareem sits squashed in the back seat of his father's red Ford Escort. He shares this space with the family's previous life, all boxed up now and headed for the new life. Fareem is curiously nervous about his future in Chatham. He has only ever known the small two bedroom terraced house in Birmingham which he shared with his grandmother, Nana. Fareem has known about the move for a couple of months now, but he hasn't really given it much thought – until now that is!

Fareem's father, Abdul, is a university lecturer; he was offered a job that was too good to refuse. So for this reason, thinking of his family's future, he uprooted them from their secure surroundings and relocated to White Road in Chatham Kent. However Nana decided that she was too old to relocate and so remained.

Chatham used to be a prosperous city, but then the dockside closed down and unemployment became the norm. The White Road Estate is one of those areas that depict the poorer side of Chatham. The majority of the houses belong to the council, and many of the residents are well accustomed to the police. Youngster's role models are their fathers who claim benefits from the government, but sell stolen goods on the side. Many of the older generation are illiterate, simply because they couldn't be bothered to learn to read and write. Wife beating is common practice and this goes hand in hand with alcohol consumption.

The community don't respond well to outsiders entering their patch - especially not educated, dark ones. Life is not going to be easy for Fareem and his family.

Fareem's father turns into White Road. It is a cold Sunday afternoon in April, and the rain is keeping most of its occupants inside. Abdul slows down to glance at the house numbers. He notices a curtain twitching and he also notices that most of the gardens are untidy. An old mattress has been discarded next to the road, and one of the houses has had its windows all boarded up and graffiti has been scribbled across its walls.

Abdul sees an unkempt man with long, stringy, greasy hair emerging from behind the boarded up door. The man's gaunt features and spotty face tell Abdul a lot – the house is probably being used as a squat for druggies.

What has he brought his family too? Abdul inwardly winces. This clearly is a deprived, neglected area, but it was all they could afford. Abdul knows that this his new work will bring in some extra money and so he is hoping that after a few years they will be able to move to somewhere more pleasant.

As Abdul turns the old Ford Escort into their new drive he only hopes that these people are more tolerant of difference than he expects, however he sensibly keeps these views to himself.

Abdul realises that the one saving grace is their religion. This neighbourhood may not accept the Khan family because they are darker than the average person, but he does know that the local mosque and its congregation will welcome them with open arms and offer them friendship.

That is one of the core values of the Islamic faith; all Muslims see and treat other Muslims as brothers irrespective of nationality or colour. This thought comforts Abdul; he knows that even if Fareem doesn't find friendship in this street, he will always make friends at the mosque. Abdul smiles lovingly over at his son who is clearly excited at the family's new adventure.

Fareem's little face is glued to the back seat window and he doesn't seem to notice the poverty around him – well what ten your old boy would? Fareem only knows about goodness in life. He has never known pain and suffering and that is the way Abdul wants to keep it. Abdul believes that a child's innocence is precious and should be preserved for as long as possible.

Abdul grew up in Chagcharan, the main town in the rather remote and isolated Ghor province, Afghanistan. Chagcharan is deep in the mountains and about 220 miles west of Kabul.

Growing up was tough for Abdul. Not only did he live through the Russian invasion of Afghanistan, but he also had to contend with a drought. Living deep in the mountains meant that it was near impossible to get food supplies to the town.

Abdul's youngest sister Aisha, died of starvation. Abdul was only five years old at the time, but can clearly remember his sister and how weak she became. She was one and a half when she died. Aisha had always been a sickly child and just didn't seem to have the strength to survive the harshness of Afghanistan. At the time Abdul didn't really understand what was happening, but he does remember the constant crying of his sister, and his Umm (Mum) permanently walking around with Aisha on her shoulder trying to calm her.

And then there was the silence, Abdul realises now that his sister eventually got to the stage where she just didn't have the energy to cry, and as annoying as the constant crying was, the silence was worse. But the image that he has never been able to rid his mind of is his Umm clutching his dead sister and howling uncontrollably. The sound seemed to come straight from the depths of her soul and was filled with so much sorrow and pain.

It was only after Fareem was born that Abdul could truly understand his mum's suffering. She blamed herself for her daughter's death, and would rather have given herself to Allah than for her child to be taken from her.

When a baby is born into a Muslim family the first thing the parents will do is to make the call to prayer in its ear: "*God is the Greatest, God is the Greatest, There is No God but Allah, There is No God but Allah, Muhammad is the Messenger of God, Muhammad is the Messenger of God, Come to Prayer, Come to Prayer, Come to Salvation, Come to Salvation, God is the Greatest, God is the Greatest.*"

And yes, this is the first thing that Abdul whispered

into Fareem's ear, as Nassir clutched him close to her chest, but then Abdul slowly lifted Fareem into his arms, and looked deep into his firstborn's eyes, and gently made his own promise to his child – Fareem would never know suffering and pain, death and hunger the way Abdul knew it.

And that is why they were moving to Kent. Abdul grew up with people dying around him; this and hunger was par for the course. Abdul survived these days by retreating into his mind. He didn't have many books, but the ones he did own were his saviour. When reading he was able to forget his hunger pangs, block out the explosions from the outside and drift into a world of fantasy. His favourite book was Peter Pan, Abdul still to this day does not know how he managed to come across a copy of this Disney story, and although he couldn't read English, his eyes devoured the pictures. Just the idea of "Never Never land" gave him hope.

About ten years later when Abdul was a twenty-year-old man who was far wiser than his years, he made the decision to leave the country of his birth for a better life. He was leaving everything he knew in order to give his unborn child the chance to live in Never Never land for real.

Fareem starts wriggling around in the back seat with excitement, "Hey Dad, did you see that boy next door – he is bigger than me, but looks kinda friendly," utters Fareem excitedly.

Abdul really does not want to damper the boy's spirits but at the same time, and more than anything else, he does not want his boy to get hurt, so he pushes his dream of Never Never land to the back of his mind and responds practically. "Oh, son, don't you go expecting too much from these folk, we are different, and not everyone appreciates that. You just keep you head down and get an education son."

"Oh, Abdul, don't be so hard on the boy, he is only ten, and he's a good boy, he will be okay, and don't forget he is British – he talks and walks just like them, surely he will be fine," expounds Nassir, waggling her finger at Abdul just to emphasise the point.

Abdul gently wraps his arm around Nassir's shoulder. "Ahh, Nassir I pray to Allah that you are right, but I fear not. These people won't take too kindly to the likes of us. Fareem may be British, but he is not white, and unfortunately that is all these people will see."

Nassir responds in her usual positive manner, "Well, Abdul, I hope that for once I am right and you are wrong – Shallah."

The Khan family spend the next week unpacking and settling into their new home. Fareem is desperate to make some friends and has been looking out for the boy next door but hasn't caught sight of him since the day they moved in. His mum mentioned she has met the boy's mother and it looks like they will be in the same class at school.

CHAPTER 3

The Easter holidays eventually come to an end, and Ryan is looking forward to getting back into his school routine. School provides a sanctuary from home and during the school term he doesn't need an excuse to get out of the house. School hours for Ryan are his lifeline.

As usual Ryan is ready for school early, so rather than sitting around the house he decides to head off. He decides he might even go down to his rock for a little while, just to enjoy the peace and quiet. And so Ryan shouts goodbye to his mum and as he slams the front door shut his eyes catch some movement in the next door garden. He raises his head and looks over and notices the new boy in his new school uniform saying goodbye to his mum. His mum is offering to walk him to school but the new boy is adamant that he is quite capable of walking alone.

Ryan recalls his mum's words and when he looks again at the new boy he notices that the toothy grin has been replaced by a nervous smile. Something in his eyes draws Ryan towards him. Perhaps it's that fearful look that Ryan feels himself when his dad goes off, or perhaps it is just that fear of the unknown that Ryan recognises. Either way, he makes a decision there and there to do right by his mother, and take care of the new boy.

He saunters over and confidently offers to walk his new neighbour to school. Betty glances out the window and beams with pride. Nassir smiles inwardly, hoping she is right and these are only ten-year-olds who don't see difference like adults.

Ryan politely stretches out his hand towards Fareem, "Hi, I'm Ryan; my mum tells me that we are the same age. I'm ten, how about you?"

"Oh, cool, I'm also ten, so we are going to be in the same class. You are so tall I thought you were much older than me. Oh, by the way I'm Fareem." Fareem breathes a sigh of relief, he has been so looking forward to his first day at school, but now that it has arrived he is petrified. Meeting Ryan has relaxed him slightly.

Ryan glances down at this watch, "Well Fareem we are way too early for school, so how do you fancy me showing you around?"

For the time being Ryan pushes the idea of going to his rock to the back of his mind – this new lad seems okay, but Ryan isn't quite ready to reveal his quiet spot just yet.

Fareem has been waiting to explore for ages but his mum was not happy about him venturing out on his own, so he eagerly accepts.

Ryan turns to Fareem and explains that they need to cross to the other side of the road. "That Fareem, is a drug squat," he says pointing out the boarded up house that Fareem's dad noticed when they arrived. Ryan continues to explain that his mum has told him never to walk past it, which is why they have crossed the road. He then goes on to describe its occupants in vivid detail to Fareem, who listens with wide eyes. Never before has

Fareem come across such a place.

"About five druggies live in there, they get into the house by squeezing through the boarded up door. And Fareem, let me tell you, you don't want to get too close to any of them as they stink. To be honest that is why I cross the road, it is more the smell that puts me off then my mum and her panicking about me being drawn into their evil lair as she calls it.

"But there is one bloke that comes and goes from the house and he is dangerous. If you see him then definitely stay away. My dad says that he is a Yardie who comes from Jamaica, but Dad also says that all Yardies carry guns and are not afraid to use them. I've seen this Yardie on a few occasions and he does look like a mean fucker." Ryan doesn't normally swear, it's something that his dad does and so Ryan tries to do everything his dad doesn't, but on this occasion Ryan wants to impress Fareem.

Fareem on the other hand is not impressed at all. He has never been in an environment where people swear so doesn't really know how to take it all, and he has also never come across drugs and guns, in fact he is starting to wish that he was back up north with his Nan. However he isn't up north, and desperately wants to fit in, so he nonchalantly kicks a stone with his brand new shoe and trying to sound as relaxed as possible he responds with, "So what does this mean mother fucker look like anyway?"

Ryan goes into graphic detail. "He is massive and black, and wears loads of gold. He always wears a dark leather jacket and jeans even in the middle of summer, so I guess he wears the jacket to hide his gun. My dad says that all blacks are bad and should be sent back to where they came from." Ryan is so busy trying to big time it that it is only after he has said it that he realises what he has done. He glances over at Fareem, whose big toothy grin is nowhere to be seen. In fact he looks kinda unhappy. Ryan realises that he has been behaving just like his dad and feels terribly ashamed of himself.

He stops walking, digs his hands deep into his pockets and looks down at Fareem. "I'm sorry mate, I shouldn't have said that. I don't know what I am talking about, I don't have a problem with black people at all, my Dad is just an arsehole. Hopefully you will never have to have anything to do with him. And anyway, I think you are kinda cool, even though we have a different colour skin."

Fareem looks up at Ryan and smiles his big toothy grin. Perhaps Ryan isn't so bad after all, and at least he had the decency to apologise. Fareem raises his arm and pats Ryan's arm, "No worries mate, no harm done."

Both continue walking along White Road in silence. Fareem is still kicking the stones, and Ryan joins in, without even realising it they have started a game – the first of many.

Ryan decides to steer the conversation towards something a little lighter, "What football team do you support?" The response that he receives is definitely not what he was expecting.

"Football, well, I'm not really into football, I prefer

rugby. Do you play rugby? With your size you would make a great rugby player."

All Ryan has ever known is football football football – in this estate football is more like a religion than a sport. Ryan personally finds it all a little boring so is relieved to meet someone who actually enjoys another sport.

"Rugby, well, to be honest Fareem I have never really watched any rugby, my Dad is such a big football supporter, he seems to think that any other sport is just a waste of time."

"Oh man, you have to learn, you would be great. Perhaps one day after school we can kick a ball around. And my dad pretty much watches all sport, so if you ever want to come over to my place and watch TV that would be great."

The conversation between the two of them flows easily, within that first half hour of meeting they have already learnt a lot about each other.

Ryan glances down at his watch and suddenly realises that they have been so caught up in conversation that he has forgotten about school.

"Shit, look at the time, if we don't get going we are going to be late for school – Mr Tindel is a real pain if you turn up late. Somehow I don't think you want detention on your first day!"

Fareem had also lost complete track of the time, but definitely does not want to get into trouble on his first day, so the two of them quickly pick up the pace as Ryan shows Fareem the short cut to school.

Fareem's first day at school turned out to be okay, but a few things did become clear to him, and he was reminded of his dad's words as they drove into White Road for the first time: "These people won't take to kindly to the likes of us."

Day one at school brought this home to Fareem. It was blatantly obvious that he was different, in fact he was the only dark boy at school, and many of them had never even seen a black man before – other than the 'Yardie' – let alone been friends with one. However the teachers all seemed really nice and Ryan had made it clear to everyone in their class that Fareem was his mate.

Ryan seemed to have a natural confidence about him, perhaps it was his size, Fareem wasn't really certain, however it did give him a kind of status at school and most of the kids seemed to like him. But what Fareem really liked was that Ryan seemed to be unaware of his popularity and really didn't seem to pay much attention to the other kids. Fareem realised that as long as Ryan was his mate, he would be okay at school.

Over the next few months Ryan and Fareem grew inseparable.

Ryan may well have come across as confident to his peers, but he shied away from this popularity. He didn't want people to know about his life at home and the easiest way to do this was to simply stick to him. His home life was not one that he would want school mates to become part of. But with Fareem it was different. Fareem was different. All the kids at school seemed to have noticed this as well, but it didn't bother Ryan; he felt comfortable around Fareem and his family. In fact, Fareem's family were so good to him that he actually felt like one of them.

And so as life at Ryan's house became more and more unbearable, he would take refuge at Fareem's home.

Ryan started to spend more and more time in the Khan household. Unlike his own, this was a home and a real family. Evening meals were eaten together and the day's events were discussed. Ryan loved every minute of it, from the strange foods that Nassir cooked, to the simply traditions of removing shoes when entering the house.

Ryan was mesmerised by Fareem's dad Abdul. His quiet and reserved manner was such a contrast to Ryan's own dad. And Abdul actually took the time out to talk to Ryan. Once Ryan realised this he would ask Abdul at every opportunity absolutely anything.

Nassir and Abdul had also noticed how close Fareem and Ryan had become. They were both relieved that Fareem finally had a close friend. Nassir and Abdul also agreed that they were happy that Fareem's best friend was a non-Muslim. They understood that the only way Fareem would ever be accepted in this Western world was by integrating. And this is exactly what he was doing.

And as for Ryan, Nassir treated him more like a second son these days than a school friend. Nassir had noticed that when Ryan was in their home he seemed softer and gentler. It was as though when he walked through their front or back door he was able to leave all of his troubles behind.

It was also very clear that Ryan had connected with Abdul. Nassir was well aware that Ryan did not quite have the most favourable father figure, and so she was pleased that Ryan felt comfortable with Abdul – a far better role model than Dwayne!

CHAPTER 4

During this time it wasn't only Fareem and Ryan that became close, so did Betty and Nassir. Theirs was a strange friendship. It started with chatting over the fence whilst hanging out the washing and then progressed to having tea at each other's houses. Although they never spoke when Dwayne was home, Betty never provided Nassir with an explanation for her cool behaviour when her husband was around. Nassir never asked for one either. She understood only too well the hardships of women. And it was for this reason that she never questioned the relationship, only sat and listened and offered Betty a comfort that both Nassir and Betty knew she would never receive from her husband.

It was in November of the year that the Khan family moved to the White Rad estate that Betty finally understood Nassir's kindness. Betty had gone over to Nassir's house as soon as the boys had left for school. She had suffered a particularly nasty beating from Dwayne the night before and just needed some comfort; Nassir was the only person she knew who would offer her that comfort.

Nassir was washing the breakfast dishes, having just put the washing on, and as the washing machine began to rumble she heard the doorbell. Reaching for the dish cloth she briskly wiped the soapy water off her hands and headed to the front door. On route she grabbed her hijab and covered her head – a Muslim custom as women are expected to cover their head, arms and legs when in the presence of a male other than their husband.

She opened the door to find Betty hunched over on the doorstep. Nassir too had heard the arguing through the thin walls the night before and so was not surprised to find Betty a little worse for wear. She quickly gathered her up and helped her to the kitchen.

"Oh Betty, look at you, come here my child, let's get you settled."

Betty allowed Nassir to usher her into the kitchen, and onto the kitchen stool. Once in the kitchen Betty sat quietly, not quite certain what Nassir must think, feeling certain that Nassir would have heard the screaming, banging and shouting that went on into the early hours. Nassir too didn't say anything and this silence Betty actually found comforting as she didn't feel it necessary to explain her pathetic state.

Betty found the natural kitchen sounds – filing the kettle with water, clanging of coffee cups and closing of cupboards oddly reassuring. It was only when a steaming cup of tea was placed in front of Betty and Nassir settled opposite her that Nassir began to speak.

"Betty, Inshallah, may Allah be with you."

Although Betty was fiercely Christian she didn't take offence to these words, she accepted them in the manner that they were delivered – from a friend offering the only form of condolence that the friend knows how to.

And then Nassir continued, "Betty, I have never spoken about my life before the White Road, Estate, I have never told you about my family and the life I come from."

Betty raised her hot cup to her lips and as she sipped up the warm sweet tea she lifted her eyes to meet Nassir. Her lower lip was so swollen that the tea dribbled down her chin so Nassir handed her a tissue – Betty felt no shame or embarrassment, just comfort, and so accepted the tissue with ease. Betty noticed that Nassir had taken a tissue for herself, and then realised that Nassir's eyes were wet with tears, and so Nassir continued her story.

"My father was not unlike your husband in a strange sort of way. He was a devout Muslim man, so you may find the similarities strange. My father did not drink alcohol, but he also had very little respect for his daughters and wife. My mother, Allah be with her, suffered a life not unlike yours. Married life for her was similar to that of a slave. She was expected to cook and clean and produce children – sons preferably. When my father brought friends home, she was expected to prepare the meals, but then disappear to her room. She was not allowed out the house unless accompanied by my father, and when she did leave she had to wear a full Burqa – which I have to say is the most uncomfortable garment. Beatings like yours, these she had to endure too. She did her best to shield my sister and me from this life of hers."

Nassir stopped briefly to sip her tea, and noticed that Betty was already refilling the kettle; Betty glanced over to Nassir and encouraged her to continue talking.

That wild trapped animal look that Nassir had recognised in Betty's eyes when she opened the front door to her had drifted away; Betty now looked on in quiet appreciation of this strange woman who was rapidly becoming her lifeline.

"My mother is still in Pakistan – she left Afghanistan shortly after we left, enduring the only life she knows and I have not seen her in five years. My mother unfortunately did not bear any sons for my father and so for that reason she has been pushed aside and another wife was taken.

"As for my sister Nazma and I, we were married off as soon as 'legally' possible. Both were arranged marriages. I was the lucky one. Abdul and I have grown together and although it was not love that brought us together it is love that we have found in one another. Abdul is a good man with a kind heart and a strong mind. He, like my father, is a devout Muslim, but is also sensible and intelligent, unlike my father. He loves Fareem and myself with all his heart. Intellectually I can never compare with him, but he does not belittle me for my lack of intelligence or ignorance, instead he praises me for the skills that I excel in. He takes pride in my cooking and the manner in which I raise Fareem, and for this I am eternally grateful – Shallah.

"Nazma, my sister, is not so fortunate. Her chosen man is not so kind or gentle. He is fifteen years her senior and once again after producing only girls he lost interest in her and that is when her punishment began – Allah be with her. Her beatings became so severe and she began to fear for her children's safety, so she made the decision to disappear. Nazma and the two daughters made their escape whilst her husband was out working. I have not heard from her since, and know that I never will. She knows only too well that any contact with her former life could lead to her death. Within our society this is known as an honour killing – she has disgraced her husband's family and brought shame to her father's family and for this reason death is the only honourable answer. I personally find this utterly barbaric, but I also understand the culture I am from and I realise that change is not going to happen. I can only pray each night that Allah will protect her and provide her and her children with some form of happiness."

Nassir pauses again and sips her tea. Betty looks at Nassir through new eyes; her respect for this woman in front of her is now great.

"So you see Betty, I am no stranger to cruel men, and I sympathise with you. But if I am honest, it is Ryan that I worry for most, and that is why I have welcomed him into my house like one of my own. Betty, our fate has been set and we simply have to cope in the only way we know how. But our children never asked for this life, and they are the ones we need to protect."

Nassir releases a long sigh, closes her eyes and mumbles softly in a language Betty does not understand, but she does recognise that this lady is uttering a prayer; a prayer for the past and one for the future. Betty responds to this act and gently lowers her aching head and says a prayer to her own God.

Later that night as Betty reads from the Bible: *"You have heard that it used to be said, 'You shall love your neighbour', and 'hate your enemy', but I tell you, Love your enemies, and pray for those who persecute you, so that you maybe sons of your Heavenly Father."* – Matthew 5:43-44.

She reflects on the day's events. Betty, a deeply religious woman, contemplates the woman next door, another deeply religious woman. She realises that Nassir, like herself only wants the best for her young. She recognises goodness in the woman's soul and more importantly she understands that Nassir's only intentions are peace and happiness.

Betty for the first time is able to appreciate the differences between religions and cultures, but also accepts the similarities. This new found light that has brightened her heart has provided her with a hope for her son, and also the knowledge that even though Nassir has Allah and Betty has God, they both have similar principals and morals and both pray for a better future. Forget colour and customs, they are both women with children who have the same fears and uncertainties about their offspring's future. Both will do anything in their power to provide for their young.

From this day on Betty encouraged Ryan to spend time with Fareem and his family. Now that she knew he was welcome and not a burden she realised that they were his opportunity for a normal life - one without fear of the man Ryan called Dad, who was no more a father than he was a husband.

CHAPTER 5

Dwayne didn't like the fact that his neighbours were dark, nor that they practised some strange religion. What God they worshipped he didn't quite know, or really care, but it was the fact that they were different that mattered to him and it always gave him plenty to talk about at the Bell Inn.

The Khan family were a bit of an exhibition for the White Road Estate, being the first non-white family to move into the area. Some were fascinated by their strange ways, others were outwardly against this "invasion" as they called it, but whether it was fascination or disgust, everyone was always keen to learn a little more about the newcomers.

Dwayne, living next door to the infiltrators, was therefore the man who gave these people what they wanted. More than once or twice he exaggerated the truth, but he really didn't give a dam to the consequences his tall stories may have for the Khan family, his only real concern was whether or not his stories would gain him an extra beer.

This newfound popularity meant that Dwayne started spending more and more time in the pub. It was where he felt most comfortable, besides he found Betty boring, and frumpy, and their house constricting. Betty was always reading her Bible and burning incense – God how Dwayne hated the smell of that stuff, and she just didn't seem to realise how infuriating she made him.

Dwayne felt that he worked hard to support his family, and he just didn't feel like Betty appreciated all he did for her these days. Dwayne had recently got some regular work, how legal it was not even Dwayne was certain, but it did mean that he was bringing in a regular income, and for this simply fact alone he believed that Betty should treat him better. Dwayne didn't think that it was right for women to work, he wanted his woman to remain at home, to look after the kids, keep the house tidy and cook the food; another fact that he felt Betty should appreciate.

A real thorn in his side was that Betty had only ever provided Dwayne with one child. And as for Ryan – well, that was a different story. The older he got the more of a disappointment he became for Dwayne. He was a pathetic excuse for a boy, who unfortunately had taken on his mum's genes.

Dwayne was well aware that Ryan was spending a lot of time with the Khan family, but he had got to the stage where he really didn't care about the boy, and so simply turned a blind eye. In his younger days Dwayne believed he could beat some character into the snotty nosed little wimp, but this seemed to have the opposite effect for Ryan – rather than standing up for himself and being a man, he tended just to sink further and further into himself. Like his mum he always had his nose stuck in a book.

Dwayne had had such high hopes for the boy; he had his dad's stature and could be a real player if he wanted to, however this was clearly not going to be the case. Yes, Dwayne had pretty much washed his hands of his pathetic excuse for a family. The pub and its clientele were his new family – especially young Sarah. Dwayne had taken quite a fancy to the pretty little twenty-year-old with the tight bum and big tits. She wasn't afraid to flaunt her bits, unlike his dour old wife, who hadn't been to the hairdresser in years let alone ever worn a short skirt and high heels.

Sarah clearly appreciated him. She would sit next to him for hours on end and listen to his stories. Her big green eyes wouldn't wander from his face, and her hand would normally be placed lovingly on his leg, whilst with her other hand she would twist that wisp of hair that always fell onto her cheek. She would never question Dwayne, or disagree with his point of view, but she wasn't scared to have a drink or two and was always up for a good time. She was also quite a pool player. In fact she was everything that Betty was not, which meant she was everything that Dwayne wanted – sexy as hell and she knew it.

Sharon sat back and watched the relationship develop with amusement from behind the bar. Dwayne and her went way back, and there was definitely no love lost between the two of them. He may have been able to fool this lovely little thing, but Sharon was under no illusion. Dwayne was a nasty man, and Betty was living proof of that. Sharon could still remember when Dwayne and Betty first got involved with each other. Betty had had a sparkle in her eye and clear ideas about her future, but unfortunately she was so besotted with Dwayne and his ideas of a wife's ambitions were vastly different to Betty's. Sharon had watched Betty's spirit get crushed over the years, and her dreams disappear.

However this was not the side of Dwayne that Sarah was seeing now. Oh yes, Dwayne knew how to put on the charm when he wanted to, and that was exactly what he was doing with young Sarah. And Sharon had to admit he was an extremely good looking man. He did have a slight beer belly these days, but his hair was a chestnut brown which he always wore a little bit long and it gave him that kind of carefree look. This look was accentuated by his lazy deep brown eyes and chiselled cheek bones – oh yes, Dwayne was a real looker, and his body wasn't too bad either. When mixed with charm and quick wit – always one to tell a joke or good story, always the centre of attention – it was no wonder that Sarah had been sucked in by his charismatic manner.

Sharon realised that Sarah was going to have to learn the hard way this time. She had been in the business long enough to know that it would make absolutely no difference whatsoever to pull Sarah aside and tell her some home truths.

Sarah, bless her heart, was what you would call not quite the sharpest tool in the box. But she was a good girl, and give her her due, she was trying extremely hard to make something of her – up until now at least – meaningless existence.

About six months ago Sarah was cutting Sharon's hair and complaining about how long the bus took to get into work each day, and how she was looking for accommodation nearer to work, but couldn't really afford what was on offer on her meagre hairdressing salary. Sharon who needed a hand in the bar in the evenings, and who had accommodation above the pub thought they might be able to both help each other out and so asked Sarah is she would be interested in working a few evenings and staying in the room above the pub.

Sharon was now beginning to think that she perhaps hadn't done Sarah any favours at all! Dwayne was going to break her heart alright; Sharon just hoped that that was all he would end up breaking. Sharon really didn't know Sarah that well. She would not describe them as friends, but from a very early stage it became clear to Sharon that Sarah respected her views and would frequently come to her for advice. Sharon realised that Sarah's mother was so much older than her that she wasn't able to relate to her daughter, which had resulted in a rather naïve young girl who clearly needed some guidance from someone that was older and wiser person but still young enough to remember what it was like to be twenty years of age.

Oh, yes, Sharon could remember what it was like to be twenty. It had been the time of her life. Parties, and getting drunk was her soul ambition, only it didn't last. By the time she reached twenty-one years she was three months pregnant, by the age of twenty-five she had two kids, been married and divorced!

However, Sharon did remind herself, Sarah did have a few more things going for her than Sharon did at that age. Sarah clearly came from a very loving family – her parents might have been too old to relate to her, but there was no lack of love. Her mum and dad clearly wanted the best for their daughter. Sarah was encouraged and supported when it came to making a career as a hairdresser. Her parents had obviously accepted that Sarah was never going to be a barrister or an accountant, but that didn't mean that she wasn't capable of making something of her life.

Sharon just hoped that this support and encouragement, and Sarah's love for hairdressing was enough to keep her on the straight and narrow, and sensible enough to see through Dwayne's advances when the "honeymoon" period wore off.

One thing Sharon was certain of though, if it didn't quite work like that and Sharon thought that for one moment that little pretty Sarah was in any sort of danger, Sharon would turn to those who she now called family. They may not be blood, but they were the only family Sharon had ever known. Sharon knew beyond a shadow of doubt that if she made the call, her "family" would make Dwayne go away – if that is what she wanted.

CHAPTER 6

Sharon wasn't the only one who believed in family values. Abdul was a firm believer in putting his family first. Family values are an integral part in the Islamic religion, and as far as Abdul was concerned a fundamental part in one's existence.

Allah said in the Holy Koran, (chapter 4:34) "...that men are the protectors and maintainers of women. The man is financially responsible for all of the women in the family."

Abdul recognised and accepted this responsibility; however, his belief went further than simply caring for and protecting the women. Abdul interpreted this part of the Holy Koran as a reference to his whole family, not simply the women closest to him. He would therefore do everything in his power to care and provide for his son as well as his wife, the two most important people in his life.

And that is why the Khan family ended up on the White Road Estate – in search of a better future. Abdul wasn't expecting this move to be easy for his family, but he knew that in the long run they would be better off.

Life in Birmingham had been ideal for Abdul; he had the perfect job and going to work was a pleasure for him. That in itself was a bit of an anomaly. Most people worked because it paid the bills, but as for actual enjoyment well work and pleasure didn't form part of the same sentence. But it wasn't like this for Abdul. He lectured on a subject close to his heart – Ancient history and classics at Birmingham University. He was also surrounded by people of a like mind, and he had his family close by – what more could a man ask for?

However, it wasn't about his happiness – the Khan family shared a two bedroom house with Abdul's mother, and on the salary he was receiving there was never going to be any opportunity to buy a bigger house, go on holiday, spoil the family, or fund Fareem's studies.

So when the opportunity arose for Abdul to take on a job in Kent, one that was willing to pay a lot more money, Abdul didn't give his happiness a second thought. This job would provide a better life for the people he cared for most.

Fortunately Abdul also enjoyed his work in Kent – an unexpected treat. His colleagues had welcomed him with open arms; they didn't even seem to notice that he was a different colour to the majority of them. Abdul soon realised that the difference between his colleagues and his neighbours was education. At work he was surrounded by educated, intelligent people and many of them also came from other parts of the world, and they were accustomed to dealing with people from a different background or culture. This was quite unlike the White Road Estate where the majority of residents had never even travelled to London, let alone Europe, and just finishing school was classed as an achievement.

So Abdul considered himself fortunate. He was once again in a situation where he was happy at work, and unlike Birmingham, he was now able to put away a couple of hundred pounds extra a month. All this money was to ensure that his family would always be provided for, and would never want for anything.

Abdul however appreciated that it was highly unlikely that the residents of the White Road Estate would ever come to see the Khan family as part of their community, but Abdul was also intelligent enough to realise that they looked on all newcomers with suspicion whether or not they were black.

Abdul knew that the next few years wouldn't be easy for himself or his family but eventually he would be able to afford a house in perhaps an area of higher standing.

Abdul also always tried to look towards the positive side of life rather than focusing on the negative, and as he sat back in his chair and surveyed the scene he thanked Allah for his happiness.

It had taken a good three months to turn the house into a home. As far as Abdul was concerned it was not the fact that the final box was unpacked three months to the day that they moved in that made the house a home – it was the manner of his family. It was clear that both Nassir and Fareem were "at home" in their new house. Nassir spoke affectionately about the neighbour next door, and mentioned just that evening that she had found a shop in Chatham High Street that specialised in Halal meat. Nassir was now also part of the Muslim ladies group that met every Wednesday in the Canterbury Street mosque. And over the past three months Abdul had come to look forward to the constant chatter from Nassir on a Wednesday evening as she recalled the events of the day. And what thrilled Abdul most was hearing the passion in Nassir's voice as she updated Abdul on the current projects that the ladies were taking on.

And then there was Fareem, the apple of Abdul's eye. He too had settled in at the school nicely – better than Abdul could ever have imagined, and it was clear that he had been accepted. Abdul realised that Ryan had had a great deal of influence in Fareem being accepted, and for this he would always be eternally grateful to Ryan, and the fact that he had taken Fareem under his wing.

And so three months to the day Abdul sat back in his chair, sipped on a cup of piping hot tea and surveyed the scene around him. Nassir was in the kitchen putting the final touches to the evening meal, Ryan and Fareem could be heard laughing and shouting with delight as they tossed a rugby ball at each other in the back yard. Yes, Abdul decided this house was now a home. And so he thanked Allah for his family's happiness.

Shattered: Sallie Baisley

PART 2

Shattered: Sallie Baisley

CHAPTER 7

September 11 2001. The Bell Inn.

"Jesus Christ." Sharon slams down the phone and urges Dwayne to turn the television on.

"Fuck me Sharon, what the hell is wrong? It is not often that I hear you swear."

Dwayne had just popped into the Bell Inn for a quick swift one and hopefully a little cuddle from Sarah, his little bit on the side, before heading on home. Betty was expecting him early and was hoping he could do a few chores around the house. Well it didn't quite work out that way. The world had turned upside down in the last few minutes. Dwayne stared at the television in disbelief as the day's events began to unfold – chores at home were the last thing on his mind.

Sharon switched the TV over to Sky News; the presenter was talking about a possible terrorist attack and a plane flying straight through the Twin Towers in New York City. Sharon was still not certain what to make of all the hype – her mind was telling her that surely it was impossible to fly a plane through the Twin Towers, and just as Sharon was considering the impossibilities, Sky News switched over to the United States and the screen was filled with images of the Twin Towers on fire. She automatically picked up a glass and poured herself a shot of whiskey – never before had she drunk whilst on duty, and it was only after she took her first sip that she

73

realised what she had done. Sharon then glanced over at the clientele. Her early afternoon regulars were the only ones who had taken up seats today. Bernie was settled in the corner, propped up as per usual against the wall. But instead of his usual drunken glazed over look, he was leaning forward and focusing on the news at hand, his eyes surprisingly bright and alert. Dwayne was also in his usual spot, staring wide mouthed at the TV, and finally there was Pete who normally sat in the corner quietly reading the newspaper. Today he had joined Bernie and Dwayne and all three of them were huddled in front of the television.

Sharon realised that she was in for a busy night. A crisis always brought in business for Sharon and what bigger crisis than this! Sharon and Sarah worked solid for the next eight hours or so. Fortunately Sharon's trusty babysitter Alice had been able to come over and get the kids all sorted, leaving Sharon to crack on with the business at hand.

The hard graft of the evening meant that Sharon wasn't able to dwell on the day's events, however it did come home to her the following day when she popped into the corner shop for milk and a newspaper. Every single newspaper was filled with pictures of pain and despair. The headlines only confirmed what the pictures were depicting. Sharon took her time to read the front page of most of the newspapers:

The Sun: "Day that changed the world"

The Mirror: "War on the world"

Daily Star: "Is this the end of the world?"

The events of September 11 2001 were incomprehensible. How was it possible that nineteen Al-Qaida terrorists were able to simultaneously hijack four commercial planes? How was it possible that 2,993 people's lives were cut short by a terrorist attack?

Sharon wasn't the only one who was asking these questions. This had taken the world by storm and people all over were wondering how this could possibly have happened. Within a matter of a few hours, the world had changed forever, and everyone was going to feel the effects of the attack on the Western world – even the residents of the White Road Estate, although for some it would be worse than others.

CHAPTER 8

Dwayne never did return home on the night of September 11 2001. Betty wasn't overly concerned, in fact in a way it was a bit of a relief and he had been doing this for a while now. Betty suspected that there was another woman, and deep down in her heart she was grateful that her tormentor had finally found someone else. However she chastised herself every time this thought crept into her mind – she was a good Christian women, how could she wish her pain and suffering on someone else? But Betty also recognised that she was only human, and it was surely natural to feel this way.

And so as she finally turned off the television, and blew out her candles on that frightful night she whispered two prayers, one thanking God that she had survived another night without a beating, and another for all those lost souls out there whose world had just collapsed.

Betty had been glued to the television all day, but still couldn't comprehend what had actually happened, although she knew enough to know that the world would pay for the actions of today – it didn't matter who was to blame, everyone would end up suffering at some time or another. A wheel had just been set in motion that would result in catastrophic events around the world. All these thoughts were running through her mind, as she quietly tided up the kitchen before heading up to bed. Her one last chore was to take the rubbish bag outside. She expertly gathered up the bag, twisted it into a knot and opened the back door then walked to the far end of the garden and placed the bin bag into the outside bin. She then turned to come back inside and tightened her gown around her waist as she felt the first chills of winter. Whilst doing so her eyes were drawn towards the Khan family home. Their kitchen light was still on and she could see Abdul pacing up and down, clutching a book to his chest. It suddenly dawned on her that the family next door who had provided her and Ryan with such comfort and love would now be the centre of attention, and plenty of fingers would be pointed in their direction. Just yesterday Betty and Nassir had discussed how well the Khan family had settled into the neighbourhood – Betty knew that all that was about to change. These thoughts seemed to send a greater chill up her spine, and so Betty quickly walked back inside. As she closed and double locked the kitchen door she whispered one more prayer for the family next door.

Abdul had been lost in thought, and it was only on hearing a rustle outside that he was brought back to the land of the living. His first thought was that the nightmare had begun; someone was already trying to get into the back garden. All sensors now on edge, he quickly slid over to the window and carefully peered outside.

Abdul's heart stopped racing, and he wiped his sweaty hands down the front of his jeans as he looked out into the back garden and saw Betty from next door quickly walking back into her house. Abdul breathed a sigh of relief, but this just helped to bring more turmoil into his mind.

Was he being paranoid? Did he really think that his family were in danger as a result of a horrific series of events that took place on the other side of the world? Surely people would understand that his family posed no threat, they believed in peace and harmony – well wasn't that what Islam was all about? And that was what sent chills down Abduls spine. Islam was all about peace, yet these key individuals had attacked the Western world all in the name of Allah. How could this possibly be happening?

Abdul realised that it would take him a long time to decipher exactly what had gone on in America today. His mind was already in turmoil around the audacity of those who professed to serve Allah. But one thought cut across the turmoil and reached the forefront of his mind with crystal clarity – how was he going to be able to protect his family from those who had just been attacked by his own people? Despair gripped his heart as he realised that he would never be able to fully protect both his wife and son, unless he actually forbid them to leave the house without him. Well, this was not Abdul's way, and so with a heavy heart he headed off to bed hoping that today was all just a bad dream.

A bad dream it was not, and Abdul woke the following morning with heavy, blood shot eyes. The bed sheets shared the same story. They were twisted and damp, soaked in Abdul's sweat. If he wasn't sleeping he was tossing and turning, and when he did manage to sleep he was plagued by nightmares of the past – war and death, a time in his life that he had hoped he would never have to reface. However this was not the case.

Nassir didn't get much sleep either that night, she too was concerned about the events of the last 24 hours, however her husband's restfulness caused her more unease. She could not change the recent events, but she could do her best to ease her husband's stress, and so she woke early, many hours before Abdul rose for his morning prayers.

Nassir wrapped her nightgown around her waist, slipped on her slippers and tiptoed downstairs to the kitchen. Once in the kitchen and after a cup of coffee she began to bake. Nassir started with bread and ended up with two loaves, a cake and batch of biscuits.

Baking was Nassir's way of taking time out; she was able to block out the world and come to terms with her own inner turmoil whilst baking. It also gave her time to be at one with Allah. Nassir had been baking for so long that all the recipes were ingrained in her memory, so instead of a cooking book she referred to the Koran. This gave her the strength and conviction to understand that she didn't always understand the reasoning behind certain acts and horrors, but by placing her trust in Allah, and ensuring that she adhered to the necessary Islamic practices she would end up in paradise alongside her saviour. And by easing her husband's stress, and ensuring that her son was brought up in the Islamic way, she was helping her family on their route towards paradise too.

And so both Abdul and Fareem woke to the wonderful smell of freshly cooked bread. Fareem, not really understanding what had happened over the past 24 hours, followed his nose towards the kitchen, whereby he rapidly devoured two thick slices of warm bread, dripping with melted butter. He was still wearing his pyjamas, and his thick, jet black hair was in complete disarray. His eyes were still full of sleep and he looked alarmingly young and innocent. Nassir had to remind her that this young lad in front of her was now in senior school and paying far too much attention to the young ladies than she would have liked. The sleepy, cuddly look was a cute reminder of the past and nothing else – Fareem was rapidly growing up, and Nassir was proud of the boy both she and Abdul had created. She had always wanted a second child, but Allah had decided against this. Nassir had for a long time battled to come to terms with this outcome, however when she did, she made a promise to herself – she would not wallow in her own self-pity by trying to keep Fareem her "little boy" for as long as possible.

Nassir was pulled out of her daydream by Abdul walking into the room, looking haggard and exhausted. Fareem was still too busy devouring the bread and did not even seem to notice his dad's distress and this suited Abdul just fine. Nassir however did notice, and caught Abdul's eye as he walked in. She was clutching a cup of coffee, and simply passed it over, placing it in Abdul's hands. In doing so they brushed fingers and their eyes met. Abdul understood that Nassir too was in a state of turmoil and decided they would sit down and talk once Fareem had left for school. Abdul was only due at the university later on in the morning, so this would give him and Nassir an opportunity to talk about the recent events. However prior to that he did feel that his son needed to have some sort of understanding as to what had happened and how that might affect their future. He did not want his son to walk into a barrage of verbal attacks simply because he was black and Muslim – he would have to give his son some form of ammunition to deal with the onslaught that was sure to come hopefully not today, but in the near future.

Events like this were indiscriminate. Thousands had been killed by the hijackings, but these same people who professed to be causing such pain and suffering on the Western world all in the name of Allah, would now be causing pain and suffering to their own brothers and sisters, who were living in the Western world. Abdul was intelligent and sensible enough to realise that every Muslim living in the Western world would suffer because of the latest atrocity.

It was human nature to attack what you felt threatened by, and at the present moment the Western world was under threat by a group of people who proclaimed to be men of Islam – and the Khan family were children of Islam.

Fareem was just wiping the crumbs off his face, and was reaching out for his school lunch, when Abdul grabbed his arm gently. "Fareem, I just want five minutes of your time before you head off for school."

"Aahh Dad, can't it wait? I'm meeting Ryan shortly, and we're going to head over to the field to do a bit of rugby practice before school."

"Son, I'm only asking for five minutes."

This response was a little more stern, and firm enough to slow Fareem down. He realised that this talk was going ahead whether he liked it or not. So he slouched back down into his chair and looked at his dad expectantly.

"Fareem, by now you will have heard bits and pieces about what happened yesterday in America."

"Obviously Dad, that is all we were talking about yesterday afternoon at school – a couple of planes were blown up, and one even flew through a massive building, pretty far-out stuff."

"Yes, Fareem, but are you also aware that Al-Qaida have laid claim to the attacks all in the name of Allah? That my son means that some of your friends might not take too kindly to you being Muslim."

"Oh Dad, don't be so dramatic, my friends are fine, I'm British after all – just like them."

"Yes, Fareem that may be the case, but I just want you to be aware, not everyone is going to feel the same way, and they may take it out on you, simply because you are a different colour and Muslim. Don't be surprised if those who you think are your friends now change their attitude towards you. But Fareem, let's hope and pray that you are right, and it will all be okay." Abdul ruffled Fareem's hair, and then leaned back in his chair.

Fareem realised the conversation was over and leant forward, grabbed another slice of bread, then legged it out of the door, giving his mum a kiss on her cheek on the way, and waving goodbye to his dad, mouth now stuffed full of bread.

CHAPTER 9

Fareem took on board what his dad had said, but was more interested in getting out into the open air, and spending some time with his mate before school.

Ryan was waiting outside Fareem's house. Fareem mumbled an apology about being late, and the two headed off down the road together. Both were unusually quiet. Fareem was thinking about what his dad had just said. Fareem may have let his folks think that he had no worries, but the reality was very different – Fareem just didn't want his folks to worry. Of course Fareem knew what happened yesterday, and was well aware of the impact it would have on him.

They had only been at secondary school for a couple of weeks, but things were not the same as primary school. Fareem had really felt accepted at primary school, he didn't feel different at all, but secondary school was completely different. Medway Secondary School was much bigger and not all the kids were keen on having a black boy in their school. They would use any excuse to pick on him, and now they had the perfect opportunity. However Fareem had Ryan – they were a team – and Fareem knew that Ryan would never let anyone hurt him.

Ryan was also thinking about the events of the last twenty-four hours and he too comprehended the implications. Ryan had woken up this morning with a sick feeling in the pit of his stomach. This was something he normally associated with his father and the attacks on him and his mother, however he hadn't seen his dad in a few days, and so recognised that today the feeling was fear for Fareem. Ryan would never let anyone harm Fareem, who was as good as a brother to him, but Ryan was also practical, and understood that he could not be with Fareem twenty-four hours a day.

Now Ryan knew that Fareem was a strong lad, and capable of giving a decent right hook if he had to. He had seen his friend on the rugby pitch, but that was sport and Ryan knew that Fareem was nowhere near strong enough to defend himself against the real bullies of the school. This caused Ryan great worry.

"Hey Fareem, I know we were going to do a bit of rugby practise this morning, but do you fancy going to this cool, quiet spot of mine instead? I go there when I want to get away from all this shit," Ryan says and indicates the neighbourhood with his hand.

In fact it had been a while since Ryan had been there; since Fareem and he had teamed up he didn't really feel the need to hide from the world, as now he had a friend to share his burdens. But today, Ryan thought it was appropriate to introduce Fareem to his sanctuary – Fareem might need it in the near future.

"What, and miss out on smashing you on the rugby pitch? No way!" responds Fareem. Fareem then punches Ryan in the arm for good measure, "Only joking mate, that sounds like a cool idea. Don't know about you, but I am not really in the mood for rugby today."

The tight knot in Ryan's stomach subsides and is

replaced by pride and a sudden surge of adrenaline. Ryan realises that for a change he is there for Fareem. In the past it has always been Fareem who has had to pull Ryan out of the deep depths of despair, when life at home just got too much. Ryan likes the feeling of being able to help others, rather than continually focusing on his own sorrow and disastrous family life.

"Come on mate, I'll race you there," shouts Ryan as he starts to up the pace.

Fareem responds with his big toothy grim, swings his book bag across his back and legs it after Ryan. Fareem knows he stands no chance of catching his tall, long legged buddy, but not one for backing down to a challenge gives it his best effort, and it feels great. For a few minutes the events of the past leave his mind and he simply focuses on Ryan now a couple of metres ahead of him. They both reach the end of the road panting and puffing, cheeks full of colour and hair wind swept.

"Man, you beat me again," exclaims Fareem, hitting his hand against his leg.

Ryan responds with an insulting remark, "It is not my fault you have the legs of a tortoise - if you ran any slower I would be late for school, slow coach!

Fareem replies with another insult, "Well, ol' speedy, you might be able to beat me on the run, but at least my brain can add two and two – thicko."

Ryan grabs Fareem around the neck in a friendly tackle and they chuckle away together, enjoying the banter.

They then cross the road and head off towards the

Coney banks. Ryan glances left and right, ensures that no one else is around and then quickly grabs Fareem's arm and leads him into the undergrowth. They battle through the overgrown shrubs and Fareem wonders where exactly Ryan is taking them, but no sooner does he start to question his mate's intentions do they reach the spot – a massive rock, that Ryan quickly scrambles up, then holds out his hand for Fareem, who grabs hold of it and then is hoisted up the rock by Ryan.

Both are silent for several minutes – Ryan is considering how much his life has changed now that Fareem is his neighbour and best mate – he used to come to this rock several times a week, and every now and again he would sneak out at night when the shouting got too bad. But he hadn't been here in a few weeks now, and although his spot brought him a sense of peace, he preferred Fareem's company.

Both boys sink down onto their haunches, and sit quietly, each comfortable enough to remain silent. Fareem can feel the sun on his face. There's a slight breeze, but not enough to bother the boys. The world might have turned upside down in the last 24 hours, but for just a few minutes Fareem is able to enjoy a feeling of peace and tranquillity that seems to engulf this hidden spot. However the feeling is not to last. Fareem is dragged out of his thoughts by Ryan tugging on his school sweater.

"Shit mate, I've forgotten to do my Maths homework, can I copy yours?"

Fareem playfully punched Ryan on the arm. "Oh

man, not again."

Ryan just laughs, knowing full well it was normally Fareem that was copying his homework. Fareem was okay at school, he would just rather spend his time on the rugby field, and so during the rugby season homework was not a priority for Fareem – especially not literature – which was Ryan's strong point anyway. So Ryan would normally do Fareem's literature for him, and every now and again when Ryan had had a tough night at home Fareem would help him out. Maths was Fareem's strong point, and Ryan's weak, so between the two of them they had quite a good homework schedule worked out!

So there they sat, on the rock, Ryan scribbling down numbers, changing the odd number every now and again so that the teacher wouldn't suspect copying. And Fareem just sat back and enjoyed the warm sun.

The rest of the day was rather eventless; there was a lot of talk about the hijackings, but the kids all seemed more interested in talking about the nearing half term holiday. Both Ryan and Fareem breathed a sigh of relief – maybe it would be okay after all.

CHAPTER 10

Abdul too breathed a sigh of relief when he realised that Fareem's day had been thankfully uneventful, however he didn't expect it to last, and that is exactly why he spoke to Nassir after Fareem had left for school that morning.

Abdul found it awkward to bring up his views, as he had always prided himself in allowing his wife to speak her own mind and do as she felt best, and as long as Nassir cared and loved Fareem Abdul was happy. In Islam the mother's role is to look after the children and develop their Islamic knowledge, and this is precisely what Nassir did.

Abdul was proud to be Nassir's husband. She was a good Muslim woman so he realised that his request would require a huge sacrifice on her part, one that Abdul believed was necessary simply to ensure Nassir's safety, but somehow he didn't think she would see it this way. And so Abdul had come to the decision that if Nassir chose to disagree, he would have to lay down the law – the Qur'an clearly states in Surah 4:34 "Men are in charge of women because Allah has made the one of them to excel the other, and because they spend of their property (for the support of women). So good women are the obedient, guarding in secret that which Allah has guarded."

Abdul knew that today he might just have to take charge! He was not willing to put his beloved wife in a position whereby she might get harmed. So Abdul gently told Nassir – whilst they were sitting at the kitchen room table, Fareem 's breakfast dishes still covering the surface, and both clasping a cup of now lukewarm coffee – that he did not want Nassir leaving the house unless it was absolutely necessary and she was accompanied by him.

Nassir sat in her wooden kitchen chair, sipping on her coffee and silently listening to her husband. She had never heard him be so forceful, and what scared her most was the fact that he managed to do so in such a gentle way. Nassir knew her husband like the back of her hand, and although the words that escaped his lips were soft, and soothing, she noticed the whiteness of his knuckles as he gripped his coffee cup far tighter than necessary. She also picked up a pleading tone that seemed to rise up from the depths of his soul. Nassir could see Abdul's love for her spilling out of his eyes, but there was also a glint of hardness, a look that Nassir knew better than to cross.

So she cast her eyes downwards in a sign of respect and took on board all what Abdul said. Of course she would follow her husband's wish that was how she had been brought up. It didn't matter what she felt, she would do as she was told.

It was a week later that Nassir realised that the sacrifice that Abdul was asking of her was not something she was willing to do any longer. She had stayed indoors for the first three days, missing out on her ladies group at the mosque, going into town with Betty and enjoying a cup of tea and a cake in the Pentagon centre before heading off to the library for some new books, she even missed doing the grocery shopping, and Abdul had clearly proven that he was not capable of taking on the extra tasks like shopping – just yesterday he had completely forgotten to collect the milk and bread from the local shop.

She was beginning to feel like a prisoner in her own home. Abdul and Fareem would return each day and she would eagerly sit them down and question them about their day – news from the outside world.

Nassir knew that she was going to have to speak to Abdul about this; she could not continue in this manner and they were going to have to come up with some sort of compromise.

Exactly one week after September 11 Nassir saw an opportunity to broach the subject with Abdul.

Fareem was out with Ryan playing rugby as usual. Abdul had returned home from work and had spent the last half hour chatting away to Nassir about the university and how fortunate he was to have such sensible colleagues. He explained to Nassir that the events of a week ago had been discussed at great length and many views and opinions were disseminated over copious amounts of coffee, but at no point did anyone point the finger at Abdul because he was dark and Muslim. He had simply joined in the healthy debate, whereby he was able to hear first-hand the views of others in a peaceful environment.

Nassir could see that he had more to tell her, but she

too needed to have her say, so she politely tapped him on the arm, and interrupted, "Abdul, I do want to hear about your work, and discuss you fortunate situation, but first you need to listen to me, and the situation that I find myself in."

Abdul sat bolt upright, and looked towards Nassir with a frown starting to etch into his forehead, but he quickly turned off the television that had been on in the background, and gave Nassir his full attention. It was only then that he noticed the sadness in her eyes. He had been so involved in the last week with work, worrying about Fareem and taking care of all the extra chores that he refused to allow Nassir to do, that he had failed to notice the slump in Nassir's shoulders, and her silence. On a usual evening it was Abdul who sat back and listened to Nassir and she updated him with her daily events, only in the last week, Abdul had been doing all the chatting and Nassir had simply sat quietly and listened to all of his news. Abdul was beginning to see that all the "conversations", if you could call them that, had been one sided. Normally they would both enjoy chipping in with the odd view. But Abdul had not had any updates on Nassir and her week, and that is when it dawned on him. He suddenly realised Nassir's dilemma, and understood that it was all his own doing. Oh yes, he wanted to protect her, but the last thing he wanted to do was crush her spirit, and dampen her soul – which is exactly what he seemed to have done!

Just as the penny dropped for Abdul, so a tear slipped down Nassir's cheek, which she tried to wipe away, but Abdul had already noticed, and gently raised his hand and lovingly wiped her cheek.

"Oh, Nassir, what have I done? I am so sorry, I truly believed that I was doing the right thing. Allah himself knows, I don't want any harm to come to you, but I realise now that not allowing you to leave our home without me is no solution. Come, my dear, let me make you a cup of tea and let's discuss our situation."

Abdul wrapped his arm around Nassir's shoulders, which seemed smaller and more fragile than usual, as he ushered her into the kitchen.

So whilst sipping on hot tea, and nibbling on gingernut biscuits Abdul and Nassir talked together about a way forward. They finally agreed that Nassir would no longer be confined to the house, and would continue as before, the only difference being, Abdul did not want her wearing her hijab (the head covering traditionally worn by Muslim women).

Abdul thought that this was a good compromise. Nassir's skin was paler than both his and Fareem's and Abdul was certain that without the hijab no one would realise that she came from an ethnic background or that she was a devout Muslim.

Nassir was so relieved to finally be allowed to leave the house that she didn't contemplate how she would actually feel being in public without a hijab – she had worn a hijab since the tender age of 12. However Abdul made complete sense when he explained that in Allah's eyes she would still be seen as a devout Muslim.

"My Nassir, wearing a hijab is your choice, and

something that has been in your family for centuries, however by not wearing it you are most definitely not showing disrespect towards Allah as it clearly states in the Koran in Surah 24:31: 'And tell the believing women to lower their gaze and be modest, and to display of their adornment only that which is apparent, and to draw their veils over their chest...'

"You see, my dear, the Qur'an says nothing about covering your head, simply about being modest – which my love, you always are."

Nassir woke early the following morning, eager to get out into the fresh air. She had called Betty last night, and they had arranged to catch the bus into town and do some shopping, followed by their usual coffee and cake.

As soon as her men had left the house she began to get ready, but try as she might, she just didn't feel comfortable about her hair. Nassir looked into the mirror and saw herself for the first time, so to speak. She had never given her hair a second thought, but today she did, and she did not like what she saw. Her hair seemed to fall lifelessly down her back; she tried twisting it into a braid, but not having done anything like that in years she really didn't know what she was doing, and only resulted in causing more of a mess.

Nassir scolded herself for behaving so frivolously – what did it matter what her hair looked like? But it did matter to Nassir, and she didn't feel like she was being vain, all she wanted was to walk outside the door and feel good about herself. But with hair like this that wasn't going to happen. Nassir eventually gave in and called Betty.

"Betty I need some help. Please can you pop over and give me a hand?"

Betty had never heard Nassir sound so out of her depth; Nassir was always the one who helped Betty calm down. But today the tone in Nassir's voice was one close to panic and Betty wondered what in heaven's name could be wrong. She quickly gathered her jacket and bag, took a quick glance at herself in the mirror and then hurried over to assist Nassir. Betty knocked on the door loudly, feeling rather anxious about her friend's fate. Nassir answered and door and looked sheepishly towards Betty as she ushered her into the house.

"Nassir, hon, what is wrong?" Betty gently patted Nassir's shoulder in an effort to comfort the woman.

"It's my hair, I can't seem to do anything with it, and Abdul and I agreed last night that I would not wear my hijab when out in public."

Betty did her best to stifle a laugh. "Is that all? I was so worried when you called. Well Nassir, you called the right person, I will sort that hair out in no time at all. Did I ever tell you that I considered going into hairdressing at one time? Well, when I realised that Dwayne didn't want me to teach, I thought he might be happier with me doing something at home, so I considered hairdressing." Betty chitter chattered away, she was thrilled that for once she was able to help Nassir as it always seemed to be the other way around.

"Right Nassir, before I get started, I think we could both do with a cup of tea. Come hon, let's get that kettle on, I'm parched."

Betty's gentle way and constant talk about nothing in particular was just what Nassir needed. The horrid feeling of trepidation that had gripped her heart was starting to subside, and she was beginning to feel the tingling of excitement about getting out of the house again.

Within an hour Betty had transformed Nassir, she couldn't believe the difference. All Betty had done was given Nassir's hair a good wash, plenty of conditioner and then blow dried it. The straight lank hair now had a shine and a bounce to it. Betty had even managed to hide the bits of grey. And more importantly Nassir was happy with the outcome, she didn't feel that it was too over the top; Betty had drawn the hair back and plaited the top half, leaving the bottom half hanging down her back and shoulders.

Finally the two ladies were ready to leave the house and enjoy a day of shopping, which is precisely what they did. And no one gave Nassir a second glance, which was what she was so used to. However, Nassir still felt awfully strange without wearing her head covering. She tried to explain to Betty how she felt, but realised that it was something that Betty simply could not comprehend. The hijab for Nassir was not just a piece of cloth, it was representative of what she was, and what she believed in, and not wearing it just didn't seem right.

Nassir did her best to push these thoughts to the back of her mind. Abdul had explained that that she was not being disrespectful towards Allah by not wearing the hijab, so perhaps she just needed to give it a little bit more time. Nassir hoped that a few more outings might help her come to terms with her new look.

CHAPTER 11

As the days and weeks went by, the world slowly seemed to come to terms with the events of September 11, and the White Road Estate was no different. However there did seem to be an electrifying current, which was bubbling below the surface, just waiting for an opportunity to explode.

Sharon from the Bell Inn had also picked up on the tension in the air. These days the general talk was not about who the police had raided, and who had some gear they wanted to get rid of. No, things seemed more volatile. The regulars would spur each other with profanities about the injustice of it all. Burt was a master at egging them all along, and as Sharon had noticed, Burt really didn't need to try that hard. It seemed to her that these tough men, who had little or no education, other than the University of Life, wanted revenge. Sharon had been in the business a long time, but never before had she seen everyone rallying together for one common cause. In times gone by certain regulars would not even sit near each other simply because they were passionate about different football teams. That all seemed to have been put aside.

Sharon should have been honoured to see everyone rally together, however there was nothing honourable about this newfound kinship. It all seemed a bit sinister. Sharon felt that the talk of these men made them no better than those Al-Qaida terrorists, however for the time being it was just talk, so no harm had been done.

Sharon also understood the effects of alcohol, and perhaps if she had drunk as much as these men had then she too might feel the need to voice her anger, because yes, she too was angry about the 9/11 attacks.

The simple fact that a handful of men had been able to cause such pain and destruction in a part of the world that seemed invincible also gave Sharon a feeling of vulnerability – if they could do it to America, then they sure as hell could do it to Britain. So maybe her regulars did have a point after all, is what Sharon was feeling as Dwayne demanded another round.

Dwayne had recently teamed up with Mark – both were as uncouth as each other and a nasty streak so it made perfect sense that the two had formed a friendship. They also both had boys of the same age, only Mark's son Shane was doing his dad proud. The older he got the more he seemed to be just like his dad – a big bully. Dwayne on the other hand was bitterly disappointed in his wimp of a son.

Sharon poured another two pints of bitter for the two men and they were off on another rant again, the beer fuelling their anger.

Sharon caught the end of the conversation, "Well, me mate, I think it is about high time that this country gets to grips with immigration, if we don't let the fuckers in in the first place, we won't have to worry about them turning on us with bombs. I tell you what Dwayne, the BNP have the right idea."

"I'd like to drop a few bombs too, a good fucking

cleansing is what this country needs. "

"Now you're talking my language, son."

This was all Sharon needed – Burt had joined in too.

"I don't give a shit what people say, as far as I'm concerned if you are not white you should not be here – this is our country and it's about time we kicked those fucking dark cunts out," exploded Burt, sending spittle across the bar.

Sharon glanced over at the clock and breathed a sigh of relief, she could call last orders in ten minutes – and tonight she was not having a lock in. She just wanted these vulgar men to leave her pub and leave her in peace and quiet. Sharon just hoped that Dwayne and Mark didn't go home and take out their anger on their wives, however that was beyond her control.

Ryan had also noticed a change in his dad, which caused him to hate his dad even more – something he didn't think was possible. For the first time in years Dwayne didn't seem to be holding a grudge against the world, and taking that grudge out on Betty and Ryan. He had become passionate about defending the rights of the Western world, and could spent hours on end ranting and raving about the audacity of those rag heads who bomb our country.

Betty would just sit on the sofa and humour him, not for one moment did she take him seriously.

Ryan on the other hand couldn't stand it. Ryan was so sick of hearing his dad bad mouth dark people. This was something that he had always done, but just not to this extent, and now he had a new group of people to target – those fucking bomb making Muslims; one of Dwayne's more tamer terms.

Ryan didn't understand why his dad couldn't see that not all Muslims wanted to destroy the Western world. He also didn't understand why his dad had such a problem with black people.

The Khan family were the kindest people he had ever met. When he was with them he felt an overwhelming sense of peace. Their home gave him a sense of security that he didn't feel at home. In his own house he always seemed to be living in fear of the next attack, his stomach was permanently knotted with tension. And now his dad, his own blood, was saying the most horrific things about Fareem, Abdul and Nassir.

Ryan had taken to hiding in his room with his ear phones on, but even then his father's booming voice could be heard through Ryan's music: "Black scum," "trash," "cunting rag heads", "fucking" this "fucking" that. It just went on and on. Ryan took each insult personally. A rage was building up inside him which he hated as much as he hated his father. He blamed his father for the burning rage. Why couldn't his dad see that the Khan family weren't bad people? They were the only ones who had even shown him any form of love other than his mother.

It was a Sunday afternoon and Dwayne had returned from the pub well tanked up and had begun his usual torrent of abuse towards the Khan family. Ryan tried to block the insults out, but no matter how hard he tried his father's voice managed to pierce through his brain. Ryan couldn't take it anymore. His simmering temper was about to boil and he wanted so badly to hurt his father the way his father was hurting him with his words. So he made the biggest mistake of his life and stood up to his father. Ryan stood in the doorway of the lounge, watching his dad pace around the room blaring out his obscenities. Ryan had his fists clenched tightly next to his side, a look of pure determination filled his face. Betty noticed too late – she tried to reach Ryan's side and calm him down, but didn't make it.

Ryan blasted out, trying to sound full of authority, but the eleven-year-old's voice came out more as a pleading shrill, "If you have nothing nice to say about them why can't you just shut up." And then he ran at his dad at full speed powering into him, and then pounding his little fists into his father's stomach, tears streaking his innocent little face. And although Ryan was larger than the average boy he looked pathetically small against his father's large frame.

Betty was frozen with fear, as she looked on in horror she found the whole experience rather pitiful. Her son venting such rage on a man who they both knew would make him pay. How could she have let things get so far out of hand? She blamed herself and only wished now that Dwayne would realise this was all her doing and that she should be controlling her son. She said a quick prayer that Dwayne would now punish her and not this young, confused son of hers who was displaying so much pain and anger.

Dwayne was dumb struck for a few seconds – maybe his boy did have a little character. Dwayne was actually impressed by his son's behaviour; maybe he was a chip of the old block after all. But, he would need to be taught a lesson. Showing a little aggression with his mates was one thing but Ryan had just overstepped the mark, who did the little fucker think he was? And with that Dwayne snapped.

Dwayne's fist caught Ryan right in the stomach, gasping for breath, and kneeling over with intense pain Ryan began to throw up. As he retched the contents of his stomach out, trying to breathe, his dad kicked him in the ribs. Ryan dropped to the floor and his head began to spin, and his vision blurred. His body shouted out at him in pain, but all he could feel was an icy sensation gripping his heart – or what was left of it. Ryan passed out before his father delivered the next blow.

When Dwayne realised that Ryan was out for the count, he simply pushed past Betty into the kitchen, and grabbed a beer from the fridge. As he passed Betty, their eyes met, he pulled up his lip in a sort of sneer, and commented, "That should teach the little twerp."

Dwayne then went out of the kitchen into the back garden, and lit a cigarette, the recent incident already long forgotten.

Betty on the other hand, rushed over to Ryan, who was just coming round. He had stopped crying, his previously determined expression was now replaced with one of sadness, and disappointment. Ryan had once again let his father get the better of him. Ryan had once again lost a small section of his heart – how much heart he had left, he truly did not know, but tonight it felt like very little.

A tiny bit of warmth finally began to seep back into his soul, as his gentle, kind mother wrapped her arms around him and tried to carry him upstairs, whispering soothing words as she struggled to move her most precious possession. Ryan raised his head to his mum, and responded with a promise of his own; "Mum, I will get you away from him, I promise." But that was all he could muster, the pain was unbearable.

Ryan and Betty inched their way upstairs. Every step seemed to drain Ryan of more energy; Betty was doing her best to carry Ryan's broken body up towards his room. Once Betty had managed to settle Ryan in bed, she returned to the kitchen for some frozen vegetables, which she wrapped into a dish cloth and then went back up to Ryan's bedroom.

Ryan held the cloth to his ribs, before long it was not only his heart that had frozen over, his aching body was beginning to feel numb. After a few minutes he returned the cloth to his mum, who handed him a hot cup of chocolate milk. They both new the routine, whether it was Ryan caring for his mum, or Betty for her son, they always recovered from the beatings in the same way – a packet of frozen vegetables to easy the ache, hot chocolate to relax and feel comforted.

Ryan knew that his mum would stay with him until he fell asleep, and even then she would check on him several times during the night – just like he did for her.

Ryan also knew that this beating was no worse than any of the others, he didn't think that anything was broken, and he knew that his dad once again had delivered the punches to positions on his body that would not be seen to the rest of the world. Oh, yes, Dwayne knew what he was doing alright– his attacks on his loved ones were not acts of passion, they were more like calculated beatings to ensure he remained top dog.

As Ryan drifted off to sleep, his mind once again returned to his paradise – a time when he could take his mum away from all of his, and they could live happily without fear, pain, and humiliation. Humiliation was the one thing that Ryan was becoming very familiar with. Tonight Dwayne had humiliated Ryan, and that is what hurt the most.

"Oh, but for a time when it will all end."

CHAPTER 12

Life wasn't going all that smoothly for Fareem either. Fareem and Ryan had only been at secondary school for a few months now, and neither of them were settling in very well. The school was much bigger than their primary school.

At Magpie Junior School, Fareem had to put up with a few kids staring at him for a couple of days, but it was no big deal. Once the majority of the kids realised that he was mates with Ryan the stares stopped. And then before long people were talking to Fareem simply because they liked him; it had nothing to do with being friends with Ryan.

But secondary school was a different kettle of fish all together. Medway Secondary School, MSS as it was generally referred to, was twice the size of Magpie Junior School. And the one thing the majority of the students had in common, just like their parents from the White road Estate and neighbouring boroughs, was that they all came from one of the most deprived places in Medway, were all white and did not appreciate outsiders invading their manor. Even though Fareem had been living in Medway for some time now, the colour of his skin meant that these students – if that's what you could call them – would always consider him to be an outsider whether he knew Ryan or not. These pale skinned boys and girls would stare at Fareem's dark skin with a mixture of fear and then curiosity.

106

It didn't take long for the stares to progress to pushing Fareem in the corridor, and name calling. The main instigator was Shane – he was in the same year as Ryan and Fareem, and had also gone to Magpie Primary school, but like all bullies, he needed an audience, and at the junior school everyone recognised him for what he was and really didn't give him so much as the time of day.

However MSS was different. Shane had a new audience, and his large frame, and ability to pick on anyone who didn't side with him guaranteed him a following. Fareem was certain that Shane's crew joined up with him simply because he was better to have as a friend than an enemy. No one wanted to be on the other end of Shane's foul mouth and large fists. The only person Shane didn't seem to have the courage to stand up against was Ryan, but then they did go back a long way. They had known each other for as long as either could remember. There was once a time a long, long time ago when they had actually been friends, but these days they both just chose to ignore each other.

Their dads on the other hand got on like a house on fire. Dwayne and Mark's relationship seemed to have strengthened after 9/11 once they both realised they had the same dreams and ideals – a white Britain. Shane's dad, Mark, had encouraged Shane to follow in his footsteps – taking the path of righteousness, not being afraid to speak out for what you believe in, to take what rightfully belongs to you, and to cast out anyone who does not belong.

Shane had become indoctrinated by his father over the last few months, and so now, he truly believed that by targeting Fareem he was triumphing over evil. However Shane may have started out believing that he was doing the right thing, but somewhere along the way he began to enjoy the power that he felt when hurting or intimidating others. And before long, he was getting satisfaction out of others pain, and that is what encouraged him to continue on his bullying campaign – not because he was fighting for what was right, but because the suffering of others excited and enthralled him.

Shane began to cast his vicious tongue and use his fists on just about anyone who was different. There was Chel who he referred to as four eyes, Becky was known as fatty and George was gay boy or homo. As for Fareem, the usual phrases were "Paki" or bomber, or just "that brown piece of shit." The bigger Shane's audience, the cruder the names got. George and Fareem got the worst of Shane's wrath; Fareem because he was black and George simply because he was , a quiet shy, rather softly spoken boy, who always seemed more comfortable around the girls.

Fareem began to despise Shane more than anything, but what he hated the most was that he did not have the courage or strength to stand up to the "wanker" - as Ryan and Fareem had started calling Shane.

Fareem soon realised that the best form of defence was to survive, and so he did his best to avoid Shane at all costs, and tried never, never to be alone with him. As for the taunts and jibes, Fareem learned to just ignore them completely. Abdul had warned Fareem about his sort and always advised Fareem to simply remain calm and restrained, no matter how cruel Shane became.

Ryan on the other hand, did not remain calm or restrained. He hated Shane more than Fareem did. Ryan would frequently comment on how Shane represented everything that he despised. Shane reminded Ryan of his own father, and although Ryan did not have the strength or courage to stand up to his father, he dammed well had the strength and courage to stand up to Shane.

It all came to a head in October 2001 – about one and a half months after September 11. Ryan and Fareem had survived the first term of secondary school, and were looking forward to the October half term. The weather was still reasonably warm, and both boys planned to spend their days out in the open air, playing rugby, fishing, and generally just having fun. And so on the last day of term, as Fareem and Ryan reached the school gates, Fareem realised that he had left his school bag in the classroom and so ran back to get it. He was in such a good mood, feeling very carefree and happy and it is perhaps for this reason that he forgot to take his usual precautions.

Fareem pushed up his pace as he headed for the classroom, he ran around the bend and straight into Shane, hitting him full on in the chest. At first he didn't realise it was Shane and simply apologised with the intention of continuing. It was only when Fareem raised his head and their eyes met that he realised and an icy fear instantly gripped his heart. Shane's eyes seemed to narrow and fill with an evil glint. The expression on his face was one of absolute delight – he very seldom came across Fareem and never alone. Shane's expression slowly turned to what can only be described as a snarl.

Fareem thought back to this day many times over the years, and the same image of Shane always filled his mind. Fareem was convinced that he was salivating, licking his lips in anticipation of the kill. For a silly second, Fareem actually believed that he stood a chance of standing his ground with the madman. He was a rugby player after all, and he was not afraid of a bit of a scuffle, but then Shane's posse seemed to appear from nowhere, and Fareem knew he stood no chance. Shane was now going to make a point, he was going to ensure that his posse remembered who was boss and Fareem was the one who was going to pay. He was determined not to give up without a fight so he braced himself in the most commanding, confident stance he could muster, and arrogantly spat back at Shane, "Yeah, so, big boy, what have you got to offer you big woozy." Fareem knew that he was signing his death warrant, but he was sick to death of hiding from this bully. Today, he would go down fighting proudly. "Fuck Shane and his posse."

Shane seemed please that his little brown bitch was putting up a fight, and so began with casual taunts – "Paki", "stinking brown shit", "go back to where you come from" – nothing that Fareem had not heard before. But Fareem was not in the mood to just stand back and take the taunts, so, as he braced himself for the biggest hiding of his life he raised his hand and prodded Shane in the chest, "Is that the best you can do, you pathetic piece of shit."

Shane could not believe his luck, this little prick, who always had Ryan to protect him, was actually making himself fair game, but as much as Shane was enjoying the banter, he wanted to get this over with.

He had a cute little bird waiting for him at the local shop, so the sooner he fucked up the little Paki shit, and got his tongue down his bird's throat the better. It was time to up the ante for this little episode which he knew would not take long, however some sick part of him wanted to ensure that he drew out Fareem's pain and humiliation for a long as possible so he slowly began to shove and push the little shit around.

Shane noticed his posse circling around them and his chest filled with pride; these boys were his, and they were showing their respect for him, by encouraging this most enjoyable beating.

Fareem on the other hand, had suddenly begun to see some sense, and he realised that goading Shane on was probably not his best move and now he had no way to escape. All of a sudden a beating was not really what he wanted, so he did his best to shut up, and pray that he didn't antagonise Shane any further. But then the posse started chanting – white, white, white is right, and this just seemed to spur Shane onto another level. By this stage Fareem was getting pushed and prodded left right and centre by Shane, who was clearly loving every minute.

111

Ryan must have heard the taunts and he appeared just as Shane spat at Fareem – the mixture of gob and snot got him right on the cheek and Shane laughed as it slowly slid down Fareem's dark skin. When he started to clear his throat for another go, Ryan charged at him like a bull. He bouldered past the posse, head down, fists clenched and hit Shane with full force in the chest. Shane stumbled back a few paces then managed to gain his footing. The posse were no longer interested in Fareem and he was able to slip away to the side out of the spotlight. All eyes were now on Ryan and Shane.

At first Shane looked as though he was looking forward to this encounter. Not only had he managed to get his hands on Fareem, but now he would get a pop at the annoying prat who had taken it on himself to protect those weaker than him – all those who Shane had built his powerful, fearful reputation on – and everyone would see who was really in charge. But when Shane saw the expression on Ryan's face his stance and composure changed and he realised he might be in for a hiding himself.

Fareem's gaze was fixed on Ryan, who had taken on a look that he didn't recognise. Ryan's face was full of anger, in fact his whole body seemed to be bubbling with rage. His eyes were focused solely on Shane, his teeth clenched. Ryan swung his right fist through the air with such speed and intensity that Shane didn't even see it coming. It landed smack on the side of Shane's cheek – funnily enough at the same place where the spit had hit Fareem. A crack like that of a gun firing greeted the air as cheek and fist collided. Fareem heard the posse inhale, clearly recognising that their leader was going to be man down. Blood spurted from the cheek, which Shane tried to wipe away and regain his posture. But Ryan didn't let it stop there. He planted a massive punch to Shane's stomach, who fell forward clenching his belly as Ryan raised his knee straight into Shane's chin. Shane's head flew back and his eyes lost focus.

Something inside Fareem suddenly clicked and he realised that he needed to stop Ryan; he had lost control and was going to kill Shane if someone didn't interfere. But at the same time, Fareem didn't recognise the Ryan that stood in front of him. The Ryan Fareem knew was peaceful and calm and would never hurt a fly. It was as though something in him had snapped. Getting in between Shane and Ryan seemed like suicide, but Fareem could and would not stand by and watch his best friend ruin his life by trying to protect him. As Fareem ran boldly towards the two of them, he whispered to himself, "Allah, may peace be upon him, protect me as I protect my brother."

Fareem grabbed hold of Ryan's arm, and shrieking at the top of his voice, he begged Ryan to stop. Shane was lying on the floor groaning in agony, but Ryan wasn't listening. He raised his left leg and as he was about to kick Shane in the lower back, Fareem lowered his voice, and in as calm and controlled manner as he could, he pleaded with Ryan to stop. But Ryan seemed to be in a different world, he clearly couldn't or chose not to hear Fareem. Eventually Fareem threw himself on top of Shane, not knowing what else to do. Ryan seemed to slow down for a second, and finally Fareem saw something register in Ryan's eyes. He lowered his leg and took a step backwards. He looked down at Fareem lying on top of Shane, and slowly his face returned to the Ryan Fareem knew.

Ryan then put out his hand towards Fareem, who accepted the gesture and grabbed hold of it as hoisted Ryan him up onto his feet, leaving Shane on the floor. Ryan took one look at Shane and then turned and walked away. Not at any stage during the whole encounter did he say a thing.

It was only when Fareem and Ryan reached the school gate and started walking home that Ryan said, "Did you get your school bag?" Fareem replied, "Yes," and they never mentioned the incident again.

Shane ended up with a broken cheekbone, and severe bruising, but he never did press charges, and by the time October half term was over and all were back at school again, he too pretended nothing had happened. From that day on Shane gave both Ryan and Fareem a wide berth.

Something came over Ryan that day, a side to him that Fareem never thought he was capable of. The Ryan that Fareem knew and loved was a quiet, thoughtful and considerate person, always dreaming about a future with his mum and not his dad. Ryan was smart too. Fareem and he would often sit and debate various issues, and on more than one occasion Fareem would be surprised at Ryan's natural ability to seek a solution from outside the box. Ryan seemed to have the wisdom of someone far older than his eleven years.

Fareem was not at all surprised that Ryan had protected him, as Ryan was a true and loyal friend, more like a brother, but Fareem had not anticipated the violence that had overcome Ryan, and this was something that bothered Fareem for many years to come.

As for Ryan, he may have never discussed the incident with Fareem, but he never forgot that day. He battled with his conscience for many months afterward. Ryan despised the way he had acted and how his body had taken on a life of its own. Ryan couldn't actually remember seeing Shane, or hitting him. But he did remember an extreme sense of anger flooding through his body as he heard the taunting and realised that his best and only friend, the person who had never brought harm to anyone, the one person in his life who had supplied Ryan with some form of sanctuary from his excuse for a life, was being hurt. As Ryan ran towards the sounds of the taunts he vaguely remembered an odd tingling sensation in his fingers, it was as if all the blood in his body was heading towards my fists, willing him to cause pain and suffering to those who deserved it.

Ryan also never forgot the sweet taste of blood in his mouth – Shane's blood. When Ryan's fist slammed into Shane's cheek bone, the blood squirted straight into Ryan's mouth. But what saddened Ryan the most was the actual enjoyment he felt at tasting his opponent's blood. As Ryan walked away from the scene of chaos he was overcome with a sense of fulfilment and achievement. It may have been the taste of blood and sweat, or the smell of fear reeking off Shane, or a combination of all three, that brought about a lightness in Ryan's heart. He had finally been able to put a stop to all the pain and suffering that Fareem had to endure on a daily basis and this filled Ryan with an overwhelming sense of satisfaction.

It was this feeling that scared Ryan more than ever. He had acted in a manner that he despised and used his fists just like his father always did. He had let his temper take control, and had caused pain and suffering by using violence.

Ryan's mother had not brought him up to behave in such a manner – he respected his mum more than ever, and realised that today he had not only let down himself but also his mum and Fareem – the two people who meant the world to him. Ryan's mum had taught him to fight his battles through words, pens and books –she always said, "You need to read and write and articulate your thoughts my son, this will take you to great places, not fists and fights." Until this day Ryan hadn't thought he had it in him to behave so violently. A small thought kept on forcing its way to the forefront of Ryan's mind, and as hard as he tried to push it back, it just kept rearing its ugly head – perhaps he was more like his dad than he dared to imagine.

Ryan tried his best to push these exploding thoughts away, he never wanted his mother to find out about that incident, and he definitely did not want to mention it to Fareem again, but he did realise that he was desperately unhappy and needed someone to turn to, someone who would not judge him, someone who would guide him and help him overcome the terrible rage that had built up inside of him.

CHAPTER 13

Nassir was also in turmoil. She was finding it harder and harder to leave the house without a head covering. Nassir hoped that with time this feeling would fade, but the opposite was happening. Nassir felt naked without her hijab. It was part of her whole being, and by not wearing it she believed that she was not only insulting Islam, but also herself. Nassir was proud of her religion, and all it stood for, why should she suffer because of the acts of others?

The incident in the Pentagon centre yesterday just reconfirmed her thoughts. She had just walked into the Pentagon centre, and saw one of the ladies from the mosque walking in her direction. Nassir had only met the lady on one or two occasions, but she immediately recognised her – she was wearing the lovely blue hijab that Nassir had liked. Nassir automatically raised her hand and waved at the lady, who just walked straight past her showing absolutely no sign of recognition whatsoever. Nassir was devastated, and began to wonder if she had said or done anything to be treated so, and then it dawned on her – without her Muslim attire Nassir was not recognisable as a Muslim women, and so the lady had most probably not even noticed her. Nassir decided there and then that she would defy her husband's wishes and wear her hijab in public! She went directly to the bathroom and pulled her hijab out of her handbag, and wrapped it around her head and neck, she then glanced in the mirror, adjusted the head covering slightly and then smiled at the reflection – yes, she was a Muslim woman, and she was not going to hide that fact from anyone.

Nassir did feel slightly guilty about deceiving Abdul, however she consoled this guilt by reminding herself that she was once again being respectful to Allah (may peace be upon him).

Abdul was none the wiser, although he did pick up on a change in Nassir's demeanour, he just couldn't put his finger on the reason for this. After their discussion Nassir had returned to her cheerful self, however this hadn't lasted and Abdul had put it down to the fact that she was concerned about Fareem and school. He did not at any time recognise that she was in fact in turmoil with herself with regards to the head covering. And then overnight Nassir once again returned to the cheery self. Abdul didn't think that for one minute Nassir would go against his wishes – she was a dutiful Muslim wife after all. So when the lightness returned to her voice, he just gave a sigh of relief and focused his attention once again on his busy lecturing schedule.

Unfortunately this carefree, cheery attitude of Nassir's did not last long. Three weeks after she had made the decision to wear the hijab again, Betty and Nassir headed off on the bus into Chatham for their usual trip to exchange library books, maybe a bit of window shopping, and then finally tea and cake in Katie's Cake Shop in Rochester High Street. It was a fair walk from Chatham High Street to Rochester, however that was how Nassir and Betty justified having a rather large piece of cake at Katie's. They would then catch the bus home.

Betty and Nassir had just about reached the Rochester train station, and were passing under the railway bridge deep in conversation about how they both wished the lady at the library would meet a nice, young man. They didn't notice the white transit van pull slowly up alongside them until the driver wound down his window and hurled a half-eaten hamburger in Nassir's direction shouting, "How do you like that, you dirty terrorist bomber, just fuck off back to your own country."

The hamburger hit Nassir right in the centre of her cheek, spattering her face with tomato sauce. She raised her arm and tried desperately to wipe it off, but only managed to spread it further across her face, and into her hijab. The vehicle then sped off, the driver laughing at the reaction of the two women.

Nassir was too shocked to speak, and all Betty could say was, "Hang on, hon. I have a tissue in here somewhere," as she frantically searched around in her bag. She eventually pulled out a crumpled tissue from her bag, and began dabbing Nassir's face, doing her best to calm Nassir down as she did.

"Nassir, you have to report this to the police, people can't get away with that sort of behaviour, come on let's go straight to the nick now. I have been told that the police have a hate crime unit that deals with crimes like this." Betty urged Nassir forward, who was still rooted to the spot. "Come on Nassir, you know how important it is to report things like these, let's get moving."

Nassir gently grabbed Betty's arm, and tried to get her attention. Betty eventually stopped talking and looked at Nassir expectantly. Nassir raised her eyes and Betty noticed them filling up with tears. In a pleading tone Nassir explained to Betty that she could not report it, as then Abdul would find out that she had been deceiving him, and she did not want that.

"Betty please, let's just forget about it, it was really no big deal."

Betty pulled Nassir into her arms and gave her a hug, "I understand Nassir, this won't go any further, let's go get that cup of tea, I think we both need it."

Neither of them said much over tea, neither of them bothered with the cake. The mood had changed and to be honest they both just wanted to get home, lock the door, and then try to forget the whole incident. However the stench of the hamburger seemed to be etched into Nassir's nostrils, giving her a constant reminder of her ordeal. She did her best to put on a show for Betty, pretending that it was no big deal, but deep down she felt dreadful. The image of the man kept flashing across her brain; he had looked at her with such hatred, and disdain. That stranger who Nassir had never met before had violated her very being. She had been singled out because of who she was and what she believed in.

Betty and Nassir finally got home an hour later. Betty gave Nassir a gentle squeeze on the arm, and promised Nassir to call her if she needed to talk. They then went their separate ways.

Nassir locked her front door, collapsed into a heap on the ground and sobbed her heart out. She cried so hard and for so long that eventually her throat began to hurt, and her shoulders ached. It was only the sound of the front gate opening that brought her out of her sorrow. Realising that Abdul was home from work, she quickly got up and hurried off to the bathroom.

Nassir took one look at herself in the mirror and groaned in despair – her face was red, her eyes were blood shot and puffy and as she didn't really wear make-up other than a little blush and lipstick, she knew she was not going to be able to hide this from Abdul. So Nassir looked into the mirror, took three deep breaths and prepared herself for the next confrontation.

As horrid as the events of the day at been, Nassir was more nervous about explaining to her husband that she had gone behind his back, defied him, and been assaulted because of it. Perhaps wearing the hijab didn't make her a good Muslim woman after all – a good Muslim woman would definitely not disobey a direct order from their husband. Nassir realised that she probably needed to do some inner soul searching. Even if Abdul forgave her for her deviant actions, it would take Nassir awhile to forgive herself.

Nassir heard Abdul walk into the kitchen calling out for her, "Nassir, honey, where are you? Do you want a cup of tea? I'm parched, I will put the kettle on. Where is Fareem? No wait, let me guess – he is out playing rugby with Ryan."

Nassir took one last look at herself in the mirror, hoping for a miracle, but not getting one. Her eyes were so puffy they were nearly closed, and her blotchy face seemed to be intensified by the paleness of her skin, the colour had drained from her face, and the outcome was not a pretty sight.

Nassir walked sheepishly into the kitchen, kept her eyes lowered, settled into the kitchen chair, and then broached the subject that she knew they were going to have to discuss. "Abdul, something happened today, we need to talk."

Abdul was still facing the kitchen counter but quickly spun around in concern. He took one look at Nassir, and panic starting rising in his chest. He grabbed Nassir's small delicate hand roughly, and uttered words that he prayed she would not answer, "Is it Fareem?"

Nassir raised her eyes and met her husband's fearful gaze, "No my husband, it is not Fareem, he is fine, it is me."

The grip of Abdul hand loosed slightly as he realised that whatever had gone on today was not good, but Fareem and Nassir were still alive and breathing. Then he glanced over at Nassir again and saw the distress, fear and sadness engulf her face. The rising panic began to subside, but was soon replaced by a feeling that he couldn't quite put his finger on. It was a mixture of fury, anger and fear. Who had caused his wife so much heartache? His natural instincts automatically seemed to take charge of his body. He was meant to protect his wife. He obviously was not doing his duty, and that is something that he too would have to come to terms with, but at that precise moment in time, he wanted revenge.

Nassir noticed the loosening grip, and could visibly see the fear in his eyes being replaced by that hard glint, a look that Nassir didn't often see in her husband, however she had seen it often enough to recognise it – his wife was in pain, and he wanted someone to pay.

Nassir quickly tried to pull him out of his 'trance' and reassured him that she was absolutely fine, just a little tearful and upset, and that she had probably overreacted.

"Abdul, everything that happened today is because of my own doing, it is not your fault. My biggest mistake has been not to do as I was told. Please Abdul, let me explain, and please Abdul before I say anymore, you must believe that I never would have disobeyed you if I had your prowess, intelligence, and clearly worldly ways. In my defence, I was only doing what I thought was best, but let me tell you, and then you can decide."

Abdul, realising that he wife wasn't actually physically hurt, and simply upset, calmed down, and promised Nassir that he would listen. Even though ever nerve in his body was demanding retribution, a quite controlled voice that came from the depths of his soul seemed to speak to him soothingly and calmly. The sensible part of him finally won and his mind stopped spinning, his muscles relaxed and he once again took control of the situation.

"Yes, my love, I will let you speak, but perhaps we

need a cup of tea first, and then you can tell me what is going on."

Nassir relieved to find that the Abdul she knew and loved was back, quickly responded and made them each a cup of tea.

They then sat down opposite each other, the old wooden kitchen table separating them. The kitchen table had become an integral part of the lives, it was a wedding present, which like Nassir and Abdul had seen better days. It was as though their lives had become ingrained in the wooden cracks; each revealing a different era, drama or success of their lives. Nassir clasped her tea cup with one hand, but used the other to gently rub the table, taking comfort in its familiarity.

Abdul settled back into his kitchen chair, which to the naked eye looked like all the others, but over the years he had managed to mould it to his shape. In fact, it had become a little family game – Fareem would switch the chairs around unbeknown to his dad, and then giggle uncontrollably when his dad sat down and grumbled as he returned the chairs to their correct "homes."

But there was no giggling in the kitchen that afternoon, both Nassir and Abdul were sitting sullenly, Nassir still horrified about the day's events, and Abdul still nervous about what Nassir was to say. He had done his best to appear calm and controlled for Nassir's sake, but he felt sick to his stomach with worry, and was doing his best to sip his tea.

Nassir began to tell her story. It took a good hour for her to relay not just the recent incident but also to convey her feelings about not wearing her hijab and the humiliation she felt when the Islamic lady from the mosque had failed to greet her. And finally she told Abdul why she chose to disobey him. At this point she broke down and once again cried uncontrollably. Abdul wrapped his arms around her and gently rocked her from side her side. He whispered soothing words, trying to calm her down. Whilst gently stroking her hair, he had time to think, and even though Nassir hadn't got as far as what had happened whilst on the way home with Betty, Abdul had pretty much realised what had happened. By the time Nassir finished her tale of events, Abdul was leaning forward, resting his arms on the table, hanging his head low, and shaking it with dismay.

He finally raised his head, reached forward and grabbed hold of Nassir's hands. "Nassir, please, now it is your turn to listen to me. What happened today is my fault. Once again I have done my best to protect you but have inadvertently caused you pain and suffering.

"Nassir, I am not surprised about the incident today, as there have been several similar attacks on Muslim students at the university. I took it upon myself to keep these attacks hidden from you because I didn't want to cause you unnecessary stress or concern. And so in hiding the truth from you, as you have hidden the truth from me, I have caused you pain and suffering."

Abdul let go of Nassir's hands and walked over to her side, he dropped his head into her lap and wrapped his arms around her legs. He wished with all his heart that he could take away Nassir's humiliation and suffering. But once again his sensible voice took hold of him, he took a deep breath and stood up and returned to his chair. The next time he opened his mouth it was in a controlled and careful manner.

"Nassir, we are living in difficult times; once again our beliefs are coming under scrutiny, and many people hate us for what we are. In some ways Nassir the wars that we have lived through were easier than the battles we are going to have to endure for the foreseeable future. Back home in Chagcharan, my biggest worry was staying warm and having a full belly, but as I look back those concerns seem trivial now. Nassir, I don't know how to protect you and Fareem from those who have chosen to hate us. And that my dear is my biggest fear – you and Fareem are my world. The events of today have opened our eyes to the truth and reality of life in Britain for a Muslim. I have realised that I cannot protect you or Fareem from this war. So where do we go from here?"

Nassir could not recall a time when Abdul had turned to her for advice on anything other than the care of Fareem. He had often asked for her views on different topics, but not actual advice, and that is when Nassir realised that today was a learning curve for all of them. Nassir's state of mind was in just as much turmoil as Nassir's. She could not answer Abdul, and so stood up and reached for the Koran.

"Perhaps Abdul it is time to turn to the great Prophet Muhammad, may peace be upon him, and seek his advice and guidance."

And so they began to pray together, Abdul chanting

the prayers and allowing for Nassir to follow.

By the time Fareem returned home, muddy and sweaty from rugby practice, life had returned to normal for Abdul and Nassir, or at least they both tried to pretend. Fareem was fortunately so excited about being chosen to play right wing in the match the following morning against Aylesford that he didn't notice Nassir's puffy eyes, or the worry lines that were creasing Abdul's forehead.

The news about the rugby match brought lightness to Nassir's heart, and she thanked Allah for her precious child who displayed such eagerness and delight that the emotion was contagious. Nassir was able to block out the earlier part of the day and indulge in Fareem's excitement. And so on hearing the news she automatically knelt down and gave Fareem a big cuddle whilst congratulating him. Fareem, quickly shrugged her off – didn't she realise he was too old for such affection from his mother?! However secretly he appreciated the gesture.

Abdul noticed Fareem shrugging off his mum, so chose instead to walk over and shake the boy's hand, whilst congratulating him. Fareem seemed to grow in stature, and felt a surge of pride as he realised that today he had not only proved to himself that he could achieve, but also to his folks, who supported him one hundred percent. He knew only too well that Ryan would not get the same reception from his family. Fareem understood that these were hard times for his family, but at least they all had each other – it was more than Ryan could say.

"Well we can't go out for a celebratory meal with you dressed like that Fareem. Come on go and have a quick shower, then give Ryan a call and see if he wants to join us for an early meal – you obviously need to get a good night's rest before your big match tomorrow." Abdul smiled at Nassir whilst shooing Fareem out of the room. After the events of the day, he felt that they could all do with a bit of a treat.

So half an hour later they all climbed into the little red Escort, and headed off for Pizza Hut in Maidstone. Ryan and Fareem had their heads locked together in the back seat, discussing rugby tactics for the big game tomorrow. Ryan was just as excited as Fareem, and it was lovely to watch such innocence and joy unfold.

On arrival at Pizza Hut, they were fortunate enough to get a table straight away in a corner as quiet as can be. The place was heaving – everyone else in Kent obviously had had the same idea. And as it was a family restaurant, there was lots of noise; a crying baby at the far end of the room, a small toddler was sitting behind them doing his best to spread the pizza all over his face and a kids' party on the other side. It was a festive atmosphere.

No sooner had their food arrived, when a tall slim man tapped Ryan on the shoulder. Abdul automatically expecting the worst took a deep intake of breath. Nassir gripped his hand tightly under the table. Ryan slowly turned around, and then his face broke into a huge grin and he tugged at Fareem who also turned around to greet this stranger.

"Well, well, fancy meeting my two best players here. Make sure you get a good feed tonight, you are going to need it for tomorrow, it's going be a tough game my boys."

Both Fareem and Ryan were awash with pride and had silly little grins on their faces. Not only were they playing tomorrow, but coach had just called them his best players.

The coach then looked up towards Nassir and Abdul expectantly. "Well, come on boys, aren't you going to introduce me?"

The boys quickly recovered their manners. "Eh, sorry coach, these are Fareem's folks," Ryan started and Fareem finished the sentence for him, "Mum, Dad, this is our rugby coach."

"Well now, Fareem I would never have guessed, if you hadn't mentioned it," chuckled Abdul.

"Pleased to meet you, Fareem's mum and dad, I hope to see you at the big game tomorrow. Now I will leave you be and go back to my own family."

Before leaving he ruffled the boy's hair, and gave them another few words of advice whilst winking over at Abdul and Nassir. It was evident to see the respect that Fareem and Ryan had for this big man, who was clearly a rugby player in his day.

The rest of the evening passed by pleasantly with the conversation was centred around the big game tomorrow. Nassir suspected that neither boy would get too much sleep tonight. She had never really been a big rugby fan, but was determined to support Fareem. It looked like she would be spending the next few Sundays standing out in the cold watching Fareem and Ryan run around the rugby field chasing an oval shaped ball – perhaps one day she would learn to love the sport!

On returning home, Ryan thanked Nassir and Abdul, and then headed back to his house, promising to knock for Fareem as soon as he was up and about the next morning.

The Khan family headed into their cosy home, which was a pleasant contrast to the icy wind that was picking up outside. They headed straight to the kitchen. Abdul put the kettle on for hot chocolate, whilst Nassir pulled out the ironing board – Fareem's rugby uniform would need to be ironed for the following morning.

Nassir was hoping to instil in Fareem the importance of preparation, so before he was allowed to crawl into his bed, he had to first ensure that everything was ready for his big day tomorrow – clean rugby boots were at the bottom of his bed and the washed and ironed shorts and Rugby shirt were folded carefully and placed on his desk. Finally Fareem turned off his light and tried his best to sleep. He was by this stage a little bit too old to be "tucked in" but this still didn't stop both Nassir and Abdul popping their heads in to kiss their son goodnight.

Fareem fell asleep dreaming of scoring a try, but for Nassir and Abdul, sleep was a little harder. Even though they had been able to spend the last few hours focusing solely on their son and his achievements, they were not able to blank out of their minds Nassir's unpleasant experience from earlier in the day.

CHAPTER 14

Abdul was devastated by the hamburger incident, and although he was grateful that Nassir had seemingly put it behind her, it still bothered him. He had also realised that something had happened at the school with Ryan and Fareem before the half term.

He had noticed the bruise on Ryan's cheek, which both boys had assured Abdul came from rugby, however they had not fooled him. He also knew that whatever had happened would have been because Fareem was dark and Muslim. But what concerned Abdul more than anything, was that all this harm that was coming to his family was as a result of nineteen suicide bombers who had taken it upon themselves to bring carnage and destruction to the Western world all in the name of Allah (may peace be upon him). These were Abdul's so called "brothers" but they had taken Islam and distorted it for their own means. At the very back of his mind was a thought that kept piercing his subconscious – how could Allah (may peace be upon him) let this happen?

Abdul returned to work on Monday and confided in a colleague, Dirk, who he had become very friendly with over the past few months. Dirk had recently moved over to the UK from South Africa. They made an unlikely pair to the outside world, but apart from their apparent differences, they realised that they were actually very similar, with the same views and opinions on life, religion (even though one was a Christian and the other a

Muslim) and they also shared a similar treatment from the outside world.

Dirk was a typical Afrikaans, South African man – he had a large frame, with big hands, deeply tanned skin and a thick accent. His usual attire was a buttoned up short sleeve shirt and shorts which displayed his brown, hairy legs that looked more like tree trunks than anything else. The whole outfit was finished off with a pair of "veld skoener" tough walking shoes that were more suited to the 'African veld' than the urban streets of the university. This gave others the overall impression that he was a man of little etiquette, who had probably seen lots of "action" in the crime ridden country of South Africa, and he obviously would not want to associate with Abdul, the black man, who he would most probably refer to as, "Hey kaffir." Well, the overall impression couldn't have been more wrong.

Abdul and Dirk hit it off immediately. Dirk was classed as a hater of black people simply because of where he came from, just like Abdul was a terrorist bomber because he was a Muslim. Unlike Abdul, Dirk had been living with this attitude for years, whereas Abdul was only just becoming accustomed to other people's discriminations. Dirk was therefore a great sense of comfort for Abdul. When Abdul relayed the recent events, rather than looking on in horror, Dirk simply patted Abdul comfortingly on the arm, and nodded his head knowingly. Dirk then proceeded to explain to Abdul how he had survived the cruel jokes, snide comments, and simple lack of understanding of who he was and where he was from. He then spoke to Abdul about what it was like to grow up in South Africa.

"I was born into a middle class Afrikaans family, however my father did marry well, so we were perhaps better off than most because of my mother's background. My father was a police officer and my mother a secretary. The best way to describe my dad is a typical Boer – he was a very strict man, who would not tolerate bad behaviour. My brothers and I grew up in fear of the man, one step out of line meant the sjambok (a heavy leather whip). I look back today and wonder what people would think if I decided to discipline my children in a similar matter – social services would be knocking on the door in no time at all. My brothers and I grew up to respect our elders; we were seen but not heard. These days we are all professional people. My eldest brother Wilfred is the manager of a large sales company in South Africa, Ben is a doctor and I am a university lecturer. Have we all achieved because we were always pushed to our limits, and expected to succeed? I don't know, but I can tell you this my friend, I feared the sjambok, and so did push myself to the limit – failure resulted in a nice red mark across our bums!

"We grew up in Port Elizabeth, the east coast of South Africa, in a large five bedroom house. This meant I never had to share a room with either of my brothers and there was also a spare room for guests. We had a huge kitchen which my mom had decorated to make it look like a traditional farm kitchen (one fairly similar to what she was brought up with). The kitchen was probably the most comfortable room in the house, it always smelt of freshly cooked food, and due to the heat the back door was pretty much always open. I would often sit at the end of the breakfast table, and feel the draft from the back door cooling my neck, whilst enjoying the smells of the next meal, and the gentle chatter between my mum and Grace (our maid).

"The kitchen led into the dining room, which was in itself a big room, but was overshadowed by the rather large, dark, oak dining room table that could quite easily sit ten. Every evening dinner was served at six without fail. We were all expected to be washed, seated and ready at the table five minutes before six o'clock – failure to any of the above resulted in—"

"No wait," interrupted Abdul, "let me guess, the sjambok."

"Ja boet, you got that right."

My two brothers and I would sit up straight at the table, looking solemn, hands clasped and placed on the top of the table, whilst waiting for my father to grace us with his presence – he always entered the room dead on six o'clock. This is when we boys would start having fun under the table. We would do our best to kick each other in the shins as hard as possible knowing full well that the first one to show any form of expression, whether that being sheer delight at hitting a brother full on in the shins, or a grimace of pain as the heel dug in, would mean stern words from my father. Being the youngest I was at a clear disadvantage having the shortest legs! Ja boet, you guessed it, I normally ended up with rather bruised shins, however I got my own back in other ways – but that, my friend is a different story, and I haven't finished this one yet.

"So, back to the dinner table; as soon as my father sat down, the dining room door would open, and Grace would walk in carrying the food. It would all be laid out on the table. Mum would usually help Grace, who would then retire to her room at the bottom of the garden. This would be followed by grace, which we were all expected to say together. I still giggle to this day at Grace our maid, and saying grace before dinner – silly I know, but it made my brothers and I chuckle at the time.

"There were occasions when this routine changed and that was generally over the weekend, when my parents were either entertaining, or were out being entertained. On the evenings when my parents were entertaining, we were expected to greet the guests as they arrived and then disappear. Now depending on the type of function would depend on what my brothers and I would then do. Our TV room also happened to be the bar, so if the rugby was showing then there was no chance that we would be allowed in the TV room as this is where all the friends would gather, the men drinking Brandy and coke, and cheering on the Springboks, and the ladies, sipping Sherry quietly and chatting to themselves.

"Therefore during the rugby session we were either expected to play in our rooms, or outside. The lounge was completely out of bounds for all children at all times and even thought there was also a massive TV in this room we were not allowed into it. My brothers being older, were quite content to disappear into their rooms, I however would head for the bottom of the garden and my second family – Grace's family!

"As a child I spent most of my time with Grace. Being the youngest brother, my mum was eager to get back to work as soon as she had stopped breast feeding me – I don't really think it was the work she missed, more the adult company. My father expected her to remain at home with the children, however he eventually had to agree that she was perhaps better off working. So from the tender age of eight months, I was left at home with Grace as both my brothers were at school by this stage – I am known as what we refer to in Afrikaans as a laat lamijie or a late lamb, so in other words I was the afterthought.

"During the day Grace would strap me to her back, and carry me around the house, whilst cleaning and polishing, and always singing to me in her native language Xhosa. By the time I was two, I was speaking more Xhosa than English. It was also at this time that Grace had her first child.

"Grace and her husband Tobias, lived at the bottom of our garden, in what we referred to as an ikhaya, but I guess what you would call a granny flat. Tobias was our gardener, he was a good man, with a big friendly smile and a body built like a bull which made him a good hard worker. However he did like to drink and gamble, and would every now and again need to be brought back down to earth by my father.

"Grace grew up on my grandparent's farm, in fact her mum cared for my mum when she was growing up, so when my mum got married, and moved out of the farm house, Grace naturally came with her. She was just sixteen when she started working for my mum and dad.

"Sorry Abdul, but this story seems to move off in tangents – please stop me if you have heard enough."

"Dirk, please continue, I am fascinated, never before have I heard about life in Africa, however I have always wondered, and this is not what I expected."

"Okay, mate, as long as you are sure. So like I was saying Grace had her first child just after I turned two. Well, to start with I was rather put out, firstly this new baby was now carried around on Grace's back, and I was expected to walk, but what I hated even more, was that this baby got to go back to the ikhaya each night with Grace, whereas I had to remain in the big house, with my two older brothers who enjoyed teasing me, and my strict father, and my mother who was by this stage so involved in her new social life that children were not of much interest to her.

"I tell you, I started to hate the little black kid, with his little flat nose, tight curly hair, and skin the colour of dark coffee. However Grace seemed to sense this, and so worked hard to include me as much as possible in helping out with the baby. She would encourage me to sing soft lullabies with her when Nkosie could not settle, all in the soft, gentle clicking Xhosa language. I was even allowed to hold him now and again, and eventually I grew to love him. By the time Nkosie was three and I

138

was five we were inseparable. We spent our days in the garden, under the hot African sky. Grace would do her best to bring us indoors during the hottest part of the day, but we never came very willingly – my garden was our playground, and boy did we play. Tobias was always about, so he managed to keep an eye on us. One of our favourite games was chasing the dogs around the garden – which never really impressed our two Labradors much, who preferred to lie around in the shade, however they could not resist chasing a ball, so we used to entice Tobias away from his work, and get him to throw the ball, whilst we did our best to catch the dogs as they chased tennis ball after tennis ball. Another favourite game was running through the sprinkler and then searching in the wet ground for isongololos (I think you call them centipedes). In that garden we learnt how to ride bikes, throw a rugby ball, and generally just have fun together.

"And so on the evenings when my folks were entertaining, I would disappear to the bottom of the garden, and sit with Nkosie, Grace and Tobias. We would huddle around a hot fire, whilst eating mealie pap and gravy. Nkosie and I would like it best when Tobias' good friend Philemon would come over. The two men would have a few cups of home brew, and always ended up telling us silly stories about life in the old days back on the farm. Nkosie and I would spend the evening either kneeled over with laughter, or starring open mouthed in sheer disbelief at the long tails of lions and elephants, witch doctors and magic. Grace would just sit quietly with a gentle smile, and look of amusement on her face, as she listened to these two grown men talk such nonsense. Nonsense it may have been, however for me it has given me the most wonderful warm memories of my childhood and Africa.

"So, Abdul, as you can see, people can say what they want about us Afrikaners. They can call us racists, and blame apartheid on us, however, just as not all Muslims are terrorists, so are not all Afrikaners racists. In fact, my dad being the typical Afrikaner, is a prime example. To listen to him, you would be certain that he is racist, well, you couldn't be more wrong. Next month Nkosie will be graduating from university as a lawyer – okay so my dad won't be there to congratulate him, but you can grantee that both Grace and Tobisi will be given money for a new outfit, and the fact that Nkosie was even able to go to university in the first place was thanks to my father's money. As for me, Nkosie is my best friend, I could speak Xhosa before English, and I still drink my tea the African way – very milky and sweet!

"Abdul, my friend, I understand how you are feeling. Every time I open my mouth and a stranger recognises my accent, they just assume I am a racist. However, I know better, and I have learnt to ignore the ignorant comments, and fortunately for me, the lime light is not on South Africa and South Africans at the moment, unfortunately for you, the focus is on the Muslim people. And that is just something that you and your family are going to have to learn to deal with."

Abdul took a big sigh and nodded his head slowly

in agreement with Dirk. "My friend, I understand what you are saying, and I am so grateful for your insight. I have to say you have not made me feel any better about my predicament however you have helped me view my dilemmas from a different angle, and I suppose all I can hope for is that within a few months, not years, the world's attention will be elsewhere, and other poor souls will be targeted because of who they are and the unmistaken belief that others have of their religion or culture.

"I have to say though Dirk, I now look at you differently and this my friend, is my insight into how you have coped with the prejudices against you. You have over the years built up layers and layers of armour – your skin metaphorically is as tough as a rhino – and this provides others with an image of a tough, white South African man who will not put up with any bullshit, which if I have to say if a pretty good description of you! However this ability to project such a hard layer and not actually forget right from wrong is because you have such strong links to the roots of your people, the only way you have been able to build up this armour and not let it affect your inner most beliefs is because of a strong family background – both yours and Grace's family, a secure trust in your God, and deep sense of respect for those older than you.

"This, my friend is not that different from the Muslim way of life. Respect your elders, trust in Allah (May peace be upon him), and first and foremost care and protect your family. My next step is to try and figure

141

out how to strengthen not only my armour but also my family's. But now after hearing your story I at least have a little hope, not that this evilness will ever go away, but that I will learn to cope with it and still enjoy a fulfilled life. Thank you Dirk, you have helped lessen the burden on my heart today, and I feel so much better for it."

As Dirk wrapped his big right arm around Abdul's shoulder he replied, "Ag, Abdul, that is what friends are for, now back in my home town I would finish this conversation with, 'come on mate, let's go grab a beer'. I realise that is not going to happen so let me make you a cup of tea?"

"I have an even better idea, why don't you come back to my house for dinner, Nassir would be delighted to meet you, and I bet you could teach my boy a thing or two about rugby."

"Well, an offer like that I simply can't refuse, an old bachelor like me never turns down a meal, I'll meet you outside in five."

And so a friendship was formed.

CHAPTER 15

2003.

Dirk, like Ryan became an extra extension to the Khan family. Nassir at first found the man a little rough around the edges, however he had grown on her. It was a different story with both Ryan and Fareem. From day one he made a good impression on them. That first evening when he came over for dinner he spent a good hour or so in the back garden throwing the rugby ball to the boys, Nassir could not fault this, so she persevered with his "vulgar ways" being certain that her husband was a good judge of character, which meant that this strange man was obviously also a good man.

But it was really the year of 2003 that Dirk's relationship with the Khan family was cemented, and he was considered part of the family and not just a colleague. In fact he spent so much time in the Khan household that Nassir would joke about him moving in. However there was a reason for his constant presence, which cemented the relationship – a common love of sport!

In June 2003 the South African cricket team left the dry African soil behind, and headed for pastures far wetter – England. Between June and September they toured England.

This obviously brought quite a bit of excitement to the Khan household, being that they now actually knew a

South African, and both Abdul and Dirk were passionate about their sport, especially cricket. And so as the two countries stood face to face on the cricket pitch, Abdul and Dirk sat side by side cheering for their respective countries.

It wasn't long before they had managed to convince Ryan and Fareem that rugby wasn't the only sport and cricket could be pretty cool too. This was no mean feat, considering that the world was preparing for the start of the Rugby World Cup.

Dirk taught the boys that a bit of cricket in the back garden would help improve their rugby – "Cricket can give your boring old rugby drills a bit of excitement," Dirk would say. "Rather than throwing the rugby ball to each other, work on your speed, agility and eye to ball co-ordination by bowling and batting to each other."

This was the turning point – anything that would improve their rugby skills was worth a try! And before long, the boys too were following the five test matches.

So Nassir would find herself coming back from her ladies group to a house full of men - all of them huddled around the TV, chomping away on bags of crisps, and anything else that they could find in the kitchen. It didn't take long for Nassir to get used to the regular banter, at first Dirk's booming voice would make her jump, but that didn't last long. Abdul and Dirk would dissect each ball bowled, ball hit, and ref decision. And depending on who won the point would decide which one of them agreed with the ref!

During the coming months, they all learnt a little

something - Nassir had picked up quite a bit about this game that had captivated her men, and by the time the final test arrived, she actually willingly sat in her lounge surrounded by crisp packets, men and smelly feet – why is it she wondered that all men seemed to have smelly feet? Well she didn't come up with an answer to that, but she did enjoy the game.

Dirk and Abdul had discovered how easy it was to change lecture times to coincide with the games that they wanted to watch, and Ryan and Fareem realised just how hard it was to actually play cricket.

In August the South African team headed down to Kent. The game had been placed in the calendar long in advance, and the Khan family with its two adopted extras – Dirk and Ryan – had planned a day out at the cricket. They all headed down to Canterbury for the last day of the test. This was a first for Nassir, Ryan and Fareem. Nassir was advised to take her book along, and the boys a rugby ball, just in case the game was a "quiet one."

Abdul agreed to drive so that Dirk could enjoy a few cold beers during the game. This was not much of a hardship for Abdul, who being Muslim did not indulge in alcohol.

When the day arrived and the sun greeted them, Dirk and Abdul were relieved as they really wanted the whole family to enjoy the cricket and atmosphere and if it had been miserable, cold and raining it would not have been much fun for anyone.

Nassir packed a picnic with plenty of packets of

crisps. She also put in a few apples and bananas hidden in-between in an attempt to ensure that her men ate at least something healthy.

They all crammed into the Ford Escort and headed down the M2 towards Canterbury with a great lot of banter between them all. Ryan had decided to back the South African team giving Dirk some extra support – Fareem and Abdul firmly backing the England team. Nassir just sat back and smiled at the excitement in their voices, as they anticipated the game to come. Dirk and Ryan left the stadium smiling when South Africa won by 101 runs. Abdul and Fareem were quite willing to make Ryan and Dirk walk home, however Nassir wouldn't have it!

No sooner had the cricket finished and the South African team returned to the hot sun of African, did the Rugby World Cup start out in Australia. Well there was no chance that Dirk was going to get a little support this time. Ryan was backing England all the way. Rugby fever gripped the nation, and it seemed that for a short few weeks differences were forgotten as all came together to support Johnny Wilkinson and the England team.

The boy's rugby club had agreed to open up the club for all of the England games, so the Khan family found themselves spending most of the World Cup at the rugby club with the other parents. All the games were recorded and many a Saturday afternoon after the world cup was spent sitting around the TV watching replays.

Dwayne, who was a firm football supporter, had

also got behind the England rugby team, and he, too, seemed to be gripped by the World Cup fever. For the first time ever Ryan actually found that he had something in common with his dad and really believed that this was the start of an improvement in their relationship.

Ryan began to spend more time at home, and would enjoy sitting around the kitchen table discussing the games with his dad. Even though his dad did not really know that much about the rules of rugby, and frequently put completely irrelevant points across to Ryan, Ryan wasn't bothered. For a change he realised that he didn't have to argue with his dad every time they spoke.

Betty too had noticed the change. She would see them sitting together enjoying each other's company, and her heart began to feel a little lighter. Maybe things could get better.

Ryan even invited his dad to the rugby club so that they could watch the games together, but Dwayne just ruffled Ryan's blonde hair, smiled and declined. Dwayne was enjoying watching the rugby down at the Bell Inn, where he had his tasty treat on the side, who would drape herself over him, rubbing her boobs against his chest whilst he wrapped one arm around her waist and caressed her tight butt, and slurped on pints of beer. Oh yes, that is what he liked about the rugby, the fact that England was doing pretty well was an added bonus.

Ryan was a little disappointed at his offer being turned down, but after giving it a little bit more thought he was actually quite relieved. He asked his dad in a rare spontaneous moment and instantly regretted it. Ryan knew only too well that once his dad had a few beers in him his mood was as fragile as a crystal goblet.

All in all life seemed to be running smoothly on the White Road Estate. Betty and the rest of the Arnold family were finally beginning to behave like a family. Betty was well aware that they had a long way to go to create the ideal family, however she was pleased with this change in things, however she did whisper a silent pray each night, praying that this was not just going to be a passing phase and the anger, violence and heartache would not return. Perhaps her prayers were finally being answered.

And as for the Khan family, they really felt like a part of England, people had seemingly forgotten that they were a different colour and worshiped a different God, during the rugby world cup, they were England supporters, just like everyone else. Yes, it was a captivating time for the English nation. The men in red and white were doing the country proud, and the people displayed their appreciation by coming together, in the name of England.

The country was reminded of the English team down under. Men, women and children were seen wearing the team's colours and flags were flown from cars. The song *Swing low sweet chariot* was on people's lips and most conversations began with an update on the team.

This world cup had managed to captivate even the wives, who would normally moan and groan when the men wanted to watch the match. However this year saw a change in the uniforms and the tough, strapping men donned tight t-shirts. The English ones brought out the best in these fit young men but the shirts seemed to have a rather alluring habit of splitting halfway through a match. This brought the ladies to the sofa, and ensured that they too were backing the England team.

Swing low sweet chariot was sung with pride and gusto, yes, this looked like England's year. Martin Johnson and his team were taking the world by storm. The big day finally arrived. England had made it to the final, and were taking on the host country Australia, a nation who knew all about rugby, and also winning. This was not going to be an easy match.

Everyone seemed unusually quiet that morning. It seemed like it wasn't just the team that was suffering with nerves, but the whole of England. Ryan and Fareem had spent the night before discussing the match, just like they did before their own games. They had researched the Australian team and had considered both teams' strengths and weaknesses.

Could England really do it? That seemed to be the question on everyone's minds.

An hour before the game the Khan family huddled into the car with Dirk, Ryan and Betty, and headed for the rugby club. Betty normally chose to remain at home. She didn't really feel comfortable with all the families, and to be perfectly honest, the thought of sitting around with other mothers having to make conversation terrified her. She had such low self-esteem that she truly believed that she had absolutely nothing of interest to say to these ladies. However today she would face her adversary, and make an effort, not only for her son but also for herself. During the games leading up to the final match she was glued to her TV, and enjoyed the games, but somehow it just wasn't the same watching them alone. Ryan and the Khan family would return home, and Betty would watch enviously from the window as they disembarked from the car full of the spirit and joy of another win. From her little house she could also hear the roar of the crowds that had squeezed into the Bell Inn.

Betty knew that she could have watched every game with the Khan family, but she really didn't have the courage to take that step. So today was a big day for Betty too. Nassir had realised that this was probably the case, so had done her best to make this friend of hers feel more relaxed and comfortable. She knew that once Betty got there she would be fine. All the families that met down at the club were great. Nassir was certain that they would make Betty feel right at home. But what really pleased Nassir was seeing Ryan enjoy his mum's company.

There were a lot of very happy English men that night. The Khan family, Betty, Ryan and Dirk stayed at the club till late into the night, celebrating the country's victory. It was a great evening. Dirk ended up sleeping in the Khan's spare room, he had drunk a few too many beers, and was clearly not in any state to drive. Betty had also had her fair share of wine, and was feeling decidedly tipsy. She had heard about Dirk, but that was the first time they had met. And for the first time in a long time she actually felt like a woman. Dirk had made it quite clear that he found Betty rather attractive, and had enjoyed flirting with her. Betty enjoyed the attention.

She climbed into bed that night feeling a million dollars. Not only had she braved the outside world, but she had also had a wonderful time. She met Ryan's team mates and their families and was made to feel completely welcome. Ryan was clearly a very popular player both on the field and off the field. This too made Betty proud. She fell asleep dreaming of a better future.

Ryan too fell asleep dreaming, however his dream was probably the same as most boys that night. He dreamt of the day when he would walk out onto the rugby pitch in the England colours with the crowds cheering for him as he scored the winning try. Fareem also fell asleep with a smile of contentment on his face. Nassir and Abdul both stood at his door smiling down at their child who was deep in slumber also dreaming of being in the England team.

Abdul wrapped his arms around Nassir and led her into the bedroom. They snuggled into bed, and both giggled at the snoring sounds coming from the spare room. Yes, Dirk was sleeping contently too.

Nassir and Abdul spent a few minutes discussing the day. Both agreed that they were extremely fortunate to have such a wonderful family, and although they did not have that much money, tonight they both felt rich beyond their means.

The quiet contentment was broken at about two in the morning. Abdul sat bolt upright in bed and listened intently. Was someone trying to break into the house? He was certain he had heard a crashing sound. Dirk had heard it too and Abdul could hear him walking softly on the landing towards the window. Abdul met him at the window and they both gazed out, searching for the origins of the sound that had woken them up. Then it came again, a mighty bang and Abdul suddenly realised what was going on.

He turned to Dirk and said, "Its Dwayne from next door, he has obviously been locked out."

They watched as an upstairs light came on in the Arnold house, and then a light downstairs. Finally the front door was opened by Betty and Dwayne stumbled inside.

As both Abdul and Dirk were now awake they decided to head downstairs for a cup of coffee. Dirk settled down at the kitchen table, clutching his head. Yes, he had definitely drunk too much beer last night and was now paying the price. Abdul rubbed his eyes, and yawned, whilst reaching into the medicine cabinet to grab a couple of paracetamol for Dirk. Even though he was half asleep, he found the sight rather amusing. Long long ago when Abdul was probably a few years older than Fareem he had indulged in too much alcohol. The following day he understood why it was forbidden in the Islamic faith. Only something produced by the devil himself could cause so much pain. And so from then on he stuck to the Islamic belief of no alcohol.

With the coffee made, they both sat at the table. Dirk was not too keen to talk, and Abdul was happy just to sit and enjoy the peace and quiet. That was not to last, for no sooner had they finished their drinks did the shouting begin. It was Dwayne's booming voice that they heard. It was so loud that it sounded as if he was in the next room. Dirk suddenly wide awake dashed into the living room, and opened the curtains. From the angle that Dirk and Abdul were standing at they could see directly into Betty's living room. She had obviously forgotten to close the curtains last night. They could see that Betty was crying but she seemed to be trying her best to calm the wild beast. For a change it wasn't Betty he had a problem with but Ryan. Betty seemed to be begging Dwayne to leave Ryan out of it, but Dwayne was in no mood to listen.

Abdul and Dirk were by now glued to the window, not really certain about what they should do, when they saw Ryan striding down the stairs. One look at his face told them that he was not in the mood to back down from his father tonight. Nassir and Fareem had also been awoken by the disturbance and had joined Dirk and Abdul at the window. Nassir had an awful feeling in the pit of her stomach. She knew that Betty and Dwayne frequently didn't see eye to eye but she had never heard his voice this loud, or directed at Ryan. What the poor child had done to cause such anger in his dad Nassir did not know.

Fareem realised that Ryan meant business, he had that determined look on his face that Fareem knew meant he was not going to back down. Nassir was focusing on Betty and suddenly saw a change in Betty's demeanour. Nassir later realised that it was at this instant that Betty understood that the man she married was going to do some serious damage to their son if she did not intervene. She suddenly threw herself in-between the two of them and began pounding her fists on Dwayne's chest. Dwayne grabbed her wrist with his fat hand and twisted her arm until Betty was screaming in agony, he then used his other hand to slap her hard across the face, then threw her aside with such strength, that she seemed to fly through the room like a rag doll, landing on the edge of the sofa, her twisted arm now sticking out at an odd angle.

This caused the Khan household to react. Dirk who had been frozen to the spot looking on in horror, suddenly started to take charge.

"Phone the police now!" he demanded whilst running out of the front door. Abdul knew that it was useless to try and stop him, and perhaps if he had been braver he would have followed, instead he grabbed hold of the phone and dialled 999 and told Nassir to get Fareem out of the room. They had seen too much already.

Betty had seemingly got her wish. Dwayne turned his attention away from Ryan and powered over to Betty who was quivering in the corner. He raised his hand again, and delivered another blow to the side of Betty's head. Betty's head flung back, and her eyes started to lose focus. Ryan was now screaming at his father, begging him to stop, but Dwayne seemed not to hear anything, his rage was now focused solely on Betty. Ryan's face was streaked with tears, as he clawed at his father's back, trying his best to protect his mother. Suddenly the door was thrown open and Dirk stormed into the room, his booming voice took Dwayne by surprise, who quickly dropped Betty and turned towards his next bit of prey.

"Come on mate, why pick on the lady, why not take on someone your own size." Dirk realised that he was playing a dangerous game, he really didn't want to end up fighting this angry man, however if the worst came to the worst he would. For the time being though, he just wanted to distract his attention long enough for the police to arrive – surely they were already on their way.

The tactic worked. Dwayne was so incensed that some strange man had the audacity to walk into his house in the early hours of the morning, and start calling the shots. "Who the fuck do you think you are?" he shouted.

Dirk slowly walked backwards, leading Dwayne away from Betty and Ryan, who was now doing what he could to comfort his mum and stop the bleeding.

Come on police, where the hell are you? Dirk was beginning to think that he might just have to fight this big brute after all.

"You fucker, what the fuck are you doing in my home, you foreign speaking wanker, no one talks to me that way. That bitch is mine, so fuck right back to where you came from you cocking sucking cunt, before I rearrange that block for you!"

Dwayne launched himself towards Dirk, who fortunately for a big man was fairly nimble on his feet. He managed to duck to the side, and miss the flying blow that Dwayne delivered, at the same time two big police man walked into the room, asps drawn, and ready to take down this bull of a man – Dwayne was known around the local nick for his hot temper and aggressive nature and this was not the first time that the police had been called to the address. In the past it had not been uncommon for a couple of coppers to limp away from the scene. These two burly big men that entered the room were not going to leave the house limping and Dwayne seemed to realise this. He rapidly calmed down as the handcuffs were slapped onto his wrists.

As the two big men escorted Dwayne out towards the police car, another car pulled up, and a young lady got out. Dirk took one look at her and realised she must be a plain clothed copper.

The ambulance arrived shortly after that. It was clear that Betty was going to need to go to hospital as her head was still bleeding heavily. It was also very clear that Ryan was not going to leave his mother's side. Fortunately it was only Betty who limped away from the scene that night, however once again another piece of Ryan's heart had been broken. How much longer could this continue? Ryan only hoped that now Dirk had witnessed the horrifying side of his dad, the police would finally be able to take him away for good. He gently wrapped his arm around his mum, and tried his best to comfort her, without hurting her. As they walked past Dirk, he raised his eyes and mouthed a thanks, Betty simply looked at Dirk through sad, tired eyes, as a tear dripped slowly down her bruised cheek, which was already starting to swell.

Dirk gave the police as much information as he could, and then finally returned to the Khan household to try and get a few hours' sleep before dawn broke. He walked in to the front door and was greeted by Nassir who wrapped her arms around him.

"Thank you so much Dirk," she said.

Abdul grabbed Nassir's arm gently, "Come on Nassir, Dirk needs to get some sleep, it's been a long night."

Nassir released her grip on Dirk, who just smiled warmly at Nassir. "If there is one thing I can't tolerate, it is men who bully women. I hope I have not caused problems for you and your family, as I know Dwayne does not take too kindly to you, and will realise that I came from your house, however I was not willing to stand by and watch those two people suffer."

"Dirk you did the right thing, I only wish I could have been of more help, but if I am perfectly honest with you, that man terrifies me."

Dirk clapped his big hand on Abdul's back, "Oh, don't be so hard on yourself Abdul, you have your own family to protect, this was not your fight, and don't forget I grew up with two older brothers and a bully of a dad. Taking on Dwayne was no big deal. However, I am glad the police turned up when they did. And if I am honest with you, I would not want to meet that man in a dark alley. So what do you say we all try and get a bit more sleep."

Everyone agreed and headed back upstairs. But before Dirk headed to the spare room, he popped his head around Fareem's bedroom door. Fareem sat up quickly, and looked at Dirk fearfully.

"Your friend is okay," Dirk sighed. "He is a tough young man, but he has had one hell of a night, and is going to need his friend tomorrow."

Fareem relaxed slightly with the knowledge that his friend was okay, and yes, of course he would be there for Ryan tomorrow. Ryan was like a brother to him, and if he needed Fareem, then Fareem would be there. Before drifting back to sleep, Fareem thought about the day that they had just shared together. This should have been one of the happiest days in their lives and it was until Ryan's dad once again ruined things for Ryan. Over the years Ryan had opened up more and more to Fareem. But up until tonight, Fareem had never really been able to understand what Ryan's home life was really like. Fareem came from such a loving home that he had difficulty comprehending the life that Ryan often described. That was until tonight. Never before had Fareem seen such anger and aggression. Fareem enjoyed the rough and tumble on the rugby pitch, and thought of himself as a bit of a hard man. He may have been smaller than many of his rugby mates, but he was not one to shy away from a tackle or an opportunity to get a good dig in without the ref seeing. And that was about as much violence he had ever come across, that and the school boy fights in the playground. So tonight's events had been hard hitting for Fareem, lying in his bed, trying desperately to fall asleep he just couldn't seem to get the image of Dwayne roughly grabbing hold of Betty's arm and twisting in until she was screaming out in pain. Fareem remembered Dwayne grabbing her, and the scream, however his attention was then diverted towards his best friend. Fareem knew with absolute certainty that Ryan wanted to kill Dwayne, and there was no doubt in his mind that one day it would happen if Dwayne continued to cause Betty such pain.

That night, Fareem realised that he had a responsibility towards his friend. Fareem owed it to Ryan to do what he could to help make Ryan's life a better life. Fareem was sensible enough to realise that he could not stop Dwayne, but he could make sure that Ryan also knew that he had a home at the Khan house. Fareem vowed to himself that from now on, Ryan would not be like a brother, he was a brother, because that it was he needed – a brother to lean on, and another family to love and care for him. And just like his family had always been there for him, Fareem would always be there for Ryan – no matter what!

The following morning, Ryan awoke with a stiff neck, sweaty and in need of giving his teeth a good clean. The hospital was not the most comfortable place to sleep if you were a relative, it was also exceedingly hot in the room. Ryan slowly uncurled his big frame out of the chair that he had fallen asleep in. He glanced over to his mum who was already awake and seemed to be watching him. Her eyes displayed pure adoration for this child of hers, but the rest of her face look tired and sad. She tried to smile over at Ryan, but instead grimaced in pain. Ryan gently clutched her hand, the one that was not bandaged up, and gave it a little squeeze.

"Don't worry Mum, you're going to be okay, the police will keep him away this time Mum, I promise, I won't ever let him hurt you again."

Betty, didn't even bother to reply, just trying to smile caused excruciating pain and talking was out of the question. Deep down she knew that nothing was going to change. She only prayed that Ryan would soon be old enough to leave home and get away from it all. He had that right but she did not. She had married Dwayne for better or worse, and if this was the worst, perhaps better days would come, but she wasn't going to hold her breath.

"Hello Betty dear, I'm Mandy, and I'm your nurse for the next few hours. Oh, hon. Look at you, let me see if I can make you more comfortable."

Ryan stepped away as Mandy lent over the bed and began to ease Betty up into a sitting position. She was being awfully caring and gentle with Betty, who really did not look very comfortable at all.

Her cheek seemed to have popped out as though she was sucking on a rather large plum, her right eye was closed and had already turned a nasty dark colour. And that was just the parts of her body that Ryan could see. Ryan dreaded to think about the bruising to her ribs.

Ryan knew from experience that Dwayne was good at hurting you where no one would see the marks. Those were the beatings that Betty and Ryan had learnt to endure in silence, but not for any longer, that animal could rot in hell for all Ryan cared.

Ryan tapped Mandy on the shoulder and indicated that he was going to get a cup of coffee, but would be back in a few minutes.

"You take your time, young man, your mum is in safe hands now. Why not go and get yourself some breakfast? I'll be with your mum for the next half an hour at least."

Ryan was tempted to take her up on the offer, but he wanted to be with his mum when the police arrived. He knew she was going to need his support. So he simply smiled gratefully and disappeared out of the door. Fortunately they had given Betty a room to herself. She was thankful for this, and so was Ryan. He really didn't want anyone seeing his mum looking like this. She was normally such a beautiful woman, now she just looked like a battered lump of pulp.

Ryan knew his way to the canteen. He normally took the lift as it was two flights up, but today he felt the urge to stretch his legs and so he rounded the corner and took the stairs two at a time at full pace. He felt the blood circulating to his muscles and it felt good. He reached the canteen and wasn't even out of breath, although he could feel a slight build-up of sweat on the nape of his neck. It was at times like this that he hit the road. After a "bust up" with his dad he would just head out and run. It seemed to be the only way for him to release his pent up anger and that is exactly what he wanted to do now. But that would have to wait, he needed to get back to his mum.

As he was walking back along the corridor towards the hospital room he recognised one of the ladies walking towards him. "Hello Ryan, look at you, you have turned into one handsome young man."

Lesley came over and ruffled his hair. Lesley, who was more commonly known as WPC Mitchell, had known the Arnold family for a long time. She had been a domestic abuse officer for the last eight years and that was how long she had known the Arnold family too!

She had brought along a new officer who Ryan could tell had not been doing the job too long. She had that nervous look about her, not quite certain about what she was going to discover during the next hour, and not quite sure whether she would be up for the job. Oh yes, Ryan had seem them come and go. Ryan didn't think this new one was up for the challenge. She did not fill him with confidence, and thought it would probably be best for everyone if she returned to the streets as dealing with domestic abuse victims was not for the faint hearted. Ryan had confidence in Lesley. Even though she had never really been able to remove Dwayne for good, she had always been there for them. One of Ryan's most vivid memories of Lesley was when Dwayne had returned home unexpectedly to find Lesley in the kitchen with Betty. Ryan can remember tugging at his mum's nightgown, trying to warn her that he was back, but

Betty was too busy trying to convince Lesley that the fight had just been a one off. She was telling Lesley she was sure it would never happen again and how it was all her own fault anyway and didn't see Dwayne but Lesley did. Well, she stood up to that big man and he didn't get a chance to get a word in. Her whole aura seemed to command respect and whether Dwayne liked it or not he had to sit down and listen to this small petite copper, who was clearly not afraid of anything.

Ryan watched on in amazement as Dwayne and Betty sat next to each other and both listened tentatively like two school children to Lesley who basically laid down the law. The bottom line was that if Dwayne did not seek anger management classes, and they did not go to counselling together, then Lesley was going put in a few phone calls to social services, and get the one thing removed that they both loved more than life itself. At the time Ryan didn't really understand what she was talking about, but as he got older, he realised Dwayne loved himself more than anything else, and Lesley would probably have done him a favour if Ryan had been taken into care.

He hoped today she would be able to make a few calls and get Dwayne removed for good. Ryan was certain of it this time because this time Dirk had seen what had happened. This time it was not just Betty's word against Dwayne's word. This time, it was going to work out.

Ryan smiled at Lesley and headed over to her. He breathed a sigh of relief, the heavy load that he seemed to be carrying lifted slightly. Lesley was like an old aunt, who always seemed to turn up in a time of crisis and make things better. Ryan supposed that in a normal family the old aunt would waddle though the door with a big cheery face, carrying jars of homemade jam and a big pasta bake. She would take charge on entering and on hearing that slightly patronising tone, "Don't worry dear, Aunt Tillie is here," everyone would know that it was going to be okay.

For Ryan there was no old lady but a petite copper, but the effect was the same. She too took charge in even the most precarious situations, and she did make them all feel okay, she just didn't walk in bearing homemade food, she walked in wearing tight cargo pants, and a baggy t-shirt, which didn't do much to hide the baton and pepper spray!

"So Ryan, first things first, how are you doing?"

"Yeah, I'm okay, you know, not much changes with my family, but I think this time things will be different. Dad did a pretty good job on mum this time, but I think you will be able to put him away for good."

"Oh, my child, from your lips to God's ears, I have been wanting to do that for a long time now." Lesley once again ruffled Ryan's hair, and introduced Ryan to Amanda, the copper that Ryan didn't have much faith in.

"So, Ryan, let's go and have a chat with your Mum, and see what we can do this time." She smiled gently at Ryan, and put her arm around his shoulder as they walked off towards Betty's room.

God, how she loved this child, she had watched him

grow up and had wished many times that she could hide this nasty world from him. But Betty had always been true to her word, and never given Lesley enough to get Ryan removed and put into care – not that that would have been any better for Ryan. Hell, Lesley knew that the majority of fosters carers were more concerned about the amount of money they were receiving than the damaged child they had been given responsibility for. But that didn't stop her worrying about Ryan, and what his future might hold. He was a good boy and smart too. Given the right opportunities he could go far. Lesley was certain of that. But as long as that brute of a man remained in his life it would be more of an existence than anything else.

As they turned into Betty's room, Ryan glanced over at Amanda. She looked like a startled rabbit caught in the headlights, no way was she going to last long on the domestic abuse unit if she couldn't learn to face the victims square on and not show even a glimmer of alarm and horror – Amanda was clearly very alarmed and horrified.

Lesley had noticed it too, and unlike Ryan, she took a different view – she had been doing this job for so long now that at times she felt like she had lost the art of really feeling, yes, she had become hard and cynical. Unfortunately that was the price she was paying for spending so many years dealing with such suffering. There were times when she wished that she could still look on in horror and alarm, however the truth was that Lesley had seen so much in her time, that there was not much to surprise her these days. However she also knew that if Amanda was going to make it as a domestic abuse officer she would need to dig deep, ignore the fact that barely looked human, and focus on the person inside who clearly needed a lot of support and comfort. And so Lesley pushed Amanda into the room, thinking, "Well, girl, you are either going to sink or swim, as I am about to throw you in at the deep end!"

"Hello Betty, I would usually say how are things going, but today I can see that things have not been too good, so, my love, let's see what we can do to make it better."

Betty tried her best to smile, but to be perfectly honest she just didn't have it in her. Her face and body hurt like hell – she too had noticed the expression on Amanda's face as she entered the room and she knew she looked bad. But the pain she was feeling in her heart was ten times worse than what her body was feeling. Her life had turned out to be a complete disaster. She just wished everyone would stop talking, and let her drift off into a long long sleep. Betty had had enough of this life, she hoped like hell there really was a God, and that he would look kindly on her, she was ready to call it a day. Dwayne had finally got the better of her, and she was done fighting.

Ryan quickly moved to his mother's side. Her face was pretty badly beaten up and her eyes were still the same, but now he saw a look in them that he really didn't like. The flame seemed to be dying behind those bright blue eyes and Ryan watched as his mum lost the will to live. A sudden flash of fury filled his body with the fuel he needed to pull his mum out of the depths of despair. Ryan knew with all his heart that one day he would make that man pay. And he was determined that his mum would be around to see it happen.

"Mum, look at me, look at me please." He had hold of her good hand, and had wrapped his other arm around her shoulder. Everything else in the room seemed to fade away, Ryan forgot about the police ladies in the corner, and didn't notice the nurses hurrying in, all he could see was his mum and her sad fading eyes.

"Mum, please, I need you, don't leave me please." Ryan's eyes had clouded over, and the tears started to fall.

Betty was in a good place. She was content. The pain finally seemed to be leaving her heart, and then a tear dropped onto her cheek and slipped down to her lips, and her tongue automatically licked the moisture away. It was the salty taste that brought her back to her senses, for she knew they were not her tears. She had stopped crying a long, long time ago. The pain was beginning to return, and as much as she tried to resist it, something deep inside her seemed to will her out of her contented sleep. Betty slowly became aware of the goings on in this world, the quiet peaceful place she was in was being replaced by bright lights and nurses shouting. She could hear what was going on, but wasn't ready to deal with any of that just yet. Her eyes had started to focus on the light of her life, and the sadness that was pouring out of his eyes. She didn't see the

167

young man standing in front of her, she saw the young helpless baby she had given birth too, and today he was cradling her like she did when the nurses first handed him over to her. Betty could recall the image as if it was yesterday. Her tiny little soul was looking up at her with his big round eyes, she could see he was trying to focus on this new world that he had just been introduced to, just as she was trying to focus on the world today. She clutched him close to her chest and whispered a promise, she nearly broke that promise today, and realising that nearly broke her heart. The tears slowly began to fall down Betty's cheeks too, she squeezed Ryan's hand back gently.

Lesley realised that it was going to be four or five days or so before Betty would be able to provide her with a victim statement and this worked both ways for Lesley. It meant that she would have to let Dwayne go as there was no way the crown prosecution service would agree to remand him in custody without a statement from the victim. However it did buy Lesley some time to work on Betty. Lesley hoped she could put her persuasive skills to the test and convince Betty to leave that son of a bitch for good! Lesley knew the chances of this happening were rather slim, ninety percent of domestic abuse victims ended up returning to their so called loved ones. The control that abusers had over their victims was quite scary, for most reasonable people receiving a broken jaw and a black eye would be enough to send you packing, however this was not the case with domestic abuse victims. More often than not the aggressors would isolate their victims from friends and family, leaving them solely dependent on the aggressor. Lesley did not like to refer to the victims as statistics but she also knew when to face the facts. Her sole role over the next few weeks would be to find a place for Betty and Ryan where they could live in safety and peace away from Dwayne. Once she had found this "magical place" she would need to pull out all the stops to convince Betty to take the plunge and leave Dwayne for good.

Lesley knew better than to rely on the law courts to put Dwayne away for a long time as it was highly unlikely that that would happen. So the first decision that Lesley made was to speak to the doctor at the hospital, Dr Herzog, and was pretty certain that she would agree to Lesley's idea.

The following day, Lesley called the hospital as soon as she arrived at work, and found out what time Dr Herzog would be doing her rounds. Lesley aimed to head down to the hospital with her side kick Amanda, who still looked like a rabbit caught in the head lights, but was rapidly proving that she might just make it as a domestic abuse officer after all, in time to see the doctor. She hadn't told Amanda what the plan was yet. This was another way of Lesley deciding whether or not the rookie was fit for the role.

"Grab your radio and kit Amanda, we are heading out of here," yelled Lesley as she leapt out of her chair and headed out of the door.

Amanda scrambled up, pen between her teeth and did her best to log off the computer and grab her kit at the same time. She resembled more a gawky adolescent than a fully-fledged copper.

Sergeant Cooper the boss of the unit just sat back and smiled. That Lesley sure was a bit of a loose cannon. She did not always play by the book and he had had to bail her out of trouble more times than he cared to remember, however, she did have passion, and she did a bloody good job. She scared the living daylights out of most probationers, but hey, it didn't do them any harm. As he leaned forward and focused on his own work load, he was pleased to not know what Lesley was up to today, sometimes it was easier that way!

They arrived at the hospital just as Dr Herzog was heading in after her cigarette break. Dr Herzog was originally from Germany, and even though she had been living in Medway, UK for the past ten years, she still had a strong German accent. This tended to make her come across as rather abrupt, and curt, but Lesley knew better. Dr Herzog was her type of woman – very good at what she did and didn't suffer fools gladly, but also open to suggestion should it be reasonable. Lesley reminded herself of these traits as she approached the doctor.

Dr Herzog spotted the two coppers first, "Vell goode morning ladies, vhat can I do for you today? No vait let me guess, you are on your vay up to see Betty?"

"Yes, Doc, we are, how is she doing today?" Lesley also remembered that the doctor did not like beating around the bush. If you wanted something from her the best way to go about it was to ask her straight out, so she continued, "Actually, doc, I was hoping to speak to you about Betty – how long do you think she will be in hospital for?"

Dr Herzog looked directly at Lesley and responded, "No, Lesley, you tell me, how long do you want her in here for?"

Lesley let a slight smile graze her face, "A week would be good doc."

"Hmmmm, I will see what I can do." Dr Herzog then strode off.

She was a tall woman, handsome women, with strong features. Her hair was severely pulled back into a pony tail, which only accentuated her sharp jaw line. Amanda and Lesley had to slip into a slow jog in order to keep up with the doctor, who with glasses half way down her nose, eyes glued to the clip board which was firmly clasped in her right hand, appeared to have already forgotten their presence.

When they reached Betty's room, Amanda and Lesley followed the doctor in, but she very quickly reprimanded them and in a short abrupt tone quickly reminded them of Betty's rights as a patient. "Oh no ladies, you vill have plenty of time to speak to Betty about your police business after I have examined her, so please remain outside until I am finished." She then smiled gently at Ryan and asked him to wait outside as well.

Lesley was not too keen on this, she wanted to hear what the good old doctor had to say, but she knew better than to argue, so she stepped outside the door, but remained close enough to be able to overhear the

171

conversation.

"Zo Betty my dear, how are you feeling today?"

Betty responded as best she could, but it still hurt like hell to talk. She had been in hospital for three days now, she thought – the first two days were pretty blurry, but she felt better today, and really wanted to go home. She hated being stuck in hospital, so she did her best to try and pull herself into a seated position without grimacing too much, and mumbled what she hoped sounded like, "Much better today."

Doctor Herzog scanned the notes next to the bed, then looked directly into Betty's eyes. "Vell my dear, you are healing well, and I could release you today."

Betty breathed a sigh of relief.

"However Betty, you are going to need quite a lot of care at home, for at least another week, have you got someone to look after you?" The doctor noticed how Betty quickly dropped her eyes, trying to avoid looking directly at the doctor as she mumbled that Ryan would help her out. "Anyone else Betty?" Once again Betty tried to mumble something. "Vell Betty, I am sure Ryan is more than competent at caring for you, however I am aware of how apt teenage boys are in ze kitchen, and if you are going to mend quickly you are going to need plenty of healthy food, and care around the clock, now I also know how much time ze average teenage boy spends at home, so for that reason I think you would be best suited to stay put for at least the next few days. Relax, take advantage of the nurses who are at your beck and call, and I am certain that in a few days you will be fit enough to go home and take care of yourself. Now I know that there are two police officers waiting outside to speak to you, are you up to speaking to them, because if not I vill send them on their vay."

Betty knew that it would be Lesley waiting to see her, and she knew what Lesley would be expecting of her – she wasn't quite ready to have that discussion yet, however she was happy to see Lesley, who Betty had become awfully fond of over the years. And as much as she wanted to go home, she was quite relieved that the doc had ordered her to stay put, because she knew deep down that she was better off where she was for the time being. So she gently nodded to tell the doc the police could come in.

Doctor Herzog walked out of the room, glanced over at Lesley and Amanda and chirped, "You can go in now, Betty vill be with us for at least another three days, so please don't rush things."

Lesley mouthed a small thanks, but the doctor was already on her way. Lesley smiled warmly at Betty as she walked in, followed by Amanda.

"How are you feeling today hon, are you ready to talk to me?" Lesley pulled a chair up next to Betty's and motioned for Amanda to do the same.

Lesley noticed Betty's brow start to frown, even in-between all the swelling, and right then and there Lesley realised that Betty was not going to prosecute. Best she start putting plan two in action, but just in case she had it wrong, she would push the matter a bit further.

"Betty, we finally have some really good evidence

this time, we have the statement from Dirk and Ryan, I really think that with your support we can put him away this time Betty, what do you say hon, how about it?"

Betty knew that what Lesley was saying made sense, she knew it would be best for Ryan too, but something deep within her just couldn't bring herself to go against the man who before God she had agreed to stay with for better or for worse. She knew that he didn't love her anymore, nor her him, but that didn't change the fact that they had said their vows to each other in God's presence, and for that reason and that reason alone, she could not bring herself to take the matter any further. Lesley would never be able to understand this, and Ryan would be devastated, but Ryan wouldn't be around much longer, he was nearly an adult, and Betty knew that the Khan family were providing him with more of a home and family life than she ever could. And that was just the way it was.

"I can't do it Lesley, I am sorry, I just can't do it." Betty's eyes filled with tears (she had done more crying in the last few days than she had in years) as she realised that Ryan was standing at the door and listening in. She could see the disappointment in his eyes, his shoulders slumped, and he turned to walk away.

Lesley noticed this too, "Oh Betty, he will be alright, he just wants the best for you, and in his mind being away from Dwayne is best for you. I do tend to agree with him love, but you need to do what is good for you, and if you don't want to prosecute, then I will just look for other ways to keep you and Ryan safe." Lesley could tell that the last ten minutes had worn Betty out, "You rest now, we will come back later, and don't you worry about Ryan, I will go and have a word with him." Lesley squeezed Betty's shoulder gently, then helped her lie down. By the time Lesley and Amanda got to the door Betty was already asleep.

"Poor girl, she has had one hell of a life, Amanda. Betty is what I would call one of life's victims. She sure as hell didn't choose this life, but now that she has it she just can't seem to get rid of it. Let's go and have a chat with Ryan before we head out of here."

They found Ryan in the canteen nursing a cup of coffee, his head hung low, the dejection that he felt seemed to be pouring out of his veins.

"Hey Ryan, let me buy you breakfast?"

"Hi Lesley, no you don't have to do that, bet you have got better things to do than hang around this hospital."

"Actually Ryan, I've been on duty since six this morning and I haven't stopped yet, so I think it is time for Amanda and I to have a big healthy fry up – what do you say? It's on me."

"Thanks, that would be nice, I've been staying with my neighbours, and they don't eat much meat, so a greasy fry with extra bacon would be a treat. Thanks again Lesley."

Lesley playfully punched Ryan in the arm, "Don't you worry about it, you can repay me with a pair of tickets to Twickenham when you play for England."

"Aaah, Lesley I don't think I'm that good, but then

you never know." Ryan smiled for the first time that day, and it felt good to talk to people about stuff other than his mum and Dwayne.

Within a few minutes Lesley and Amanda returned with three plates full of grease and cholesterol! Ryan devoured the food as if there was no tomorrow. It was the one thing he missed whilst staying with the Khan family – he did like pork, which was a big no no for Muslims.

Lesley had paid a visit to the Khan family before she agreed to allow Ryan to stay there, so she was aware that they were Muslims. Obviously she had checked them through the system as since 9/11 every Muslim seemed to pose some sort of threat or another. But they had come back clean. What Lesley had appreciated about the visit to the house was the feeling on entering that it was a home, and a real family. These were obviously good people who cared deeply not only for each other but also Ryan. So Lesley agreed to let Ryan stay with them, in fact she thought it would do him the world of good to spend time with a real family – he certainly didn't have a real family!

Amanda had finally seemed to come out of her shell a bit, and was in deep conversation about rugby, confessing that she was also a keen rugby player. The two of them chatted away about the recent world cup, Lesley who really didn't follow rugby took the opportunity to gather her thoughts – what exactly what she going to be able to do for Betty and Ryan?

Amanda and Lesley headed out of the hospital half

an hour later. As Lesley got up to leave she leant over to Ryan and gently told him not to be too hard on his mum. "You just hang in there son, things will work out for the best."

Ryan wasn't so certain, but they were the police, the ones who were meant to protect, so he hoped with all his heart that Lesley was right.

The two coppers walked out to the car in silence, Amanda really was quite lost, she had been in the job long enough to realise that there came a time when you just had to move on, the cases were starting to pile up, and everyone knew that in domestics if the victim wasn't willing to play game then it was a non-starter – so what they hell were they doing still hanging around? But this was also the first time that Amanda had worked on a specialist unit, and things did seem to work slightly differently, so she just kept her mouth shut, and just hoped that Lesley knew what she was doing and they weren't just wasting valuable time, which could perhaps be better spend on a victim that was willing to help the police. Perhaps she wasn't cut out for this type of work after all. In the last unit she was on all they were interested in was numbers and detecting crimes, and that is why she had wanted out – she was sick of playing the numbers game, but perhaps she was wrong, maybe petty criminal damage and drunks on a Saturday night was what she should be dealing with. It sure as hell was easier than this!

And so while Amanda was contemplating her career as a domestic abuse officer, Lesley was considering her next move. She knew what was going through Amanda's mind, but that was not going to stop her. When she joined the domestic abuse unit she'd made a little promise with herself that figures and bureaucratic would not get in the way of helping a victim. She had kept this promise and she was not planning on breaking it now. So how the hell was she going to help Betty?

Well, Lesley still had a few tricks up her sleeve, and she was going to work those tricks. It was highly unlikely that they would agree to charge Dwayne with assault without a statement from Betty agreeing to prosecute, but it had been done before, so Lesley's first stop would be her friendly Crown Prosecution lawyer; he had helped her out before in more ways than one, and perhaps he would help her out again.

Failing that it would be on the phone looking for a refuge for Betty and Ryan. That meant ringing around the country and hoping that a refuge would have a space for them – that plan also depended on Betty agreeing to give up her life in Medway and start over completely in another part of the country. This was a big step to make, many of Lesley's victims had taken the step before, but it was not an easy one, and Lesley wasn't convinced that Betty would go for it. The main reason for this is that it would mean taking Ryan away from everything he knew, and Lesley just didn't think that Betty could do that, even if it meant that Ryan would continue to suffer at the hands of Dwayne, or at least watch his mother suffer the same fate.

So that led Lesley to her third and final option;

putting things in place as best she could to keep Betty and Ryan as safe as possible in their own home with Dwayne returning as soon as his bail conditions ended. This meant panic alarms, coded mobile phone calls, and a getaway suitcase stashed away somewhere safe just in case things got so bad that Betty and Ryan had to get out.

Three days later Amanda was banging her head against a brick wall while Lesley continued to waste valuable time on Betty, who in Amanda's world was really becoming a pain in the neck – they had offered her just about everything other than a private jet and new identities on a faraway island, where the sun always shone, but still she refused to play game. She was adamant that she would not support a prosecution, and would not consider refuge. Lesley had even managed to find a house up north for her, but no, she would not hear of it. Meanwhile their cases stacked up, but still Lesley continued to work with this mad women, who Amanda was beginning to think should perhaps be sectioned into the mental hospital – Dwayne had just about killed her, but she was willing to go back to him, even if it meant risking her son's life.

Funnily enough the sergeant didn't seem to mind, he would just smile knowingly at Amanda, as it was clear that she was getting rather frustrated, and as for the rest of the domestic abuse team, well they were just as mad as Betty – they too didn't utter a word of annoyance, or frustration at Lesley's lack of being able to realise when it was time to close the door – they quietly worked away, keeping an eye on Lesley's work load, and taking over cases as and when they could manage.

The one thing the rest of the team knew, as well as the sergeant, was that Lesley did one hell of a job, and she never gave up on a victim. This was a great trait, and one that the sergeant was not going to try and change. The rest of the team also knew, that as long as Lesley was willing to take on all of the real hard to crack victims, then they wouldn't have to. And that is why the sergeant would always place a new attachment with Lesley, because if they could last with Lesley for a month, then they would more than likely be able to cut it as a domestic abuse officer.

And so the day finally arrived for Betty to get released from the hospital. Dwayne was still on bail conditions, and so was not allowed to return home for another three weeks – Lesley hoped that this would give Betty enough time to recover from her physical injuries and get Ryan settled back into his routine. It also gave Lesley a couple of weeks to make sure that Betty was as safe as she possibly could – this meant putting in quite a few measures in order to pre-empt a worst case scenario. Betty had allowed Lesley to help her set this escape plan up and so the hard work continued.

Lesley's first job was a visit to the Khan family. She had enjoyed meeting them earlier on in the case, the house was a real home, and the family were clearly a "family" - she liked that, and hoped that one day she would have a similar set up. As for the whole Muslim thing, well, they didn't seem all that different from her own family. And more importantly Betty was friendly with Nassir, and it was that friendship that Lesley was relying on helping Betty should the need arise, oh, and also the fact that Ryan was more comfortable in the Khan home than his own. Lesley was pretty certain that the Khan family would do as much as they possibly could to help out Ryan and Betty.

Lesley had phoned beforehand, so the Khan family were expecting her. Abdul opened the door and welcomed Lesley and Amanda into their home. Prior to the visit, Lesley had done a quick check on the internet about Muslim etiquette – she briefed Amanda on the way over.

"So, what socks are you wearing?" enquired Lesley.

Amanda was a little taken aback, and really was not too certain about where this conversation was going, Lesley did not have much of a sense of humour – or not that Amanda had seen! "Ummm, I'm not quite sure, and can't see the relevance of it," Amanda responded in a rather terse manner.

"Well, before heading out of the police station I did a little bit of research on the Muslim faith, and we, as a sign of respect are going to remove our shoes when we enter the Khan household, so I hope your socks don't have holes in them, or have anything inappropriate printed on them!"

"Well, Lesley, I will have you know, that I never wear socks with holes in them, and as for inappropriate print, I don't own any such socks!"

"Jeez, you are lucky, I have been hunting around

my gym bag searching for a pair of respectable socks – which fortunately I found. Only down side is that they are the same socks I was wearing for my five mile run yesterday! I also learnt another couple of pointers – it is disrespectful to shake the hand of a Muslim woman, and did you know that Muslims are expected to prayer five times a day! Oh, and here we are, so remember, remove your shoes as you enter! Let's hope this goes accordingly to plan."

Amanda knocked boldly on the door, trying to portray a confidence that she didn't quite have – walking into a strange house, and hoping that you didn't insult them by doing something wholly inappropriate was not her idea of fun, but hey, somehow this domestic abuse attachment was not that fun!

Abdul opened the door for them and warmly welcomed them into the house. Both Lesley and Amanda quickly removed their shoes on entering, Abdul noticed this small gesture, and appreciated it. He then ushered them into the lounge, which looked tidy and clean, but homely. Nassir walked in and offered them both tea and coffee, to which they both accepted.

"It is awfully quiet, I would have expected Fareem to be glued to the TV," commented Lesley to Nassir.

"Oh, if only. TV is not a problem with Fareem, it is rugby – he is out in the garden as we speak kicking the ball around with Ryan; those two boys live, eat and sleep rugby!"

Nassir then disappeared to the kitchen, to presumably make the tea. Abdul was sitting expectantly opposite Lesley, so she decided to explain the visit.

Abdul quickly interrupted, and apologised for this, "Sorry, eh PC ", Lesley, please call me Lesley, and this is Amanda."

"Ah, continued Abdul, thank you, I was not quite certain what to call you, this is a first for us, having the police coming to visit." Abdul then turned towards Lesley, "Sorry, Lesley, what I was going to say, can we please wait for Nassir, she won't be long, and I would really like her to be present."

"Yes, of course." Responded Lesley who was surprised by this, she was under the impression that Muslim women were very much not seen and not heard! However this did not appear to be the case with this family. After a few minutes Nassir returned with cups of tea and biscuits and they then got down to business.

"Mr and Mrs Khan, firstly I need to thank you for all the support you have given Betty and Ryan over the last few weeks, something they desperately needed, and I have to say, it makes my job a lot easier knowing that Betty and Ryan have friends like yourselves. This I suppose brings me to the reason why I have asked to see you today. Just to let you know, prior to arranging this visit I did discuss the reason for the visit with Betty, and she has agreed for me to speak to you both."

Lesley noticed Abdul give Nassir's hand a gentle squeeze, and they both visibly seemed to relax with the knowledge that Betty was aware and in agreement with the visit.

"Just to give you an update, Betty has decided not

to support a police prosecution, which therefore means that it is more than likely that Dwayne will be returning to the home within the next few weeks. I have spoken to Betty long and hard over the issue of prosecuting, as I am sure you have as well." Lesley glanced at Nassir, who nodded in agreement. "And I have to respect her views for not wanting to take the matter any further, which means that I have naturally been looking into other ways to keep both Betty and Ryan safe – which brings me to our visit today!"

Abdul leaned forward and with a quizzical expression questioned Lesley, "I don't really understand what we can do to help Lesley, as much as I care for Ryan, and appreciate Betty's position, it is not our way to get involved in another's domestic situation."

Nassir nodded in agreement, and Amanda just looked on in awe - what exactly what Lesley playing at?!

"I understand your confusion, and yes, you are quite right, I would not, and do not expect you to get involved in the relationship between Betty and Dwayne, however what I would like you to do is call the police whenever you hear them arguing, or you think that Dwayne may be hurting or about to hurt either Betty or Ryan. Betty knows that if she fears for her safety, she should shout/scream loud enough for you to hear, and that you will call the police. Secondly, and Nassir this one is for you, I would like you and Betty to agree on a 'password' so to speak, and should you receive a text message or call from Betty and she says the password then this is another cue to ring the police, as it means that she feels

184

in danger."

Nassir, Abdul and Amanda all started nodding at a similar time, it was as though they all suddenly realised where Lesley was coming from, and yes, how it could work.

"And as for Ryan, well, what more can you do for him?" questioned Lesley in a rhetorical manner. "You are both doing so much for Ryan, you have clearly made him feel like part of the family. And I have absolute certainty that you will continue to provide him with the care that you do now. And that is exactly what Ryan needs."

Lesley leaned back, took a sip of her tea and wondered how they would respond to her "plan." She thought it had gone pretty well, but was never really certain. Some people called themselves friends, and offered their support until they were actually called upon to act on that friendship and support, and then all of a sudden, it was – too close to home, or, not something that we really want to get involved in, or, Billy is still friendly with Bob so it would make it a bit awkward for us to call the police blah blah blah. Lesley had heard it all and she hoped that the Khans would not come up with a similar excuse.

Nassir was the first one to speak up, but whilst doing so, she did appear to glance over towards Abdul in a look that hoped she had his approval. This husband and wife were clearly a team. Lesley liked that for she believed that that was what marriage was all about.

"Lesley, as you are aware, I am very fond of both

185

Betty and Ryan, and yes, I will do as you ask, it is the least we can do to help them." Nassir looked as though she was going to going to speak further, she was clearly speaking from the heart, and she answered Lesley's question with a strength that came from deep within the soul, but her voice quivered just a bit, which indicated to Lesley, that abuse was no stranger to her. Lesley was thinking perhaps her parents led a volatile life or maybe she had a brutish bother, or even a sister who had married into an abusive relationship – one way or another, Lesley was certain that Nassir knew what she was talking about.

Lesley also noticed the look in Abdul's eyes; she caught a glance of sympathy, and protection, he clearly knew where Nassir was coming from, and was obviously determined to protect her from her past perhaps and the ugliness that domestic abuse can bring to all that it affects.

Yes, she had their support – time to move on.

Lesley took one final sip of tea, handed over her card to Nassir, and made her promise that she would call her directly should Nassir have any concerns about either Betty or Ryan's safety. Lesley then nudged Amanda, in an attempt to politely tell her that it was time to leave. The nudge was not so subtle, and both Nassir and Abdul tried to stifle a little giggle. Amanda was actually too engrossed in the TV and the rugby highlights showing!

Lesley finally managed to get Amanda out of the front door, and after thanking both Mr and Mrs Khan, and remembering not to shake hands they headed for the car.

Lesley carelessly handed the keys over to Amanda, "You can drive, I have a phone call to make."

Well, Amanda nearly lost her footing, the two of them had been crewed up for nearly a month together now, and never before had Lesley let her drive!

As they pulled out of White Road Estate and headed down City Way towards the nick, Lesley made her call, "Sergeant, yes, it's Lesley. First round is on me, will be at the Coopers Arms in 20, tell the team will you!"

Well, Amanda was amazed, it was a kinda ritual for the domestic abuse unit to head over to the Coopers Arms on a Friday afternoon for a few "quiet ones" before heading home for the weekend – but the whole time Amanda had been attached to the unit, Lesley had never joined them. And now all of a sudden she was offering to buy the first round! What was going on? Oh, and, Lesley had let her drive!

Lesley had noted the look of astonishment on Amanda's face as she a) threw her the car keys, and then b) offered to buy the first round at the nicks' local – so she decided to give her an explanation for this strange behaviour.

"Well, Amanda, as you heard the first round is on me, best you enjoy it, because as of Monday we start a new case!"

Later on in the evening when a few of the team were still enjoying a few "quiet ones" in the Coopers Arms, Amanda was to learn that Lesley would never join them for a drink whilst in the middle of a case, but once

187

it was over, she would join them and buy the first couple of rounds as a way of saying thanks for putting up with her and her determination to help those not capable of helping themselves.

And so on that Friday night when Amanda finally climbed into bed she felt absolutely exhausted and rather pissed, but also with a weird sense of achievement floating through her veins. The past month had been hard work, but today, she actually felt like she had done all she could to help another, and strangely enough she remembered that that was exactly why she joined the police – to help others. Perhaps the domestic abuse unit was for her after all!

Betty too climbed into bed feeling a little better. She was back at home, Ryan was snoring away in the room next door, and she had survived another month as Mrs McDonald – not quite what she had planned, but she would cope, because that is what she had promised herself she would do.

And as for Dwayne, well, the beating that he had given Betty was long forgotten, in fact he was quite enjoying the bail conditions of not to go back to the house, or contact with the frigid bitch and pathetic son. He could actually spend all evening in the pub and then shag his little, pretty, Miss blonde bimbo all night long – now and again the police actually did him a favour!

And so life on White Road Estate returned to

normal, if that's what you could call it. Dwayne came back home, Betty did her best to keep him happy, Ryan stayed away as much as possible, and the Khan family did all they could for both Ryan and Betty.

No change there then!

Shattered: Sallie Baisley

.

PART 3: 2005

Shattered: Sallie Baisley

CHAPTER 16

It finally seemed that for the Khan family life had settled down. The events of 9/11 and the horrendous months that followed seemed to be a thing of the past.

Abdul could confidently say that they were beginning to feel like Kent was their home, and a welcome home at that. He was still not too keen on the area, but once again, money was not something that came to them easily, so for the time being the Khan family had to be content with the White Road Estate.

On the whole though, Abdul was not complaining, he was still working at the university, and still found the job challenging and motivating. Abdul knew only too well, that not many people got such job satisfaction as he did.

And as for his family, well they too seemed to be content. Nassir was heavily involved with the ladies' groups at the mosque – she was forever helping out with different functions and events. She had also thrown herself heart and soul into the new youth group that was up and running – something that was not available to Fareem a few years ago.

Nassir enjoyed the work at the mosque, now that Fareem was a little older he didn't really need or want his mum about that much these days. And so Nassir turned her focus towards the mosque, and just like everything else in her life, she gave it one hundred and ten percent, and finally the benefits were starting to be seen.

Fareem would be 15 years old in May. He was a good boy, perhaps not as religious as Abdul would have liked, however Fareem did seem to be popular at school, and seemed to be accepted.

Abdul continued to battle with his desire to protect his family, but still allow them a fulfilling life, and on the very dark days he began to question Islam, and how the Prophet Mohammed (peace be upon him) could allow such acts of atrocity. But fortunately the dark days were far and few between for the time being.

On the other side of the fence however, it was a different matter. As Ryan had got older and more independent, Betty hardly ever saw him these days, if he wasn't at the Khan household he was out with Fareem. It seemed to Betty that he only ever came home to sleep these days.

And as for Dwayne, not much had changed with him, which is perhaps why Ryan spent so much time away from home. Even she had to admit to herself that the Arnold home was not a pleasant place to be in. So she couldn't really blame Ryan, however his absence also meant that Betty had lost her direction; as long as she had Ryan to focus on and care for she had some purpose in life. With this gone she found herself withdrawing deeper and deeper into herself.

Unfortunately unlike Abdul, Betty's darker moments were getting more regular. Betty still had good links with the church, but even she had lost interest in this. A few years ago she helped out every Sunday in the

Sunday school, and was also in charge of the flowers. She thrived on these little extras that at the time provided her with a sense of worth and satisfaction.

Over the years her flower arranging had got quite respectable, and on a few occasions she had been approached to prepare and arrangement for Valentines days, and the odd birthday. She wasn't quite confident enough yet to take on a wedding, however she did hope to progress to such in the future, and maybe one day even open her own little florist.

This however was a few years ago now. And Betty had long since given up on any such dreams. To be perfectly honest, during the last few months she had been so caught up in her own dark thoughts of misery that she had all but forgotten about her dreams. That all changed today, and that is perhaps why tonight she was wrapped up in her house, lights turned down low, sipping a small glass of whiskey – something she had started doing more frequently these days, especially during her dark moods.

Earlier on in the day, she had ventured out into town, not Chatham town centre, but Maidstone, a little further. Betty enjoyed the bus trip and was in the mood for a change of scenery.

The bus dropped her off at the Checkers Centre, and she begun to wander aimlessly around the shops, popping in and out of the odd one, but more just for interest rather than actually looking for something to buy. Betty enjoyed window shopping, she found that it gave her the opportunity to disappear into another world, even if just for a short space of time. Whilst wandering through the shops she was able to block out the misery of her life and simply focus on the new fashions and colours, and every now and again she would really let her imagination wander. This would happen mostly in the more "elite" shops, should we say, the ones that Betty could only in her wildest dreams shop in.

On this particular day, she was in one of those "elite" shops, admiring a silk evening dress, a deep tantalising blue colour – one which matched Betty's eyes perfectly. It was a strapless dress that tightened at the waist, and then flowed down into a voluptuous skirt. The deep blue colour complemented her golden blonde hair, and strapless style meant that her sun kissed skin would have ample opportunity to show off as well.

Yes, Betty would have looked beautiful in that dress. Betty had lifted the silk skirt up to her face and was rubbing the soft, cool fabric over her freckled cheeks. Her eyes held a dreamy expression and her mind was filled with images of a candlelight dinner with a good looking charming man who clearly adored her, while she looked stunning in the tantalising dress, and was just admiring the glittering diamond ring that her man had gently slipped onto her finger.

"Betty, Betty, is that you?"

Betty was brought back down to earth by a familiar voice. She opened her eyes, quickly placed the dress back on the rack, and straightened her own cotton dress in an attempt to compose herself.

Maureen was an old friend of Betty's. They both use

to do the flowers for the church, but then Maureen had met a nice young man, got married and moved out of Chatham and the church. The last Betty had heard was that she was living in Bearsted, the better part of Maidstone, and she could afford to shop in the "elite" shops"! Maureen had chosen well, her man was a very rich, successful business man. Maureen was now a woman of means. She was still heavily involved in a church in Maidstone, but now also ran her own florist.

"Betty, I didn't recognise you, look at you."

Betty could hear in the tone of Maureen's voice that Betty was perhaps not looking as good as she could.

"I haven't seen you in years honey, how is life treating you? Have you got rid of that rotten husband yet, and how is that good looking boy of yours, Ryan, is it?"

The questions just kept on coming, every now and again Betty tried to respond, but was gobbled up by another wade of questions that were flowing out of Maureen's perfectly made up lips. Yes, Betty had to admit it, Maureen was looking good.

"Are you still doing flower arranging? I could always do with some extra help – here is my card, give me a call sometime."

As Maureen put her purse back into her designer bag, she glanced at her sparkling watch, and gasped, "Oh heaven is that the time, sorry hon, got to run, please call me some time. Kiss, kiss, so good to see you."

And then she was gone, Betty breathed a sigh of relief and turned to leave the store that she clearly could not afford to shop in.

It was the image that she caught sight of as she was leaving the store, which had brought about her dark mood that evening.

Whilst quickly sipping on her whiskey, she brooded. How could life be so unfair. Seeing Maureen after all these years just reminded her of her pathetic existence. And after seeing her own reflection in the mirror, it was no wonder that Maureen didn't recognise her. Hell nor did Betty. The dreamy image of the women in the silky dress was not the same woman that stared back at Betty.

Her hair was no longer a shimmering blonde, it was dull and going grey rapidly. Betty had pulled it back severely into a pony tail at the nape of her neck. In times long ago, when Betty swept her hair back, it had accentuated her high cheeks bones, these days it only accentuated the wrinkles. She didn't even bother with much make-up these days either. And as for her dress, well, there was really no excuse for her to wear something so old, faded and frumpy looking! She did have some money, and could definitely afford a new dress or two, perhaps more likely form "Asda's" clothing range George, and not the elite store. However she chose not to.

Betty got up to fill her glass, and swayed slightly as she headed to the kitchen. She had drunk more than usual tonight, but the normal two tots had not eased the dark clouds that were thundering through her mind.

Today she realised that she was a pathetic fool, who

had turned into a middle aged timid women, who scurried around like a mouse, wore clothes certain not to attract any attention, and generally had given up all hope of happiness.

Where had the young vibrant twenty-year-old gone? Saying that, where had the vibrant 30-year-old gone? The problem was that even though Betty recognised what she had become, she could still remember her dreams of a better life, as well as the days when she had a life. She knew only too well that she just did not have it in her any more to try and find that lost soul. She was ready to give in to this boring creation of a woman that she had become. Old before her time, sad, and lonely. There was a small corner of her heart that wished she had the courage to phone Maureen up and offer to help in the florist, hell, she had the time these days, but unfortunately the majority of her heart was battered and bruised, and the fight to survive had long since disappeared.

Betty ended up having another couple of whiskeys that night, and finally fell asleep on the couch with the glass still in her hand. The Bible lay next to her, but had not been opened. It was Ryan who found her like that. His heart grew heavy as he gently lifted the glass out of her hand, pulled a blanket over her and turned off the little light. He too wondered how his mum had gotten to this stage. There had been a time when he had always known that she would be there for him. These days he realised that this was no longer the case, he was the one who had to look after her more and more.

As he climbed the stairs to bed, dragging his heavy heart, he reminded himself that it wouldn't always be this way. He would take her away, and give her the life she deserved, he just needed a little bit more time.

CHAPTER 17

July 8 2005.

It was chaos in the Khan household that morning. The family were all still in shock about the events that had not only rocked London, but the whole of the UK, and also the world. Once again Al-Qaida, in the name of Islam, had brought pain and destruction to the Western world. Abdul really didn't know whether he was coming or going, he was convinced that any minute now he would wake up and find that it was all a bad nightmare.

Abdul had finally fallen into a deep sleep in the early hours of the morning, so when the alarm went off at six o'clock, he slept straight through – so did Nassir and also Fareem.

It was Fareem who finally raised the household. He had forgotten to close his curtains the night before, in fact, he had also gone to bed without dinner, which was a first. Since the news of the bombings, his mum and dad had been in a state of shock and he too could not believe what had happened. So last night closing his curtains had been the last thing on his mind, and fortunately it is what had woken the family from their deep slumber.

In July sunrise was pretty early, which is why it had become a habit of Fareem to shut his curtains at night – it meant that he could sleep a little longer in the darkness. It was hard enough getting back to sleep after morning prayers without having to worry about the sun.

However with the angle of his window, it meant that with the curtains open the sun (if it was shining) would come streaming through his window and straight onto his bed at around seven o'clock – which is what woke him up.

He too had been hoping that the day before had been a horrid nightmare, but when the sun streamed in on him he realized that it was no nightmare, it was life. His folks had never slept through the alarm either. His dad was a real stickler for time. This in itself was quite out of the norm for people from his culture, who always turned up late. It was for this reason that his dad made a point of always being early and he had drummed it into Fareem over the years. "Son, if you want to get on in this world, then you need to play by the rules of the country, and that my boy, means being on time."

Abdul would then start to reminisce on his days in Afghanistan, "Oh, Fareem, my father always made a point of being a few minutes late, as this was the right way in our land, blah blah blah." Fareem had heard the stories many times, and always after the lecture on time keeping, Abdul would refer to the Koran, and how it clearly stated that a Muslim is expected to take on the law of the land.

So when he awoke, he realized that he was late. Fareem rubbed his eyes and headed towards his folk's room. They had remembered to draw their curtains and their room was still in darkness. Abdul was snoring deeply and Nassir was snuggled up next to him. Fareem opened the curtains and let the light pour in and gave his dad a shake.

"Dad, Dad, wake up, you are going to be late."

Abdul woke with a start, the sick feeling deep in his stomach was still there, his eyes felt like sawdust, and his body ached with tension. But he was now running late, and that was not acceptable, especially today of all days. He was determined to make a stance. He was a good Muslim, and the events of yesterday were not a reflection of all Muslims, so he would turn up at work as usual and face the music, which was sure to come, if not from his fellow work mates, then from his students.

So Abdul jumped out of bed, thanked Fareem, and at the same time asked him to put the kettle on, it looked like he was going to have to rely on caffeine to get him through the day. Nassir stirred, and then she too woke with a start, and so the Khan household spent the next half an hour running around like headless chickens trying to make some sense of the day.

Abdul made it out the door in record time, toast still in his hand, leaving his coffee cup on the table next to the front door. He grabbed his "lecture bag" and headed out of the door.

During the mad rush, he failed to notice the deep scratches to the side of his car. It was only when he arrived at work, and had to squeeze into a tiny park, which meant getting out of the passenger door, rather than the driver's door, that he spotted the graffiti – to be fair, there was no chance that he could miss it. All along the passenger side of the car someone had scratched in "Muslim bomber".

Abdul sunk to the ground, covering his face in his hands, the realisation was starting to set in and Abdul knew that this would be the first of many attacks. As he knelt beside the car, he closed his eye and said a silent prayer to Allah (May peace be with him).

"My family, how do I protect them? Please guide and protect me and my family."

After a few minutes Abdul slowly rose up off the ground, took three deep breaths and then strode with confidence and pride into the university.

"I will not let the events of yesterday get it me, I am Muslim, we believe in peace, I will survive this, I will survive this."

Ryan ended up going over to the Khan household that morning. He had realised that all was not well when he saw Abdul rushing out the house with the curtains still drawn – this was very unlike the Khan family.

Ryan knew that it probably had to do with the explosions from yesterday. Ryan had spent the night before hidden in his room, with his ear phones on and his music turned up full blast. His dad had spent the evening ranting and raving about Muslims being terrorists etc. etc. He was so sick of his dad and his obnoxious ways. And to be honest, Ryan was just looking for an excuse to go next door. So when the curtains were drawn, he headed over under the impression of concern, when actually he just wanted to be with the people who he felt closest to. At this moment in time it was definitely not his dad – even his mum was driving him mad. Recently she would just sit and listen to his dad rant and rave. Ryan knew that it meant she didn't get a beating, but he found it so hard watching her allow him to say such awful things about the Muslim people. Nassir was probably his mum's best friend, and one thing his mum had always taught him was to look out for your friends, and always stand by them no matter what! Why couldn't she do that now? Yes, he was sick of both of them, and just wanted to be with the family he felt closest to.

Ryan ran around through the side gate and walked in the back door. Nassir looked up for the kitchen table where she was sitting with her night gown wrapped around her and clutching a cup of coffee.

"Good morning my child, and how are you this morning?" Nassir smiled warmly at Ryan as he walked in.

"Okay, but starving, was hoping to steal some of those delicious biscuits of yours before heading off to school." Ryan leant over and gave Nassir a kiss on her cheek and a little cuddle.

Nassir smiled inwardly. That boy is no fool, she thought, that gentle kiss and little cuddle was his way of giving the Khan family his support. "Oh, Ryan, you won't be able to get through the day on my biscuits, go up and say hello to Fareem, and I will make you some toast – how does that sound?"

"Yippee, not only do I get to eat some biscuits, I also get to have some of your delicious homemade bread!" Ryan disappeared out of the kitchen door and up the stairs – Nassir heard his feet pounding up the stairs two at a time.

"Hey bro, how are things going?" Ryan flopped onto Fareem's bed. Ryan's relaxed state was the complete opposite of Fareem, who was normally the chilled out one.

Fareem was stuffing books into his school bag as he responded, "Late mate, that is what, can you believe it but my dad actually overslept this morning! And now I am rushing around trying to avoid a detention by being late to school. And on top of that I am starving."

"Chill bro, we have plenty of time, your mum is making us some toast, and then we can leg it to school, well, at least, I can, I will once again whip your slow butt, and avoid a detention – you my friend need to learn to run faster!"

Fareem strode rapidly over to Ryan, who was lying stretched out on his bed, hand behind his head, legs crossed, looking as those he had no cares in the world. Fareem planted one almighty punch into the side of Ryan's leg – giving him one hell of a good dead leg. "Now, my friend, let's see who beats whose butt to school."

And with that they both raced downstairs, Fareem chuckling away, Ryan howling in pain, but with a big, broad smile caressing his face. How he loved this family. And he had enjoyed making both Nassir and Fareem smile today.

Nassir, stood at the door, with two doorstep sized pieces of toast in her hands. As the boys dashed past her, she handed them each a piece.

"Thanks Mum, love you always."

"Thanks Nassir, love you always too."

Nassir closed the door and took a big breath. The whirlwind of the morning was finally over. Her eyes were gritty with lack of sleep, and she was desperate for a long hot shower whereby she could slowly consider the events of yesterday and how the family were going to be able to move forward. Because forward was the only way they could go!

CHAPTER 18

November 2005.

In the months that followed the 7/7 attacks the Khan family's life was made a living hell. If someone had told Abdul that his family would be persecuted in so many different ways he would have laughed at the impossibility of it. However he was not laughing now.

His car had been scratched four times now and was costing him a fortune to repair. When someone at work at asked if it was worth the bother, Abdul looked directly at them and responded, "Would you really want to drive your family around with terrorist or bomber displayed along the length of the car for all to see?"

The reply was something along the lines of, "Well, now when you put it that way, I guess not."

As it so happened, Abdul was actually being polite when he described the words scratched onto his car, as he would never have voluntarily repeated what was the actually there.

But that was not all he had endured. He had been spat at whilst walking along the street and sworn at. Generally it was just mindless yobs that treated him so disrespectfully, but on occasion he had been sworn at by well-dressed business men!

However even that he was willing to put up with, it was the attacks on his home and his family that he feared the most. The police had done their best to help, but even they could not guarantee his family's safety. And to be honest, there were times when he felt that some of the police officers who had responded to his calls for help had also looked on him and his family suspiciously.

Letters had been placed in the letter box threatening to burn the house down. Pork had been thrown onto the door step (this might seem insignificant to many, however for a Muslim family pork is believed to be unclean.

Their door bell had been rung in the middle of the night, and red paint had been thrown across their house.

Nassir had willing stopped wearing her hijab as it was now a matter of safety more than anything else. She personally had not been attacked in the street, but some of the other ladies from the mosque had. In fact a friend of theirs had been so badly beaten up that she had spent three weeks in hospital. Abdul did not have to lay down the law. Nassir willingly went about her daily business these days doing her best to look 100% British.

And as for Fareem, Abdul did not know what effect this was having on him. Abdul was certain that Fareem was doing his best to hide any issues from his folks. Fareem was a care free easy going boy, and it seemed to Abdul that he was just taking it all in his stride, dealing with whatever came his way. Once again Abdul thanked Allah (May peace be upon him) for the friendship that had developed over the years between Fareem and Ryan. Ryan was a good boy, Abdul knew that as long as the two of them remained friends Fareem would be okay.

Ryan was very different to his father – another thing

that Abdul thanked Allah (May peace be upon him) for, however Ryan did have a sort of status at school simply because he was an Arnold – a name that the neighbourhood knew and respected, even if it was for all the wrong reasons. And this certain respect gave Ryan and Fareem a bit of "protection" to say the least – or that is what Abdul thought.

Abdul did suspect that life for Fareem was not as easy as he portrayed, this just added to his many concerns – there was the constant worry about the house being damaged, or set alight, Nassir spending time out of the house, and to add to the list, all the students at the university seemed to treat him with great suspicion.

It was making for a very stressful life. For the first time in a very long time Abdul was desperately unhappy. He wasn't enjoying his work, he was continually expecting a call from Nassir or the police to say that one of the family was either in hospital, or the house had been burnt down. The police had assured Abdul that it was highly unlikely however in the same breath they also advised Abdul to change his letter box to a fire safety device!

The police had also installed cameras, and were in touch with Abdul on nearly a day-to-day basis. Did this make Abdul feel safer? No, it just made him realise that even the police thought his family were at risk.

And so it was for all of these reasons that Abdul was not sleeping at night. However there was one more issue that disturbed him even more. He had noticed a change in the mosque since 7/7. There seemed to be an underlying current channelling its way through the younger Muslims. It wasn't so much the events of 7/7 that had caused the change. It was more the response of the Western world to all Muslims as a result of firstly 9/11 and then 7/7. The Western World seemed to be tarnishing all Muslims with the same brush – in the eyes of the Western World, all Muslims were terrorists.

Abdul did not like what he was seeing, and what scared him even more was the radicalisation that he was witnessing amongst the younger generation, this was causing him to question his faith, something he never believed could happen, but it was. And it was this questioning of his faith that was causing him such turmoil.

In the end it was Dirk who came to his rescue. One Friday afternoon after a particularly hard week – both at university and at home – Abdul was near breaking point. Dirk had recognised the suffering that Abdul was going through and decided to take the bull by the horns, and get the man to share his burden.

So at four on Friday afternoon Dirk phoned Nassir and told her that he was taking Abdul out for the night – they would be home a lot later. Nassir breathed a sigh of relief. She had also recognised the turmoil that Abdul had been going through and was extremely worried about him. She knew that if he was going to open up to anyone then it would be to Dirk.

Dirk caught up with Abdul as he was returning from Friday prayers. Canterbury Street mosque was within walking distance of the university. And as Friday

211

afternoon prayers were obligatory, Abdul would do his best to attend the mosque for prayers. The congregation was slowly growing again as many men had stopped attending the mosque for afternoon prayers after 7/7. Abdul had discussed this with his brothers – in the Islamic faith, Muslims refer to all other Muslims as brothers or sisters. The other men had expressed their concern at walking into the mosque during daylight hours – there was so much suspicion against all Muslims that they just didn't feel safe.

But a few months had passed, and people were obviously feeling safer about attending the mosque for afternoon prayers. But this rise in numbers also seemed to fill the youngsters with confidence. They were starting to question the committee who were all old men. This was not something that Abdul approved of even though he had always felt that the committee should be representative of all Muslims – not just the old men. Abdul would have willing seen some young faces as well as women joining the committee, but it was not under these circumstances that Abdul wanted to see these young men take charge of the mosque. There was one young man in particular that Abdul did not like, and he appeared to be the natural leader. He was also clearly very intelligent and well versed in the Islamic faith, however Abdul did not necessarily agree with his interpretation of the faith. His name was Aarif; he was dynamic, handsome and smart – it was easy to see how he was able to draw the younger men would be drawn to him.

The older men seemed to appreciate and accept this new young man and his exuberant ways. They would comment that it was good to see the younger community taking more of an interest in the faith, and if this young man was going to help them do this than so be it. For this reason everyone was happy to ignore Aarif's "interesting" interpretation.

Abdul wasn't so sure about this! And it was this thought he was pondering when he bumped into Dirk.

"Hello my old mate, you look like you were miles away."

"Oh, ummm, yes, sorry Dirk, I didn't see you standing there. Yes, you are quite right I was miles away – and it was not happy thoughts, so I am pleased that you interrupted them." Abdul patted Dirk on the shoulder in a friendly gesture.

"Well, then my friend, I think you are going to like what I have to say next – I have phoned Nassir, and told her that we are going out this evening, and so not to expect you home anytime soon."

"Oh, that is unexpected, have you got some news for me or something?"

"No, Abdul, nothing like that – I am concerned about you and I think it is about time that you got everything off your chest so we are off to a quiet little spot that I know. You can have a cup of tea, while I have a few beers – which might mean you have to drive me home, but Abdul, one way or another, we are going to talk things through tonight so get your bag and I will meet you in the car park."

Abdul hurried off, quite pleased about this unexpected "date" if you could call it that. A good chat with a friend might be just the thing he needed.

Dirk and Abdul headed away from the university just after five in the evening which meant that they hit the rush hour traffic. They crawled along through Chatham, bumper to bumper with every other person trying to get home for the evening. The air outside was bitterly cold, and Abdul's heater was taking its time at warming up. Dirk was rubbing his hands together and blowing into them in a bid to warm up.

"Gees Abdul, I hate this sodden weather, when God made me he had the sun in mind. This African blood does not do well in these Baltic temperatures."

Dirk continued to complain about the weather. Abdul was so used to hearing Dirk moan and groan about the cold that he switched off, and once again his mind began to wander back to the turmoil he was facing.

"Earth to Abdul! Are you still in the same planet as the rest of us, you have just missed the turn." Dirk gave Abdul a playful prod on the shoulder and brought Abdul back into the land of the living.

"Sorry Dirk, I was once again miles away - where should I go now?"

"No problem boet, just take the next right and we will be back on track."

After another 20 minutes of fighting the traffic Abdul's car, which had finally started to warm up, turned down a quiet country road. "Where exactly are you taking me Dirk, I know things aren't going too well on the girl front at the moment, but if you are planning on taking advantage of me in these dark woods you should think twice," said Abdul in mock humour.

"Aaah, Abdul you my friend are really not my type."

As Abdul smiled at his friend, he began to relax for the first time in weeks, just as they rounded the bend and turned into the car park of a typical country pub - The Robin Hood.

Both men climbed out of the car, pulled their jackets tighter and bent their heads in an attempt to keep the icy air off their faces.

"Move it mate, it will be warm inside and I need a beer."

Abdul didn't need any encouragement from Dirk, he too had picked up the pace. Abdul opened the door and hurried inside, only to be met with every single person sitting at the bar turning to stare at the new comer.

Oh hell, here we go again, maybe this was not such a good idea. Abdul's heart sank as he saw the looks of hostility on these people's faces. Abdul was just about to turn around and leave when Dirk entered, and now all eyes were on Dirk. A few men raised their arms, nodded their heads in recognition, and then they all turned back to their drinks and continued with their conversations. However Dirk had seen the look in Abduls eyes and realised what had happened.

"Don't you worry about this lot Abdul, they view all strangers with equal suspicion - do you know how much beer I had to drink here, and how many Friday nights I had to spend in this place before I too became a local?!"

Abdul smiled, and tried to relax, as he chose a table closest to the door - if he did need to get out quickly then at least he was sitting in the most opportunist spot!

However true to his word, Dirk disappeared off to the bar, and chatted to a couple of the men whilst ordering our drinks, and everyone seemed to forget that Abdul was there. Whilst Abdul was waiting for Dirk his gaze drifted over to the massive fireplace in the corner of the room, Abdul could feel the heat coming off the blazing fire that was crackling away, and could just be heard above the banter from the "locals" hugging the bar.

It was then that Abdul noticed the couple snuggled up on the sofa that was placed right opposite the fire. They were quietly chatting together, whilst sipping their drinks - hers a red wine, his a pint of beer. He was stroking her hair, she was resting her hand on his thigh - they were in a world of their own, and had definitely not paid any attention to Abdul, the dark man who walked into the pub 20 minutes ago. "The dark man" then slowly scanned the rest of the pub, and realised that actually there were quite a few people present who had not paid him any attention whatsoever. He breathed a sigh of relief and tried hard to relax, reprimanding himself for being so paranoid.

Abdul was pulled out of his thoughts by Dirk shouting over to him, "Hey, Abdul, come over here I want to introduce you to a friend of mine."

Abdul raised his eyes and took in the man standing

next to Dirk - a big jolly man, who by the size of his belly and ruddy complexion spent a lot of time in the pub! Abdul headed that way, was handed a large coke by Dirk and then introduced to Gerry. Gerry now lived in Chatham but was originally from Northern Ireland. He had met Dirk in the pub, and the two of them had spent many an evening chatting about this and that over a few beers. Gerry appeared to hold no malice towards Abdul, and his cheery, easy going nature, and very humorous outlook on life made Abdul laugh - a big hearty laugh for the first time in ages.

Abdul was not quite sure how long they sat in the pub for, but it did do him the world of good. Firstly meeting Gerry, and then chatting long into the night with Dirk, Abdul slowly shared his fears and concerns with Dirk - he even had a beer or two! It was completely against the Islamic faith, but somehow it just felt right on that night. What Abdul did remember was that he stumbled into the house way after both Nassir and Fareem had gone to bed. He also remembered that Dirk had told him to take a break - to go away for a few weeks with the family. He also then told Abdul that he was welcome to use the family holiday home in South Africa. The more Dirk spoke about it the more it seemed like a good idea. So as he collapsed, exhausted onto the bed he rolled over, wrapped his arms around Nassir - who was snoring gently, and promised himself that the first thing tomorrow he would look into flights to South Africa.

True to his word, he awoke the following day,

feeling slightly under the weather, but with this small ball of excitement growing inside his belly. In fact he actually woke before both Nassir, Fareem and Ryan (another sleep over - they were happening more and more often, in fact it was odd over the weekend if Ryan was not about).

Abdul crept quietly down the stairs trying his best not to wake his sleeping family. But the stairs were prone to creaking, which he knew, so if anyone had actually seen him it would have looked rather humorous - Abdul creeping down the old stairs, wearing nothing but a pair of jogging bottoms, hair in disarray, feeling a slight headache, and tiptoeing down each step. He looked more like Shaggy from Scooby-Doo than a highly intelligent university lecturer. He reached the ground floor successfully - the snoring could still be heard above the creaking stairs! And so he headed firstly into the dining room-library and switched on the computer, then made his way into kitchen to get that kettle boiling - he needed a strong cup of black coffee!

Abdul returned to the dining room armed with a steaming cup of coffee and a couple of biscuits - he was starving – as eating had not quite been part of Dirk's agenda last night! After a few sips of coffee, and gobbling down the biscuits he felt ready to hit the computer and find out a little bit more about South Africa and this holiday house that Dirk had offered.

An hour later Nassir walked into the room. Her nightgown was wrapped tightly around her waist and her hair swept back, but a few strands kept escaping. She absent mindedly pushed them out of her eyes and glanced into the dining room.

When Nassir awoke to an empty bed she was rather confused. Abdul seldom rose before her, and especially not over a weekend unless he had work to do or was stressed. Her first thought was so much for the "night out" with Dirk, great lot of good that did. So she was not at all surprised to find Abdul in the dining room in front of his computer. What she was not expecting to see was his bare top half - Abdul seldom walked around the house without a shirt on, even on a hot summer's day. He had a gentle smile that seemed to be caressing his jaw line.

What in the name of Allah was her husband up to?

Abdul glanced up on hearing the door slide open, "Aah, the love of my life, come my dear, come and sit next to me." Abdul pushed his chair away from the table, opened his arms and beckoned towards Nassir. He was grinning like a five-year-old in Harrods! It was just so good to see Abdul smiling that Nassir rushed towards him and fell into his embrace. She sat on his knee and ruffled his hair.

"Now my dear husband, please, I know I am the love of your life, but it has been a while since you have whispered such words, and you haven't smiled in so long that I thought you had forgotten how to - what in the name of Allah were you and Dirk up to last night?!" She concluded the sentence with a brief kiss to the top of his head, which was slowly turning grey. How she loved this man, and how she hurt when she knew he was in pain. It

219

was good to have him back - so to speak!

Before Abdul got a chance to explain his plans to Nassir, they were interrupted by two very sleepy 15-year-olds walking into the room. They were both rubbing their eyes, and still had on their pyjamas. If it wasn't for the size of the two of them they could have passed for five-year-olds as they both had that innocent look of the young. Nassir sighed at the sight of the two of them, it was good to see such innocence, but she knew it would not last, as soon as they had both had a chance to fully waken their expressions would change as they too remembered "life" - Ryan more so than Fareem. These days Ryan's gentle good looking features were a thing of the past - he was still a very good looking boy, but his eyes were hard and cold, and his seemed to be permanently clenching his teeth together.

"Come come, boys," Abdul ushered the boys into the room with the broad smile still plastered to his face, the tone of his voice seemed to be bubbling with excitement.

Just like Nassir, the boys were surprised as well as delighted in Abdul's manner. Abdul also noticed the look in his family's eyes. These days he considered Ryan part of the family and he finally was able to realise how much stress he had not only put himself under but also his loved ones. It was time to end it all. Abdul also realised that he really should discuss his plans through with Nassir first, but realised that it was not going to happen - he was desperate to fill them all in on his news, and it was not going to wait a second longer.

"Nassir, boys, I have something to tell you all." The three of them had now all awoken fully and were learning forward expectantly.

"Well come on Dad, what is going on, or are we going to have to tickle it out of you?!" It was an old game the family used to play.

Abdul let out a big throaty laugh, "No Fareem, no tickles today. As you know I went out with Dirk last night and we chatted long into the night. Basically he has offered us the opportunity to go away to South Africa for a few weeks and stay in his family holiday home."

Ryan's shoulders slowly began to slump as he realised that he was not actually part of this conversation - holidays were not something that he did, let alone a holiday abroad. That was what real families did - not families like his.

"Well, naturally, I thanked Dirk for the offer, but also was certain that something like that would be far too expensive, however, this morning I thought I would have a look at flights on the internet. And boys, do you know what - I think we can do it!"

Fareem was thinking just what Ryan was thinking, how could his Dad be doing this in front of Ryan. Fareem glanced over to Ryan and could see the sadness engulfing his face. He was blinking rapidly, and Fareem realised that he was trying to get rid of the tears that were rapidly filling up in his eyes. A big lump started rising in Fareem's throat. More than anything else, he hated seeing Ryan sad, and unfortunately it happened more often these days.

Abdul glanced from boy to boy and looked confused. "What is up with the two of you? I thought you would be excited."

Fareem raised his big brown eyes and reminded his dad that there was no way Ryan would be able to afford to come on holiday to South Africa. Abdul let out another big throaty laugh, and now it was the boys turn to look confused - had Abdul gone crazy because he sure as hell was acting crazy. Nassir too, was alarmed at his odd behaviour, and stiffened as she moved off Abdul's lap and looked him sternly in the eye.

"Abdul, I think we need to discuss this later. Now these boys need to get ready for rugby practise." She turned towards the boys and gently told them to hurry along and she would sort this out with her husband.

"No, no, you have it all wrong - Nassir, my love, Ryan and Fareem - I can afford for all of us to go. Ryan, my boy, come here. I consider you a part of this family, and would never not include you. Now I understand that we are going to have to speak long and hard to your mum and dad about this, and they might not be happy about it, but don't you worry my son - I will try my best, and Ryan, if they are not happy about it, well then, we will think of something else! And that is the way we do things in this house - it's all of us or nothing."

Well this changed the expressions on the boy's faces - Ryan felt a sudden surge of love for this family, his family, and now his eyes were filled with tears, only this time his heart was not aching, for the first time in his life he actually felt like he was a part of something -

something special. This family really loved him, so much that they considered him a part of that loving family. Fareem too, felt a surge of love for both his dad and his best friend, who yes, was more than just a friend, he was like a brother. He tugged at Ryan's arm and started dragging him out of the room.

"Come on 'Bro' best we get ready for rugby, then we can decide how to tell your mum that we are going on holiday!"

The boys disappeared up the stairs, and Nassir, who was still a little concerned about all these plans that Abdul was making, ushered him into the kitchen, sat down expectantly at the table and informed Abdul in no uncertain terms that he would make her a cup of coffee and then tell him exactly what he was planning! But not even her stern and determined tone could wipe the smile off Abdul's face. He gently rubbed both her shoulders lovingly and sighed.

"Okay, okay, my dear, let's just get that kettle on."

Half an hour later, Nassir also had a little tight ball of excitement sitting at the pit of her belly. Abdul was right - they could afford this! He had stumbled upon some last minute deals to South Africa. It would mean they would be leaving in two weeks, and the boys would miss a week of school, but this was clearly an opportunity that would be ludicrous to miss out on. And a break is exactly what they all needed - some time away from this town and country where they could all just breathe a little easier and sleep a little better. The stress of the last few months had taken its toll on all of them, including Ryan, who had enough problems of his own without having to worry about Fareem as well. Yes, this was a good idea.

Nassir wrapped her arms around her husband and gave him a long, deep kiss. He responded by pulling her closer and kissing her urgently back, he could feel the bulge in his trousers beginning to grow. It had been months since the two of them had felt this close. It was not that they were drifting apart, more like finding the time to get together, and the stress they had both been under had meant that, to be honest, neither of them really had the energy to "bond." So it was good to feel the sense of urgency throbbing through their bodies again. It gave them both hope that things would eventually return to normal, and more importantly that they both still enjoyed the other's body.

Yes, Nassir loved this man, and loved how he made her feel. It was good to have him back. Gently, and reluctantly she pulled away from him. She reached up and placed her finger on his lips.

"Save these thoughts for tonight my love, unfortunately we have two 15-year-old boys upstairs who will be bounding down the stairs any minute and demanding food!"

Abdul tried to tug onto Nassir and playfully whispered, "Come on, you can't leave me like this, look what you have done to me." He pressed himself fully against her, and growled in desperation. Nassir chuckled, and pulled away, which was lucky too, no sooner had she stepped away from Abdul did the boys come running into the room.

"Food, food, Mum, we need food," boomed Fareem.

And food is what they got - four thick slices of toast each, covered with butter and cheese, jam, honey and anything else the boys could get their hands on. They scoffed down the food with a pint of milk each!

Guess I'll have to do some shopping today thought Nassir as the boys riffled through the fruit bowl and left it near empty as they legged it out of the front door and were off. She knew she wouldn't see them until much later that afternoon, or until they got hungry!

Hmmmm, she wondered if Abdul would now be keen to finish off where they had left off early, gosh it had been ages since they snuck off to the bedroom during the day and fulfilled each other. But just as she was thinking such "wicked" thoughts, Abdul shouted from the front door.

"I'll see you later love, I am off to Dirk's to just confirm what he said last night. Will you try and speak to Betty later on? Love you always."

Nassir leaned around the kitchen door, smiled happily and blew a kiss back at Abdul, so much for that she thought. She was now the only one wandering around in her nightgown, so decided to head upstairs for a shower - it might help cool her down. She was really quite hot and bothered by the feeling of Abdul pressing up against her. The mess in the kitchen could wait for later.

As Nassir headed upstairs she sent Betty a quick

text message. "Hi, are you around today, and if so do you fancy a cuppa? Ryan and Fareem have just headed out the door for rugby practice."

Just as Nassir was slipping into the shower she heard the beep beep of her mobile phone and knowing it would be Betty, she quickly dashed into the bedroom and checked the message.

"A cuppa sounds good, when?"

"Give me an hour and then pop over," responded Nassir. It was very seldom that Nassir went over to Betty's house, you never really knew when Dwayne would be around, and it was best not to give him any extra ammunition, so instead, Betty would come over to hers.

The two ladies had become firm friends over the years and Nassir felt a closeness to Betty that she hadn't felt with any of her other friends before. And yes, it was true that they had been through a lot together, and Nassir did understand that that in itself brought about closeness, but with Betty it seemed different. With the ladies at the Muslim ladies group Nassir always felt like she had to watch what she said; someone was always waiting to criticise, or belittle another.

At times Nassir felt sorry for the ladies, they all seemed a little bit bitter about the card they had been dealt with, and all they seemed to have in their lives was the caring for the children and husband, and then the ladies group. To sum it up they were all very bored, old ladies who had never really had the opportunity to do anything more with their lives than be a glorified housewife. The only difference being, they were all rich, and used their money to try and buy themselves some form of happiness. Because one thing was certain, there was not much happiness in their marriages. This resulted in a lot of very bitter women, who gossiped and took great delight in others' misfortunes.

Nassir scolded herself quietly. They were not all like that. Some of the ladies, like herself, were happy, however these were the ones that like Nassir kept themselves to themselves at the usual Wednesday ladies circle. Nassir wondered if they too had friends outside the mosque. She hoped they did.

CHAPTER 19

December 2005. South Africa.

It hadn't been nearly as difficult as Nassir and Abdul had expected to get Dwayne to agree to allow Ryan to travel to South Africa. In fact it had been alarmingly easy. When Nassir had first approached Betty, Betty had become overwhelmed with a sense of joy, mingled with slight sadness. How lucky was she that Ryan had been accepted as part of such a strong secure family. They were able to offer Ryan everything that she had dreamed of offering him. But she realised that being married to a man like Dwayne meant that any chance of a strong and secure family life was non-existent.

That day she told Nassir just how grateful she was and also that she would find a way to convince Dwayne that Ryan should go. She also promised Nassir that she would ensure that Ryan had enough money to pay his way (how the hell she was going to do this she didn't know, but there was no way she was going to let Ryan miss out on such a great opportunity).

Betty spent the rest of the day planning ways to tell Dwayne that Ryan would be away over Christmas. As it so happened, Dwayne walked in a great mood, so whilst he was gobbling down his dinner as fast as he could so he could get down to the pub, Betty broached the subject. Well, Dwayne appeared delighted, he even pulled out his wallet and handed over £500 for the air ticket, promising to get more out the bank tomorrow. It was only later on in the evening after Betty had time to consider the out of character behaviour that it dawned on her - Dwayne was pleased to get Ryan out of the house for a couple of weeks, even if it meant handing over some money. Less stress for him, less responsibility for him and more time at the pub with his bit on the side. And as for the money, Betty was not really sure what Dwayne was up to at the moment, but he always seemed to have plenty of money on him - she was wise enough to not ask questions to which she didn't want to know the answers.

So although she was elated at the opportunity that Ryan was about to experience, she was desperately aware that it was more than likely illegal money that was getting him there and because of a father who really couldn't be bothered. It all made her realise just exactly how depressing life in the Arnold house had become!

The result was that three weeks to the day that Dirk and Abdul had gone out for a "few quiet ones" the Khan family and Ryan were heading down the M25 towards Heathrow, the old little Ford packed to the tilt. Abdul and Nassir were doing their best to keep a lid on their excitement, but the boys were out of control. If you can imagine two 15-year-old boys on speed, well that was what Abdul and Nassir had to contend with in the back seat! There were yelps of delight, and yelps of pain as the two of them took turns in punching each other's arms, in a friendly game of "we have too much energy, and just want to get to South Africa". This was not just the first time the two boys would be travelling to another country, but also the first trip on an aeroplane! As a punch was landed directly on the arm, the boys seemed to automatically kick out at the seat in front of them; this resulted in Nassir and Abdul having an incredibly noisy and bumpy drive all the way to the airport. On a normal occasion they both would have probably lost their temper and demanded the boys calm down, however not today. Today was about the future. Today was the start of the break all five of them desperately needed. Today was the first step in getting not only their lives, but also their minds back on track.

Nassir was looking forward to some hot weather, a break from the "bitchy ladies" at the Muslim ladies group, and just an opportunity to unwind. Abdul on the other hand was planning on focusing on his religion. These few weeks were going to give him time to reflect on his Islamic roots and remind him of the goodness of Islam - not what people perturbed it to be.

And then there were the two boys. Fareem, was planning on learning how to surf and hoping to meet a few "hot" babes or perhaps even get the opportunity to kiss a girl! His mind recently seemed to be consumed with the girls in his class, and their rapidly developing bodies! Ryan, well, he was just pleased to be out of the stifling house for a while, and really looking forward to being part of a normal family. And so the car continued to speed towards the airport, filled with bags, excitement and a great anticipation for what was to come.

The flight over to South Africa was long, and so by

the time the Khan family and Ryan finally arrived in Durban they were exhausted, however on stepping out onto African soil, with the African sun beating down on their backs, all of them pushed the exhaustion to the back of their minds and a sense of excitement started to well up inside of them. And if the truth was known Nassir and Abdul were also rather nervous. Not only were they visiting a strange country for the first time, but they also had two 15-year-old boys with them! To top it off South Africa was not exactly renowned for being a safe and crime free country!

Well neither of them had the opportunity to ponder their nervous situation. No sooner had they arrived they collected their luggage, passed through immigration, received their hire car and were heading down the motorway towards Balito.

Balito was a small holiday town on the outskirts of Durban, in fact it was only 20 minutes from the airport. Dirk had arranged for Abdul to collect the key for the apartment from the caretaker, who was hopefully expecting them! Dirk had also given Abdul very detailed instructions on how to reach their destination - he explained that they really did not want to take a wrong turn! The Phoenix township, or perhaps better known as a shanty town, was not far from Balito, and as Dirk joked, gently patting Abdul's cheek, "You might be the same colour as the Blacks, but trust me boet, you don't want to end up in a township." And so Abdul followed the details exactly. He got beeped several times as a result and a few drivers made use of their hands whilst swearing at Abdul as they sped past them, probably because of the slow pace Abdul was travelling. Each time a horn beeped, he just turned to Nassir and smiled, "There is nothing wrong with driving slowly if it saves us from taking a wrong turn!" Nassir on the other hand was not paying any attention to the drivers or Abdul, she was fascinated with the land around her. It was not yet ten in the morning, but the sun was already beating down onto the scorched earth. Nassir was amazed at the colour of the ground – it was red, as though too much blood had seeped into it. And then every now and again they would drive past someone walking along this hot road, barefoot and carefree. No one seemed to be going anywhere in a hurry other than the cars! These dark barefoot people appeared to be at one with the earth and sun. The pure simplicity of it took Nassir's breathe away.

As for the boys in the back, well, for the first time since they had left Chatham the day before they were quiet. They too seemed to be overwhelmed by the climate, county and people.

Abdul spotted the off ramp that they needed, and signalled politely, this was something he came to realise that only he did! He commented to no one in particular that he thought they were nearly there, but no one responded. Abdul took a right, then a left down a sharp hill, and came face to face with a troop on monkeys. Well this got everyone's attention, and they found their voices. Nassir shrieked in fright, the boys shrieked with delight and Abdul laughed at them all, including the monkeys, who really did not seem nearly as interested in the "English" people, as the "English" people were in them. Abdul remembered Dirk giving him strict instructions to keep all the windows and doors locked when out and about, "Those monkeys will trash the place, they will eat all your food and shit on your clothes." Abdul had laughed, not for one minute believing him.

Abdul turned to the boys and told them that this was their stop.

"What?" said both boys in horror. Yes, they had turned off the road, but there were still not many houses in sight.

"Come on my two monkeys, go and join your brothers," giggled Abdul.

Fareem sighed deeply, and responded in that annoying 15-year-old, bored tone, "Daaad, you are so laaame."

Ryan just sat in the back grinning from ear to ear, he was having the time of his life.

"Okay, okay, children - that means you too Abdul," said Nassir mockingly, "I am dying for a cup of tea, so can we find this holiday home please."

A few minutes later they arrived at the complex. "Wow, can you believe this place?" shouted Ryan and Fareem as they ran around in awe.

Nassir and Abdul stood there wide eyed with even wider mouths. The "holiday" home was unbelievable, definitely not what any of them were expecting. The three bedroom holiday home was the most beautiful house Ryan had ever seen. Not even in his wildest dreams did he imagine that people actually lived in such homes, let alone call them holiday homes.

"And there was I expecting to lug dirty washing down to the Laundromat every other day, imagine that not only am I going to get to use a top of the range washing machine, but there is also a tumble dryer," laughed Nassir.

Abdul walked over to the curtains and slowly begun to pull them apart - he too then stood speechless, just as the rest of the family did once they too caught a glimpse of the view. The lounge opened out onto a balcony the same length as the house, and being on the second floor, meant that they had the most spectacular view of the sea.

This is paradise thought Abdul. "Thank you Dirk," he whispered to himself.

It didn't take long for the family to get into some kind of routine. This basically meant that Ryan and Fareem were out the house pretty much as soon as the sun rose, and only returned when their bellies started growling at them. Nassir and Abdul would spend the morning lounging in bed, enjoying the magnificent view of the sea which they could see from their big comfy bed. They would each take it in turns at making the coffee in the morning. Nassir would then potter about in the kitchen and get some breakfast ready. The boys were eating plenty and Nassir knew that all that fresh air made for a big appetite, but it was so good for them. Ryan's skin had quickly adapted to the scorching sun, and before long he was as brown as a berry. The salt water was turning his hair a lovely sun kissed blonde. The tan and the hair accentuated his deep blue eyes, which were looking kinder and more gentle these days - or was that just Nassir's imagination?

As for Fareem, well he didn't really need the sun to darken his skin, but even his dark skin started looking healthier after a few days in the sun, and as his skin got darker, so his dark hair started to also get bleached by the sun and sea. Nassir knew she was biased, but this hot climate definitely brought out the best in him and she thought he was looking extremely handsome. In fact, Nassir had noticed that she was not the only one that had thought Fareem was looking rather good. The boys had quickly made friends with another couple of families who were staying in the same complex. This new group of friends included a few girls and one in particular seemed to be rather taken by Fareem and his dark looks and English accent! Nassir smiled to herself as she recalled catching Cindy sneaking glances at Fareem - aah, first love, what a wonderful time. Nassir could still recall her first love. In fact, they actually made a lovely looking couple. Cindy was Argentinean, and so also had a dark skin, and lovely long wavy dark hair.

One of the other girls, Tanya, seemed to be rather taken by Ryan, but he didn't seem all that interested, in fact as the group of friends started spending more and more time together Ryan appeared to be pulling away from them. He seemed to be more content to spend time talking to Abdul. Nassir's heart bled for that child, who she loved as if he was her own. The child had shadows and Nassir didn't know if he would ever really be able to push those shadows away. She was certain that that was the reason he had started to shun his new friends and favour Abdul's company - the boy had never really had the opportunity to have a father figure to be proud of. And so this was a first for him. Fortunately Abdul seemed happy to have this "lost" boy follow him around like a devoted puppy. Abdul also realised that the boy was just desperate for the opportunity to spend quality time with a man. And so Abdul took the boy under his wing so to speak.

Abdul was using this time away from Britain to reflect on both himself, and his religion, which he had begun to question over the last few months. He therefore spent a lot of time reading through the Koran. Ryan seemed to be fascinated by the holy book, and more than once Abdul had seen Ryan reading the book himself. This in itself brought about an issue, which Nassir and Abdul discussed at length one evening - both the boys had gone into town to watch a movie and get something to eat with their new friends. Ryan hadn't been too keen to start with, but Abdul had encouraged him to go because he really wanted to discuss Ryan's fascination of Islam with Nassir.

Nassir and Abdul settled down into the chairs on the balcony, and watched the sun drift below the sea. The sea was angry tonight, or rather in turmoil. The waves rapidly changing direction and crashed into other waves. There seemed to be no direction or pattern, just confusion and Abdul sensed something similar in his soul. This he had noticed was happening a lot. His mood often seemed to be portrayed by the sea, or perhaps it was the sea that portrayed his mood. Either way, he knew it was time to speak to his "better half" and seek her advice.

Abdul finally broke the silence, "Nassir, my dear, was it such a good idea to bring Ryan with us and accept him into our home?"

Nassir lent over and gently rubbed Abdul's shoulder, "Aah, Abdul, don't you ever question what we have done for that boy? He has 'blossomed' over the past week like never before. Can't you see the change in his eyes? They seem to be far softer and more gentle these days, and that my love, is because of what we have been able to offer him." Nassir then turned her chair to face Abdul directly. She leant forward and placed both her hands on his knees, "But, what we really need to discuss is his fascination with Islam and how we are going to deal with that!"

And that is why Abdul had first fell in love with Nassir, and was still deeply in love with her. She was not as intelligent as Abdul, but her insight into life was far greater than his, and this is how the two complemented each other.

"Yes my dear, once again you have hit the nail on the head, I take it that you too have noticed Ryan's new interest."

"Well, you may be a university lecturer, but you are absolutely useless at matters of the heart. Yes, Ryan's fascination with Islam is a concern, but his fascination in you is so understandable, we just need to figure out how to manage it best. And I think the first step will be for me to call Betty and discuss the matter with her. She is fiercely Christen, and if she does not want us to explore the Islamic faith with her son then we have to respect that, but, my dear husband, it is not point losing sleep over the matter. I will call Betty right now and discuss it with her, whilst you my dear can go and make me a nice ice cold cup of something sweet!" And with that Nassir lent forward and planted a kiss on Abdul's nose.

A gentle smile started to form in the corners of his lips, he wrapped his arms around his waist and pulled her closer. "Oh Nassir, I do love you so, and you have already put my mind at rest, perhaps we should just disappear to that big lovely bed of ours and I can show you how much I appreciate you before the boys return!"

Nassir pulled away and teasingly wagged her finger at him, "Oh no you don't Mr Khan, you know the way this family works, we solve a problem as and when we can - we don't go to bed on it! Perhaps if you play your cards right you might just get lucky tonight - but first I am going to make that call, and you best get into that kitchen and make me something cold and sweet!"

With that Nassir walked off towards the lounge and dialled Betty. It was seven rings before she answered, in fact Nassir was just about to hang up.

"Hello," murmured Betty.

Nassir could tell straight away from the tone of Betty's voice that things were not good. "Aah Betty, my friend, what is going on?"

Betty's voice perked up a bit at the sound of her

friend's voice, "Oh hello Nassir, I am okay, it has just been a long day. How is my boy? Is anything wrong?"

"No, not at all, I just phoned to run a few things by you and check up on you, it can't be easy having Ryan away from you."

"Aah, Nassir, don't you know it, I am so glad he is with you, and his phone calls every morning are the highlight of my day. I can hear by the tone of his voice how happy he is. But yes, you understand, I do miss him terribly, and it is not as if I have much to keep me busy over here."

Nassir realised that Dwayne was more than likely the reason for Betty's sombre mood, but that unfortunately was Betty's life. Dwayne was a constant thorn in her side. But this conversation still had to go ahead, so Nassir continued, "Well, actually Betty, I did want to discuss something with you, are you happy to chat, or should I call back?"

"Nassir, I want nothing more than to chat with you, Dwayne left half an hour ago - he has gone down to the pub I think, and yes, we did argue as usual but at least this evening my face is still intact - so, my friend, you chat way, what is concerning you?"

Nassir proceeded to update Betty on Ryan's fascination first with Abdul which came as no surprise to either of them, and then his sudden interest in Islam. Nassir explained that Abdul was more than happy to spend time with the boy, answer his questions and teach him about the Islamic faith, however, first they needed Betty's consent. Nassir spoke to Betty about her own faith, Christianity, and how both Abdul and herself respected Betty's faith, and naturally did not want Betty to think that they were trying to in any shape or form convert Ryan to the Islamic faith.

Betty was silent for a while. Nassir could hear her moving about the house, and sipping on her drink. Nassir kept quiet, and knew that Betty would respond when she was ready.

Finally Betty broke the silence, "Nassir, I understand exactly what you are saying, and I appreciate you calling me, but can you give me a little while to think this through. If you are still going to be awake in half an hour I will call you back then."

"Oh Betty, of course, I understand, and yes, we will be awake. Abdul is busy in the kitchen as we speak trying to make me something cold and sweet - my dear, you should see the mess he has made. I am going to up for the next few hours at least cleaning up the mess! So, you just give me a call back when you are ready. Oh, and Betty, you take care of yourself."

Betty sighed deeply into the phone, murmured a, "I will," and then hung up.

Thousands of miles away, Betty placed the phone gently back onto the receiver, clutched her glass of wine closer, and then sank into the arm chair, which was conveniently next to her. A tear slowly rolled down her cheek. She absently brushed it away, and took a sip of her wine. Betty thought about the tears that were now falling softly from her eyes. She wasn't crying because her son was showing an interest in another faith, not at all, it was the fact that the Khan family were providing Ryan with everything that she should be providing him - stability, love, and now a following. Once again she was reminded about how different she had hoped her life would turn out. And so the tears were for herself and her loss. She allowed herself some self-pity, and then decided that she needed to pull herself together. It was only right that she call the Khan's back this evening. She also reminded herself that this life of hers was her choosing, and not Ryan's. The fact that Dwayne had never actually caused the child any really serious damage was a miracle. And more importantly the fact that he had not been shipped off to foster care was a credit to Betty and that is what she would focus on. In some strange way, during all the hardships that Dwayne had put them through, she had managed to keep them all together.

Betty finished her wine, slowly stood up and walked through to the bathroom. She had to turn on the lights as she went, because as usual she was alone in the house, and so only had the reading lamp on. She gave her face a good wash, trying hard not to look in the mirror. The image that was reflected was not one that she cared to look at much. These days she looked old, tired, and past her sell buy date. She then walked into the kitchen, grabbed her wine glass on the way and topped it up. Respectable wine was her one luxury these days, and in fact, because Ryan was out in South Africa at the moment, she had decided to buy herself some nice South Africa wine hoping that it would perhaps make her feel closer to him.

She then headed back to the arm chair, turning the lights off along the way, and settled back down. She then picked up the phone, which she had left on the corner table next to the lamp and her latest book, and dialled the South African number that had become so familiar to her over the past week - Ryan and Betty had made a deal that they would speak to each other each day without fail. So far so good.

Nassir answered the phone on the second ring. She was feeling slightly apprehensive and wondered if they had they done the right thing by bringing Ryan over with them. When she heard Betty's voice she relaxed - the tone that she was greeted with was that of her best friend. Betty and Nassir had gone through a lot together over the past few years, and it had resulted in a solid and lasting friendship. And just like their boys, even though they both came from very different backgrounds, they didn't let this interfere with their friendship. On hearing Betty's tone, Nassir realised that this little concern would be no different.

"Amah, Nassir, my friend, how can I ever thank you for what you have given Ryan." Betty did not expect an answer, but she still wanted to make sure that Nassir knew how grateful she was.

"Oh Betty, it is just the way it is, no need for thanks, and by the way, you have brought up a lovely young man, he is polite, intelligent and very good looking - that my dear is all down to you, in fact it is his enquiring mind that has brought about the Islamic issue."

"Well, Nassir, I can't think of anyone better than Abdul to teach my son, we both know that he won't learn anything good from his own father. So, yes, Nassir, does that answer your question, you have my blessing to explain the Islamic faith to Ryan. And over the years I have realised how similar both Christianity and Islam actually are. And any faith is better than no faith at all, and to be fair Nassir, you can't blame the poor child for not having faith in my beliefs."

"Oh, Betty, don't you be so hard on yourself. You have done a good job with him, and I promise you we will take good care of him. Now this is costing you a fortune and Ryan will be expecting to speak to you in the morning, so my dear, you go and get a good night's sleep and we will speak tomorrow."

"Aaah, yes, a good night's sleep, I am looking forward to that, if I could just put this book down!" Betty heard Nassir giggle in the background.

"Aah, so that is where Ryan gets his love of reading from! Well you get back to that book then. Till tomorrow my friend."

"Till tomorrow Nassir."

Nassir put down the receiver and smiled over at Abdul. He was sitting on the couch looking at her expectantly, Nassir walked over, settled down next to him and snuggled into his arm which wrapped around her small shoulders.

"Well my dear, I think you heard enough of the conversation to realise that we really had no need to worry so much. You have Betty's blessing."

Abdul sighed deeply and squeezed Nassir gently. "That is very fortunate, as I was not quite sure how I was going to have to fob him off."

In the meantime Fareem and Ryan were enjoying the company of their new friends - Fareem especially! Cindy, Tanya, Fareem, Ryan and Paul (Tanya's younger brother) had all gone out to the local shopping centre in the late afternoon. The plan was to watch a movie and then head to the local Spur for something to eat.

It was a good 30 minute walk, and Abdul had offered to take them, but they all seemed more than happy to walk, even though the sun was streaming down, however Abdul did suspect that even though the walk could quite easily be completed in 30 minutes, it would take these new friends much longer!

However both Abdul and Nassir had put their foot down at walking home in the dark, fortunately the other parents felt the same. So it was Cindy's mum that was going to do the collection run tonight.

And yes, Abdul was right, the walk had taken far longer than 30 minutes!

CHAPTER 20

Fareem had most definitely fallen in love. He had never before experienced such a wonderful feeling. His thoughts were constantly filled with images of Cindy. She was the most beautiful and intriguing girl Fareem had ever met. And what amazed him even more was the fact that she fancied him - not Ryan. In fact it was Ryan who had told him that Cindy liked him.

They had been mucking around on the beach one evening with the rugby ball, when Ryan spotted Tanya and Cindy walking over. Ryan had bent over to pick up the rugby ball, and as he raised his head he came face to face with the two girls. He gave them both a big smile, whilst brushing his hair out of his face. Tanya returned the smile, but Cindy wasn't even looking at him - her eyes were making a bee line for Fareem. Ryan had also never had a girlfriend, and to be perfectly honest he was not really interested in having one either. However he had had his fair share of admirers over the years, and was also surprised to realise that Cindy, who he had to agree with Fareem, was beautiful, did not even give him a second glance.

Ryan was pleased for Fareem, he had gone through such a miserable time at school the last few months - both girls and boys alike had called him names or simply ignored him simply because he was dark and Muslim. Ryan was pleased that Cindy could clearly see past this.

And so as Ryan and Fareem headed back to the

holiday flat that evening, Ryan commented on Cindy and her attraction to Fareem.

He wrapped his arm around Fareem's shoulders and gave him a knuckle cuddle on the head. "So, my mate, are you going to make the first move with Cindy or what?"

Fareem stopped dead in his tracks, and looked up at Ryan with astonishment. "Yeah right mate, as if someone that hot would really go for me!"

"What, Fareem, you really are a thick shit. She digs you man, have you not seen the way she looks at you? I am telling you Fareem, you are in there."

Fareem pushed Ryan playfully, "Yeah right, should I be so lucky."

And that is when Ryan realised that he really had no idea that Cindy was keen on him. So Ryan sat him down, on the rocks, and told him straight! Basically the message was - If you want her she is yours!

Fareem felt like the world had come to a standstill, this was surely a dream come true - actually now that he was thinking about it, it was quite a few of his dreams coming true! And with that Ryan and Fareem headed back to the house - Fareem with a goofy smile on his face and dreamy eyes, and Ryan just happy to see his friend so clearly besotted.

Well, Fareem had been up most of the night contemplating just how he was going to "make the first move!" Every scenario he came up with just seemed to dumb or way to lame, or just stupid.

As it so happened, Cindy did it all for him. The

following day they all met down on the beach as usual. Paul had promised to teach both Ryan and Fareem how to surf, Tanya who was not too bad herself had promised to help out. Cindy had made it quite clear earlier on that she would not be surfing - it was not her thing. So just as they were all about to head into the water for their first "lesson" Cindy grabbed hold of Fareem's arm and shouted over to Paul.

"Surely you don't need to take both of them at the same time. Fareem can keep me company while you teach Ryan."

Tanya responded with a quick, "Great idea Cin, come on Ryan, let's hit the waves."

Ryan caught Fareem's eye, gave him a quick wink and then headed into the sea.

Fareem's skin was tingling. He could still feel the pressure of her hand on his arm. His mouth was suddenly ridiculously dry and his stomach had clenched into a tight knot. He turned to Cindy and attempted to say something clever or funny, but all that came out was a garbled group of words that made no sense what so ever. Cindy didn't seem to notice, or maybe she was just too polite - more like she was used to boys getting tongue tied in her company!

She, on the other hand seemed to be completely at ease. She kept holding onto Fareem's arm and dragged him back up the beach, she then plonked herself down onto the sand, and pulled Fareem down next to her.

They were sitting so close to each other that Fareem could feel the heat from her body. The wind was

247

blowing quite a bit, this caused her hair every now and again to blow into his face, "Gees it smelt beautiful."

Cindy was chatting away to him about school and how much she hated it, and how she couldn't wait to leave. Fareem really was not paying any attention to the chatter at all, his ears seemed to be ringing, and his whole body was on fire as having Cindy sitting so close to him was really rather disturbing, in fact he realised that he was going to have to get some of the delicious images of Cindy that kept flashing though his mind out of his mind, otherwise the bulge in his swimming trunks was going to get progressively larger - perhaps not the best way to impress Cindy he thought.

That was when he realised that Cindy had asked him a question. Fortunately this rapidly brought him back to earth - if he wanted this girl he was going to have to pull himself together and do his best to impress her. So he quickly changed his thoughts to his science teacher - Mr Hickle - the oldest, grumpiest, most boring teacher in the whole world! This worked, and he felt the bulge in his pants returning to normal.

"Gees Fareem, have you even heard a word I said," pouted Cindy, playfully folding her arms across her chest in mock irritation.

"Aah, come on Cin, of course I was listening to you, but I was slightly distracted by the pathetic effort that Ryan is putting in - look, oh no, don't worry, he has fallen off again."

"Well Fareem, let's just wait and see how you do - it is harder than you think mate, and that is why I stick to the solid ground. Surfing is just not my thing."

Fareem and Cindy spent the next hour or so chatting and Fareem realised that they actually had loads in common. Yes, she was hot, but she was also fun to be with. They were both passionate about sport - her thing was gymnastics, his rugby. But just like all South Africans, she knew a fair bit about rugby too. Fareem found that so cool - a girl that actually understood rugby. He apologised time and time again to Cindy about his lack of knowledge about gymnastics. This was a sport that he had never really come across before. He also quickly realised that it was also a sport that his folks would probably not approve of - young woman performing with not too many clothes on. This would not sit well with the Islamic faith and women covering up!

However, his folks had seen both Tanya and Cindy wandering about in their bikinis and nothing had been said. And to be perfectly honest, this was perhaps one occasion where he would go against his parents if they suddenly decided to get all holier than thou with him! He was in with a chance with this hot chick and nothing was going to get in his way, not even Islam. Fareem realised that just thinking such thoughts was so "un Islamic", but so be it. He was a young man who had the opportunity of getting close to a woman other than his mum. Religion was not at the forefront of his mind!

Eventually Ryan dragged himself out of the water, looking shattered. Paul and Tanya chuckled away. Ryan flopped down on the sand next to Fareem.

"Well mate, respect to Paul and Tanya - this surfing stuff is hard!"

Paul, who although was a few years younger than the rest of them, was pretty cool, and seemed to enjoy hanging around with them. "Don't be too hard on yourself Ryan, it took me three weeks before I could stand up on the board properly - not like my sister here who is a real natural."

Tanya pushed Paul playfully and blushed slightly. Ryan realised that she was also hoping for a summer romance like Cindy, and she too had made it quite clear that she was interested in him, but he just didn't have his heart in it. Relationships just seemed a bit pointless to him. He hoped that this would change one day, but at the moment girls were the last thing on his mind. Other than his mum that is. It was great to be with the Khan family, and he had to agree, he was having the time of his life, for the first time ever he felt like he belonged to a real family. But these feelings of love and security were also masked by the sick feeling that was constantly lurking in the pit of his stomach. He was terrified that his dad was going to do some serious damage to his mum while he was not there to protect her. Every morning it felt like he was holding his breath in anticipation for her phone call, and praying that the call would come and Mum would sound fine. So far it had been okay, well kind of as there were a few mornings when Mum sounded really down and sad. Ryan could hear by the tone of her voice that she was doing her best to sound cheerful for Ryan, but he knew better than that. But at least she had answered the phone!

The only time he seemed to be able to quell the sick feeling in the pit of his stomach was when he was reading the Koran. He had always enjoyed the Bible stories, but somehow reading the Koran seemed to engulf him in peace. Just like Fareem was fascinated with Cindy, he was fascinated with Islam and the calmness it brought him.

And so as Fareem nervously began to explore new love, with lots of fumbling and awkwardness, Ryan turned his attention towards the Koran and the one person who could satisfy his desire for greater knowledge of the Islamic faith - Abdul.

Fortunately for Tanya, a new boy arrived in Bilito that same week, and he rapidly turned his attention towards Tanya. This gave Ryan the perfect excuse to turn down evenings out as he really didn't want to feel like a spare part.

The rest of the holiday seemed to fly by for Ryan and the Khan family. Abdul had found that introducing Ryan to Islam had been a great faith restorer for him. It had given him the opportunity to explore the religion through new eyes. And Ryan was an excellent student. He questioned everything for he was a child who came from a mother with strong religious beliefs. Over the years Betty had tried her best to educated Ryan the "Christian way". The result was that Ryan had a thorough understanding of the Bible, as well as Christianity. Abdul therefore had to really dig deep for his answers. For the first time in ages he actually had to provide explanations and the reasoning behind these, not just the usual, "because the Koran says so", or "that is what Allah - peace be with him - says." The two of them had spent hours sitting on the rocks watching the sea crashing down around them and examining the various surahs (chapters of the Koran).

Yes, it was definitely a holiday that Abdul would treasure. He became reunited with his faith, and at the same time seemed to be able to ease some of Ryan's heartache and pain. Yes, Ryan seemed more content these days. Abdul thought that it was perhaps more about the father figure than the Islamic teachings, but either way, Abdul was happy to help.

Nassir too had thoroughly enjoyed the break. She had not found friendship, nor new love or a rekindling of her religion, but she did find herself. What she enjoyed most about the holiday was to sit on the balcony, overlooking the sea, reading her book, or just simply enjoying the peace and quiet. It was the first time in a long time that she was able to spend time alone. This could produce either positive or negative results, because by spending time alone, getting the opportunity to get to know yourself again, you could just find that you didn't actually like the person you have become! Fortunately this was not the case for Nassir, but it was a good reminder that she really needed to make more of an effort to find time for herself. For the first time in years she felt invigorated. She enjoyed spending an extra ten minutes soaking in the bath, taking time in choosing her clothing for the day and applying the little bit of make-up that she did wear with care. Back in the UK she seemed to be in a constant rush, there was never spare time for herself. Well, that was going to change.

All too soon they found themselves packing up and returning to the airport. It had been a fairly emotional good bye for Fareem and Cindy, who had been clinging to each other constantly for the last few days of the holiday. They had exchanged email addresses and had both promised to mail each other daily. Ryan and Tanya had also exchanged email addresses, as although they had not become "an item" they had become pretty good friends. When Ryan had not been spending time with Abdul he had taken to the waves, and had over the past few weeks actually become a half decent surfer. Tanya and Ryan had spent hours in the water together waiting for the next set of waves to catch. Ryan had learnt that her folks had split up when she was really little, and now she had to put up the variety of men that her mum managed to "fall in love" with. Ryan liked to listen and Tanya liked to talk, so over the weeks their friendship developed.

CHAPTER 21

January 2006.

Ryan and the Khan family left sunny South Africa on Friday 5 January. They arrived at Heathrow Airport, London on Saturday 6 January and were greeted with two inches of snow!

The drive back to Chatham seemed to take forever. The usual 90 minute trip took closer to three hours. The snow seemed to bring everything to a standstill. Abdul did his best to keep control of the car on the roads that were decidedly icy. The other three had fallen asleep. The long flight had taken its toll on all of them. Nassir had tried her best to stay awake, but she too eventually drifted off. Ryan woke first and Abdul was relieved for he too was battling with tiredness and needed someone to chat too, only Ryan was unusually quiet. It seemed that the nearer they got to Chatham the more he withdrew. Abdul watched with sadness as he saw the haunted look return to Ryan's eyes. It was only as they pulled into the drive and Ryan saw his mum charge out of the door and head for the car with a big smile on her face that Ryan's dark expression changed.

The shriek of excitement from Betty woke both Nassir and Fareem from their slumber. Nassir gave a big sigh of relief, she, like Ryan, was pleased to see Betty still in one piece - so to speak!

Betty ran over to Ryan's side of the car and yanked

open the door, and then for such a petite woman she showed remarkable strength at pulling her son out of the car and then enveloping him in a big bear hug. Ryan straightened up as best he could, and returned the hug. God he had missed her. This was the longest he had ever been away from his mum and the emotions he felt at seeing her again surprised him. But Ryan realised that deep down he had been terrified at what his dad might do to her whilst he was away, so perhaps his emotions were really more a relief that she was safe and sound more than actual home sickness.

Betty finally pulled herself away from Ryan, however still holding him at arm's length she looked him up and down, then stood on her tiptoes to ruffle his hair.

"My word Ryan, look at you, that African sun most certainly suited you." She continued to beam proudly as she slowly turned her attention to the rest of the Khan family.

Nassir walked over and gently hugged her friend closely. "We took good care of him. He is a good boy, you should be proud."

Well, Betty's smile seemed to grow even bigger. Her life might be in ruins, but here was this woman who she respected so much complementing her on the upbringing of her child. It was a good feeling. Nassir with her arm still around Betty's shoulders ushered her into the house.

"Come on Betty, let's get into the warmth and make a cup of tea. The men can unpack the car. We have got plenty of catching up to do."

So as the ladies caught up, the men did their best to unpack the car as quickly as possible. The icy wind and freezing temperatures make for a rather unpleasant experience - all three of them were wishing that they were still back in sunny South Africa.

Nassir updated Betty on the holiday, she talked about Fareem and how he had fallen in love, and how Ryan and Abdul had formed the most wonderful friendship. She mentioned how much Abdul had appreciated Ryan and his enquiring mind.

"But Betty, that is enough about me, tell me how you coped without Ryan, especially over Christmas, it can't have been easy."

Betty smiled gently at her friend, and took a sip of her piping hot tea before answering, "Actually, Nassir, it was not too bad, to be honest Dwayne seemed calmer without Ryan around, and for the first time in years we were able to have a few civil words, in fact he took me to the pub for a few drinks on Christmas Eve. Don't get me wrong, it was not all plain sailing, but on the whole he seemed to be a different person."

What Betty didn't realise is that Ryan, who had been coming down the stairs had overheard the conversation. Part of him was relieved that his dad had not harmed his mum while he was away, but a part of his heart seemed to shut down even further, and he couldn't help but think that perhaps his mum was better off without him.

This thought came back to Ryan later on that night. Not much had changed for him at home. It was the usual

Friday evening argument between his folks and once again Dwayne was drunk. He stumbled in from the pub at six in the evening and didn't even acknowledge Ryan - actually that was not quite true, his acknowledgment went something like this, "Hey you little shit, it is lucky you have got blonde hair as I might have mistaken you for a fucking koon like your mates next door." Dwayne then seemed to ruffle Ryan's blonde hair. This to any bystander would have seemed like a touch of affection, however there was no love in that touch. Ryan's body turned colder than the freezing temperature outside. He had also noticed his mom's face going at white as the snow outside.

God he wished he had the courage to tell this big lump of a man to, "Fuck off and leave him alone." In his mind he was running the statement over and over but just couldn't bring himself to front up to the "old fucker."

His next moved may have seemed cowardly, but his mum saw it as a sign of strength and courage - Ryan grabbed his coat and walked out. Dwayne seemed a little deflated, in a strange sort of way he was really hoping Ryan would stand up to him. The boy was nearly sixteen, he needed to start acting like a man!

As Ryan walked outside he noticed Fareem and Abdul getting into the car.

"What's up mate, what the hell are you doing outside? It's freezing out." After uttering the words Fareem wished he could take them back, he knew exactly why Ryan was walking out of the house. He too had heard Dwayne returning home half an hour earlier.

Abdul intervened, "Come on Ryan, come with us, we are going down to the mosque for prayers - how about you join us, I tell you what, I will send your mum a text message to let her know you are with us."

That voice was his life line. Ryan felt the calming feeling that he always did when around Abdul. His heart stopped beating so rapidly, and the buzzing in his head seemed to subside as he climbed into the back seat and strapped the seat belt on.

Abdul explained that they were going to the Chatham Hill mosque. It was not his usual one, however the road conditions were so bad that he thought it was not such a great idea to drive the extra couple of miles to the bigger mosque on Canterbury Street, Gillingham.

Abdul realised that he was babbling away, but he had also just realised that he had agreed to take Ryan to a mosque without even consulting Betty. Discussing the Islamic faith whilst on holiday with the boy was one thing, actually taking him into the mosque was a completely different story. He sure hoped Betty realised that he was simply trying to protect Ryan from his dad.

Two hours later Ryan returned home. The house was quiet and so he was able to sneak upstairs without any confrontation. He guessed that his dad had probably gone out for the night and would not be back.

Ryan climbed into bed twenty minutes later, but he mind just wouldn't rest. He kept on going over and over his visit to the mosque.

The first thing that happened was he was told to remove his shoes; he should have been expecting this as he always removed his shoes when entering the Khan household. However this was different - there were rows and rows of shoes lined up, not quite like in a house at all. Typically he was also wearing socks with holes in them! It was very difficult trying to tuck up your toes under your big size seven feet! When Ryan realised Fareem's socks were holey too he let his toes relax.

This was also the first time in his life that he was the odd one out. The majority of people at the mosque were dark skinned like Fareem and Abdul, and just like realising that his socks had holes in them, so he started feeling self-conscious. However there was no need. He was made to feel welcome, everyone seemed to treat him as an equal and the colour of his skin didn't seem to make any difference at all.

The rest of the evening seemed to fly past for Ryan. The Imam started speaking in a strange language - Ryan had absolute no idea what was being said but he was simply fascinated by the tone and lilt of the voice. The Imam appeared to be reciting words in a rhythmic tone - it wasn't quite singing, but not far off it. A wonderful feeling of peace seemed to engulf Ryan. It was such a good feeling to be surrounded by so many calm, respectful men - so unlike his dad.

Yes, Ryan had had a wonderful evening, better than he could ever have imagined. He stretched out on his bed, pulled his duvet closer around him and then closed his eyes, his mind finally began to slow down, and eventually he drifted off to sleep with a contented smile gently creasing the corners of his lips.

CHAPTER 22

May 2006.

The boys only had a few more months of school, and then would be out in the real world. Neither of them really had any idea of what they were going to do. But one thing they knew for certain was they would be doing it together and it would involve rugby. Over the past few years both boys had turned into strong young men. Ryan's size was a great asset to rugby, and as for Fareem, he wasn't tall, but he was fast and was not afraid about getting stuck in, in fact he was generally the one who came out of the rugby matches the worse for wear. It was not uncommon for Fareem to be seen sporting a black eye!

But that was not quite at the forefront of their minds. More importantly they would both be turning sixteen soon. For the past few years they had celebrated their birthdays together, and this year would be no different. Naturally whatever they decided on would involve the rest of the rugby team, but Fareem had recently become rather "friendly" with a girl from school, he kept on dropping hints about wanting to include her in the celebrations. However unfortunately for Ryan, Dwayne had other ideas!

Yes, for the first time in years Dwayne had spent time thinking about his son, and the fact that he would soon be a man. Ryan was clearly a great disappointment to Dwayne, he just didn't seem to have that "White Road" blood in him, so Dwayne decided that in true "White Road" tradition, Ryan would be introduced to the real world when he turned sixteen. Basically this would mean taking the boy down to the local and letting him have a couple of beers with his old man. In fact just last month Shane had turned sixteen, and both Dwayne and Shane's dad Mark had enjoyed a great evening with the young man, downing a few pints. Dwayne truly believed that the boy would come around and see the error of his ways, surely he just needed a little help along the way!

So while Dwayne was planning a night out with his boy, Ryan and Fareem were working on a rather more subdued evening, probably a meal with their mates and girlfriends at Pizza Hut followed by a movie. Unfortunately Dwayne didn't bother to mention his plans to anyone until the day before Ryan's birthday!

Friday morning. The day before Ryan's 16th Birthday.

Ryan had walked downstairs, dressed for school. He was hoping to grab a quick bite to eat and be out the house before his dad decided to grace the world with his presence. Not so lucky! Ryan walked into the kitchen to see his dad hunched over the table, nursing a cup of coffee and sucking on a fag. Ryan was not quite sure what time Dwayne stumbled into the house the night before, but it had clearly been a rough night - he looked like shit, he hadn't bothered to shave, and his eyes were bleary and blood shot. Ryan could smell the alcohol fumes as soon as he entered the kitchen. That mixed with the cigarette smoke was enough to make him retch. All of a sudden he was not so hungry, and so made an excuse and tried to leave the room - not so lucky!

"Aaah, my boy, so, who is turning sixteen tomorrow then?"

Startled, Ryan looked up at this father - this was the most Dwayne had said to Ryan in a while, and not something Ryan was expecting.

"Come on son, have a seat, let me tell you about me plans for your big day."

Ryan reluctantly walked over and took a seat, doing his best to hold his breath. Betty, was in the lounge trying to clear up the empty beer cans, and ashtrays and overheard the conversation. She too was surprised, so joined them in the kitchen to find out about the "big plans." Betty was aware that Ryan had already made his plans and was desperately excited about tomorrow night, but the knot in her belly started to tighten, as she realised that Dwayne, once again, was about to ruin the weekend.

"Well, my boy, I have a full day planned for just the two of us, sorry Betty, but the afternoon entertainment is just for us boys!" Dwayne glanced over at Betty, whilst pulling something out of his pocket, he then proudly slapped two tickets for the Gillingham football game onto the kitchen table. "And after the game, my son, we will pick up your mum and then head over to the local for a couple of pints - yes, Ryan, you heard me right, you can come and have a few beers with your old man."

Ryan's heart sank, he knew that there was now no way he would be spending the day with his mates - not if he valued his life at all! So he took a deep breath, plastered a smile on his face and tried hard to sound appreciative.

Betty could see the disappointment in his eyes, and a small part of her heart broke. She did her best to get Ryan out of the house as quick as possible, just to give him some space.

"Wow, Ryan, isn't that fantastic, guess we will just have to move our plans to another weekend - now hurry along, I don't want you to be late for school."

Betty ushered Ryan out of the room and walked with him to the front door. As Ryan opened the door, Betty grabbed his shoulder, "I am so sorry Ryan, I had no idea he was planning all this, I will make it up to you, I promise my love."

Ryan ripped his arm away from her and spoke with more aggression than he actually meant, "Don't bother Mum, just don't, we both know what he is like, and neither of us clearly have the courage to stand up to him, so just leave me alone." Ryan stormed off down the path, and instantly regretted his words, but it was either that or cry, and there was no way that was going to happen.

God, he had been looking forward to this weekend for so long, how could life be so unfair? If he could get his hands on a gun, he would most certainly use it on his dad - why oh why, did his dad always manage to ruin his life?

Ryan was so caught up in his own thoughts that he

didn't hear Fareem behind him, and Fareem knew straight away that something was wrong - Ryan was striding along the road, shaking his head from side to side, and clenching and releasing his fists.

Fareem ran up alongside Ryan and tapped him on the shoulder. "Hold up mate - we clearly need to talk."

Ryan finally stopped pacing and suddenly feeling completely exhausted, he turned towards Fareem, and explained.

"Man that sucks!"

"Tell me about it, I have had fifteen birthdays and not once has my dad been at all interested in them, and now the one year that I am really looking forward to it he decided to fuck it up!"

"Aah, mate, maybe we can change it all to next week, how does that sound?"

"Nice try Fareem, but no, we can't do that, the table has already been booked, and to be honest if we change the date then we will have to tell everyone why - and there is no way I want anyone to know that I have been to a football match! No Fareem, as far as you are concerned - I will be as sick as a dog tomorrow."

"Aah, mate, that sucks, it just won't be the same without you."

"Don't worry, I will get my own back one day. My dad can't keep ruining my life - his time will come." Ryan started cackling in a rather sinister way.

Fareem glanced at Ryan out of the corner of his eyes - something in the tone of Ryan's voice sounded a bit too serious.

CHAPTER 23

"Come on you old bag, get that fat arse of yours moving." Dwayne was in his element. Gillingham had won, and now they were off to the pub. Dwayne had not actually noticed that Ryan had sat silently next to him the whole afternoon. He had been more interested in his mate Mark and son Shane. The three of them in their Gillingham shirts had spent most of the match slagging off the visiting supporters than actually watching the game. Ryan had been absolutely horrified by their language which appeared to be completely acceptable. They had sat in the cheap seats, which his dad had explained was the best place to sit as it meant they were right next to the visitors and would have ample opportunity to hurl abuse at them - which is exactly the way it went.

Now that the game was over, Dwayne was eager to get to the pub. His voice was hoarse from so much shouting and he was in desperate need of a pint. Mark, Shane and Angie were going to be meeting them at the pub.

Ryan was hoping that his mum would have come up with some excuse or another so that they could both avoid this next outing with dad, but once again, she had let him down. They arrived back from the football and there she was sitting in the front room all dressed and ready.

As Dwayne walked into the house, she jumped up

and gave him a peck on the cheek, "Thanks for doing this, it means a lot to Ryan and I."

Ryan realised that she was doing her best to keep the peace, and if that meant dragging them both down to the pub, then that is what she would do - he had to agree that his dad was okay when he was like this, the problem was that his jolly mood was because he was doing exactly what he wanted to do, and once again had not taken into consideration anyone else's thoughts. If Dwayne had actually just stopped to think for one moment, he would have known that the last thing in the world Ryan wanted to do was go to a football match and then the pub. But then again Dwayne really didn't know Ryan at all.

Ten minutes later they were heading out the door and walking down the road to the Bell Inn, the walk would only take a couple of minutes, but Dwayne already had a can of Fosters in his hand that he was gulping down.

To any passer-by they would have looked like an ordinary family, but there was nothing ordinary about them at all! Ryan saw Abdul drive past, and stifled the urge to wave - that would have wound his dad up no end. He realised that Abdul was probably off to the mosque.

They could hear the music blaring long before they arrived at the pub, and the closer they got the bigger Dwayne's grin got.

"Can you hear that son? Not only did I manage to get us tickets for the game, but I also managed to wangle a band at the pub!" Dwayne put his arm around Ryan's shoulders and squeezed him just a little bit too tightly. "I had to call in quite a few favours Ryan, I just hope you appreciate all I've done for you."

Betty quickly picked up on the change in the tone of Dwayne's voice, and rapidly tried to squeeze her way between the two of them. She slipped her arm around Dwayne's waist, gave Ryan a quick glance, then assured Dwayne that they were both awfully grateful for all he had done for them, and they were both looking forward to the evening.

Well, it clearly looked like everyone in the White Road Estate wad making the most of tonight's entertainment at the Bell Inn. The place was heaving, Dwayne took great delight in ushering the two of them through the crowds and everyone on his way through. Right in the corner of the pub Ryan noticed Mark and Angie propping up the bar. Mark was gesturing over to Dwayne, letting him know that he had saved them a couple of seats.

Ryan took a deep breath, and said a little prayer, "God, make this night fly by."

The band hadn't started playing yet, but "Crazy" by Gnarls Barkley was blaring out of the speakers - quite apt thought Ryan as he hummed along to the song 'Does that make me crazy'. Ryan knew that if he didn't get out of this place soon he would be going crazy! Mark had ordered the first round, and Dwayne took great delight in handing Ryan a pint of beer.

Betty wasn't feeling all that comfortable either, she had tried so hard to make an effort with her make-up, hair, and deciding what to wear. In the luxury of her own home, she thought she looked pretty good. She had applied a little bit more make-up than usual, and had curled her hair up at the ends, so it was not like her usual curled under look. And as for her outfit, she had decided on a royal blue silk top that was fairly low cut, exposing more flesh than Betty was used to, but she was going to a pub, and so thought it would be okay. She also had on a pair of black trousers and some nice black high heels. She knew she could do with losing a few pounds, however she thought she looked rather slim, and well, good. The blue top accentuated her eyes, and the high heels and black trousers seemed to slim her down a bit.

Well, let's just say that on entering the pub she realised straight away that she was well over dressed, and looked rather conservative and frumpy compared to the rest of the ladies. Not that she would ever come out dressed like the majority of them, but she did feel awfully self-conscious all the same.

"Betty, love, you alright." Angie gave Betty the once over. "You are looking lovely dear." She then lent over and gave Betty a quick kiss on the cheek, without actually making contact with her skin - which Betty was quite relieved about as the lipstick no doubt would have left marks on her cheek. But it wasn't so much the thick coated lip stick, or over powering perfume that caught Betty's attention.

Angie was basically not leaving much to the imagination when it came to her low cut shirt. She had a pair of massive boobs and seemed intent on sharing them with everyone. The shirt was skin tight clinging not just to the tips of her boobs but also the several rolls of fat that graced her waist. And as for the jeans, they too were skin tight, however to give Angie her due, she did have a pair of fantastic legs, which seemed to stretch up to the sky! And as for her make-up, well, her face looked more like it had been plastered than just a bit of foundation.

Betty realised that this was obviously in an attempt to cover up the wrinkles - well she was probably on the wrong side of forty.

Ryan realised that she was feeling just as out of place as him, what he couldn't understand is why she continued to put herself through this hell. Ryan knew without a shadow of doubt that the moment he left school would also be the day that he walked out. Well, that's what he imagined, but deep down Ryan knew he wouldn't be able to leave his mum behind.

"Oi, Ryan, come over here mate, I've got someone who wants to meet you."

Ryan was pulled out of his day dream by Shane wandering over and thumping him on the back with such force that Ryan ended up spilling the pint of beer. Shane apologised, but Ryan was not fooled. Shane was loving every moment of this. Shane and Ryan had not said a word to each other since Ryan had beaten him up all those years ago before summer break. But now, Ryan was in Shane's territory, and Dwayne had mentioned it more times than once to Shane and Mark that he wished Ryan was more of a man like Shane. So tonight Shane would get his own back - Ryan was his for the night, and

Shane knew that Ryan was just going to have to grin and bear it, because that it was Dwayne wanted, and everyone knew that Dwayne got what Dwayne wanted.

Dwayne was certain that after tonight, Ryan would be the son that he expected. So far it was looking good - Shane had treated Ryan like an old mate. Now Shane just needed to get Ryan to relax a little, drink a few beers and then show him the ropes. Yes, Dwayne was certain that tonight would be the night that Ryan transformed from the fucking pansy of a boy into a force to be reckoned with - just like his old man.

Shane had a plan all of his own - he was going to get the nigger loving brat wasted and then humiliate him in front of Chloe, who was the hottest chick at school. She was also meant to be quite, well, how can you put it, experienced in the sack, or back of the car, or behind the shed, well, basically Chloe had had her fair share of "men" in just about anywhere you could imagine, and Shane wanted some of that. Tonight was going to be his night, oh yes, he was going to finally get his own back on Ryan, and then finish off the evening with a bit of boob, and anything else Chloe was willing to share!

Ryan played the game as best he could. He spent most of the evening standing in the beer garden with Shane and his mates. Chloe was there with a couple of her friends and as far as Ryan was concerned it was actually quite embarrassing watching Shane doing his best to "woo" Chloe. They were all getting rather drunk while Ryan did his best to pour his beer into the garden when he hoped no one was looking. The stuff tasted absolutely gross.

About three hours into the night he saw his opportunity and took it. Shane obviously couldn't handle his alcohol as well as he professed, as he suddenly stumbled away from the group and headed for the back of the beer garden. A few minutes later a mighty roar was heard coming from his direction. He was hunched over and puking his guts out! Well, his mates took this as an ideal opportunity to grab their phones head to the rear of the garden and video the site.

Ryan made his move. He headed back into the pub, and over to his mum who he expected to find her engaged in conversation with Angie. Unfortunately that is not what he found. His mum was sitting on her own dabbing her eyes and he could see that she was doing her best not to cry. It was then that he saw his dad entwined in the arms of some young blonde women. It was very clear to see that they were more than just friends. Ryan's heart broke for his mum. Although both Betty and Ryan knew, or at least suspected that Dwayne was seeing someone else, he had never been so blatant about it before.

Ryan went from feeling perfectly calm to furious in a matter of seconds. He could feel the blood starting to boil. Enough was enough, and Ryan had finally had enough. He was not going to take this anymore, and why the hell should he. Ryan made a bee line for his dad, but fortunately Betty saw him just in time, and managed to pull him away.

God, the last thing she needed now was to see her

271

husband beat up her son -she was already humiliated beyond belief, and Ryan may think he was strong enough to take on Dwayne, but Betty knew better. No, all she wanted to do was go home. She quickly grabbed hold of Ryan and pulled him over to the side.

"Come on Ryan, leave it alone, it is not going to make any difference. Please can you just be a gentleman and walk your old mum home?"

Ryan turned towards his Mum and realised that she was right. The tone in her voice scared Ryan more than his dad cuddling some other woman. Betty sounded completely defeated, her voice was flat, tired and resigned. She clearly had lost the energy to fight any longer. Ryan realised that if he didn't get his mum away from this place soon she would shrivel up and die.

He quickly wrapped his arm around her and led them both out the door. Spring had not quite arrived and there was still a wintry feel to the air. It was only once the two of them had made it outside that they realised their coats were still hanging over the chairs, but neither of them had the energy to go back in, so they just huddled together and headed home. Ryan didn't even try and talk to his mum, it was clear that she was in no state to talk. He could feel her shivering under his arms, but then realised that she was crying, a slow quiet sob which racked her shoulders. Ryan really didn't know what to say, so just did his best to comfort her.

Hell, how he hated seeing her like this. God, he wished his head would clear, the small amount of beer that he had drunk had made his head all fuzzy. He was still so mad with his dad, and was relieved that his mum had rescued him before he had lost control completely in the pub. God, he needed to get out of this shit hole called Chatham.

Finally they got home. It seemed to take an age to do the short walk and Betty was struggling with the key in the door, she too had obviously had too much to drink and between the wine and the crying, there was no way she was going to get the door open. So Ryan gently took the key from her cold hands, which he squeezed, then unlocked the door and ushered her in. On closing the front door behind him he realised how badly he needed to get out. The house suddenly felt like it was closing in on him, and if he didn't get out he was going to sink. He knew that he should probably stay long enough to get his mum sorted, but he just didn't have it in his heart.

His head was pounding, and his blood was pumping, he was still so furious with his dad. God how he wanted just to get away from this mess. So he kissed his mum softly on the cheek and closed the door behind him. As Ryan walked away from the house he glanced towards Fareem's house. It was all in darkness. How had Fareem's evening gone?, he wondered. Certainly much better than his.

Ryan wasn't really certain as to where he was going, he really just needed some time to sort his head out, and calm down. He dug his hands deeper into his pockets and stuck his head down low, hoping to block out some of the wind. The air was bitter, so much for spring being on its way. But Ryan liked the cold weather, it was helping to clear the fuzziness from his head. Slowly he found himself relaxing, and starting to think a little bit clearer. A thought was beginning to grow at the back of his mind, and the slow walk and fresh air was giving him an opportunity to allow the thought to develop. He wasn't quite sure where he was going, but his legs just seemed to be carrying him, and he was happy just to "follow".

Ryan had been saving his money for years, and his recent trip to South Africa had given him an idea, and perhaps the time was right to finally do the right thing and take his mum away. He obviously had to finish school first, but only had a couple of months to go, and anyway he was going to need a few months to prepare. Yes, the more he thought about it the more he thought it would work. Ryan would email Tanya in South Africa tomorrow morning and ask her to find out if the local pub/restaurant in Billito was still looking for staff, and could he have a contact number/ email address. He knew that there was accommodation available above the restaurant for staff - no it would not be a house like here, but he was certain that his mum and he could make do with just a room for a few months, and anyway, to be perfectly honest anything had to be better than living with his dad. Yes, he knew it was a big step, but he also knew that it was the only way both he and his mum could have any sort of decent future. His dad was not the type of person to give up a possession, so there is no way on earth that he would let Betty leave.

For the first time in ages Ryan felt invigorated, it

felt good to finally have a plan, and to know that within a matter of months he would be free from his dad's clutches. Ryan's sunken heart was starting to lift, he felt a new found confidence rising inside of him. Ryan suddenly realised that he was standing outside the Chatham Hill mosque. He had not been back to the mosque since that cold day in January, however he had been to the other mosque in Canterbury Street a few times with Abdul, and on each occasion he had left feeling a great sense of peacefulness. Ryan noticed a light on in the mosque, and with his added confidence he plucked up the courage to knock on the door. It seemed to take an age for someone to answer, and Ryan was just about to give up when he heard footsteps, and the door creaking open slightly. A young dark man peered around the corner and demanded to know who was waiting. Ryan's confidence was long gone, and he suddenly felt very silly and embarrassed.

"Er, sorry, I came here a couple of months ago."

"Ryan, Ryan Arnold, is that you?"

"Er, yes."

"Come in brother you must be freezing."

The door opened wider and Ryan recognised Mr Ahmed, the new teaching assistant at the school. Ryan was led down the corridor, into a small room, where four other men were sitting around the table. None of them looked too impressed with Ryan joining them, however this didn't deter Mr Ahmed.

"Come in, come in Ryan, take a seat and I will get you a cup of hot chocolate, you must be freezing. We have just finished our meeting, so don't worry, you are not interrupting us."

Ryan didn't notice the knowing look that passed between the men who were rapidly putting "paperwork" away. It didn't even cross Ryan's mind to question why they were meeting so late at night. It was only once he was in the warmth that he realised how cold it actually was outside and how cold he was. He was looking forward to the chocolate milk.

"So Ryan, what brought you to our mosque a few months ago?" asked Mr Ahmed.

Ryan began to explain about the Khan family, and his interest in the Islamic faith. The other men seemed to relax a little when they realised that Ryan did actually have some understanding of the Islamic faith, and was not just there to cause trouble. Mr Ahmed was quite impressed with Ryan's knowledge and eagerness to learn more and made a mental note to himself to speak further with Ryan.

Ryan was not quite sure how long he sat in the mosque for, but once again, on leaving he had a wonderful sense of peace wash over him. Mr Ahmed also insisted on driving him home, which Ryan was quite relieved about. The events of the day finally seemed to have caught up with him. As he climbed into Mr Ahmed's little red Golf, he felt absolutely exhausted, and was battling to keep his eyes open. Ten minutes later Ryan was climbing out the car, thanking Mr Ahmed for the lift and heading for his front door. He quietly crept in, not wanting to wake his mum. As soon as he walked in he realised that his dad was not home, and so breathed a sigh of relief. Ryan then dragged himself up to bed and finally fell fast asleep.

CHAPTER 24

A few weeks had passed since the sixteenth birthday incident. Ryan had spent most of his spare time locked in his room on the internet. He had been in touch with Tanya who had passed on the details of the pub in Billitto to him. He had emailed them and was now waiting to hear back from the manager about the possibility of taking both Ryan and his mum on. Ryan hoped that as Tanya was now working there she would pass on a good word. Once he was certain that they would have somewhere to stay and at least one of them could get a job he would then tell his mum.

Ryan had found some good flight tickets, it wasn't a direct flight, but then they would not be in any rush. He had also already decided what they would say to his dad – there was a rugby tour coming up that Ryan knew his dad would not be interested in tagging along to. Dwayne would see it as a weekend of no nagging from Betty or agro from Ryan. This would give Betty and Ryan the weekend to get out of the country and by the time Dwayne figured out that they were not coming home it would be too late! Yes, Ryan had thought of everything. The only concern was the money. He had been saving for years for this occasions, but ten years of birthday money and a little bit of pocket money did not actually add up to all that much when you were hoping to leave the country for good! However he did know that his mum had a little bit saved away which they could probably get their hands on without Dwayne noticing. Yes, it was all coming together. The rugby tour was a month away, so Ryan had plenty of time.

As for Fareem, well, his sixteenth birthday party had been a great success, the young lady from school who was rather fond of him did end up coming along, and they were now officially an item. Yes, Fareem was delighted with the way his life was turning out. Something had happened to him in South African that he couldn't quite explain, but whatever it was, it had made him far more sure and confident of himself. This new image that he was now projecting seemed to have a positive effect all around. All of a sudden he didn't feel like he was the odd one out, he was just like the other kids at school – actually no, rephrase that, he was turning into quite a good looking lad. Most of his peers were covered in pimples, and were kinda gawky looking, or overweight – Fareem on the other hand had perfect skin, and all the rugby training over the years had ensured that his body was far from gawky! Yes he was handsome alright, and the girls were starting to notice this!

In fact, Fareem was so caught up in his new life that he had failed to notice the change in Ryan. Ryan had noticed this too, and under normal circumstances Ryan would have felt rather let down, however he was grateful not to have Fareem asking too many questions – the last thing he needed now was someone trying to talk him out of leaving with his mum, and to be fair, he was not certain that Fareem would talk him out of it, but at the same time he didn't want to take that chance!

Ryan has also been spending time with Mr Ahmed, the school teaching assistant that he had seen at the mosque. Mr Ahmed had promised to help Ryan out with a school project, so a couple of times a week Ryan would forgo his lunch break and sit with Mr Ahmed. Nine out of ten times they would end up talking about the Islamic faith, and the project would get left for another week. This didn't bother Ryan in the least, he really was not that fazed about the project, but was thoroughly enjoying conversing with Mr Ahmed, who he found fascinating. Like Abdul, Ahmed was extremely knowledgeable about Islam, however that is where the difference ended – Abdul was so quietly spoken, whereas Mr Ahmed somehow seemed to fill the whole room when he spoke. He talked with such passion and enthusiasm that Ryan tended to just sit back and listen in awe. However every now and again Mr Ahmed would put his foot down and insist that they worked on the school project. This is exactly what happened on this day.

"Aah, Ryan, you came. The weather is so great outside that I thought you might choose the sun rather than an hour stuck in this classroom with me!"

Ryan was in a world of his own when he walked in and only caught part of the conversation. "Sorry Mr, Ahmed, what was that about the sun?"

"Oh never mind my boy, you were obviously miles away - anything I can help with?"

Ryan was once again going through the "escape plan" in his mind, and he really would have liked to talk it through with someone, but once again just wasn't willing to chance it, so declined Mr Ahmed's offer. However he had been going over and over some stuff that Mr Ahmed had told Ryan last week about the Islamic faith, and Abdul seemed to have rather different ideas - they had been discussing the concept of Jihad.

"Well, now that you mention it, I have been thinking about our talk around Jihad last week, and am slightly confused as Abdul's explanation is slightly different."

"Aaah, Ryan, come come and sit down, Abdul is a good Muslim man, who I have known him for many years, and the brothers speak highly of him, but, how do I put this - let's just say his views are old fashioned. Now Ryan, don't get me wrong, that it not to say that his views are wrong, just a little outdated. Let me put it another way - would you let your mum buy your clothes for you?"

"What, my mum, no way, I would look ridiculous, she still thinks that bell bottoms are in fashion!" responded Ryan.

"Well there you have it, and sometimes what the older generation don't know doesn't hurt them. But young man, today you are not going to side track me again! We are working on your project, however I did bring along some pamphlets about Islam for you which you can take away and read - if you want of course?" Mr Ahmed bent down and dug some magazines out of his brief case and handed them over to Ryan. "Best you put them in your bag Ryan, you probably don't want too many people knowing that you are interested in the Muslim faith - I don't think I need to tell you how difficult it has been for us, we are a good people, but not everyone sees it like that."

Ryan nodded in agreement, he knew only too well what Mr Ahmed was talking about. The Khan family were the most peaceful loving family he had ever met, and he knew exactly what they had had to endure because of the likes of thugs like his dad.

"Aah, Ryan, you are doing it again." Mr Ahmed patted Ryan's head while smiling, "you are too clever for your own good, but today, I am not going to be distracted, we have to work on your project, but, I tell you what, why don't you come down to the mosque tonight at six. The brothers are meeting and you are welcome to join us, perhaps then some of your many questions about our faith will be answered."

Ryan's eyes began to sparkle, "Oh yes, please, I will be there." Ryan was trying hard to hide his delight. The thought of spending more time with people like Mr Ahmed was too tantalizing for words. When he was talking to Mr Ahmed he really felt like he was worth something, and capable of actually doing something with his life. Yes, he would definitely be at the mosque tonight.

Ryan went straight home from school that day. Fareem was hanging around by the gate waiting for Megan as he had started walking her home. Normally Ryan would join them, but today, he made his excuses and left. He didn't hear Fareem say that he would see him later for rugby practice. All Ryan could think about was the magazines in his school bag from Mr Ahmed. He was desperate to get home and look at them before his visit to the mosque that evening.

As he opened the garden gate he saw Abdul driving in. They waved at each other, before Ryan quickly scurried inside.

That's odd, thought Abdul, Ryan would normally have come inside for a cup of tea and a chat. Abdul continued to ponder on Ryan's strange behaviour until he walked over to the passenger side of the car and noticed all the paperwork that he had brought home to do. Ryan and his lack of communication was pushed to the back of Abdul's mind, as Abdul lifted the heavy load out of the car. He last thought was perhaps it was a blessing in disguise that Ryan didn't want to chat - Abdul really didn't have the time today, but never wanted to push Ryan away.

Ryan on the other hand was not quite sure why he didn't stay for a chat, but he knew that if he had stayed to chat he would have more than likely having ended up telling Abdul that he had been invited to the mosque, and for some reason or another he just wasn't willing to share that information just yet.

Ryan slammed the front door closed, shouted hello to his mum and then ran upstairs. He had about an hour before he had to leave for the mosque and really wanted to look through the stuff Mr Ahmed had given him before tonight - he wanted to make sure that Mr Ahmed realised that he had made a point of reading the information provided as soon as possible. He also did not want to look stupid by asking questions that perhaps had the answers in the literature.

So he ignored his mum's shouts about food, and having something to drink, closed his bedroom door and plonked himself down on the bed - but not before grabbing a few rugby magazines that he could hide the Islamic stuff in. An hour later Ryan was so engrossed in the magazines that he didn't hear Fareem knocking on the front door and then heading up the stairs. Fareem barged into Ryan's room as usual, and looked on in surprise at Ryan who was still in his school clothes.

"Come on mate, we are going to be late for rugby!"

Ryan had completely forgotten about rugby, and even if he had remembered he would rather go to the mosque - these days rugby just didn't seem to be as important as it had in the past.

"Ahh sorry mate, I am really not feeling very well, might give it a miss tonight."

Fareem couldn't believe what he was hearing, he had never known Ryan to miss a rugby session, he must really be feeling rubbish. "Okay, no worries, I'll tell the coach that you aren't feeling too good. Just make sure you are ready for the match on Sunday mate!" Fareem playfully punched Ryan on the arm and then left the room.

Abdul gave Fareem a lift to rugby and was also surprised to see that Ryan was not joining them, but then remembered the odd behaviour earlier and so realised that it wasn't odd at all, just that Ryan really wasn't feeling too well. Fareem and Abdul both commented on the fact that they had never really known Ryan to be sick, so he must really be out of sorts.

Twenty minutes after Fareem left Ryan headed down the stairs and popped his head around the kitchen door. "I'm going out for a couple of hours Mum, so don't worry about tea for me, I'll make something when I get back in."

"I didn't realise you were still here, thought you had gone with Fareem to rugby. What's up Ryan? It's not like you to miss rugby." Betty headed over to Ryan with a concerned expression on her face, and gently placed her hand on his forehead, just like she used to do when he was younger, checking for a temperature.

"I'm fine Mum, really, it's just that one of the teachers at school has promised to help me with a school project, he says that if I really focus my studies then I might even get good enough grades to get into uni. Imagine that Mum, who would have ever thought I might be capable of that!"

Betty's heart swelled with pride, she knew her son deserved better than the life he had ended up with, and finally it seemed like someone else had also recognised that there was more to him than just another oik from the White Road Estate. She gave him a quick hug, ruffled his hair, and sent him on his way.

"That's my boy, I also knew you were university quality - just like your mum! I'll leave something in the oven for you, and am looking forward to hearing all about this project when you get in, now hurry up, you don't want to keep the teacher waiting."

Ryan grabbed his coat and then headed out the door, it was very seldom that he lied to his mum, and it didn't really sit well with him, however, on this occasion he didn't really think it was a lie, as Mr Ahmed was helping him with a project, and did comment all the time on how well Ryan could do for himself if he just focused more. And perhaps he could do his project on Islam, and then tonight would be studying! Yes, Ryan might just mention that to Mr Ahmed.

CHAPTER 25

Ryan was ready to reveal his plans to his mum. They had a week and half before they left. Ryan had heard from Tanya, and the boss had agreed to give both Ryan and Betty a job, as well as accommodate them above the restaurant. Things were going even better than Ryan could have imagined. All they needed to do now was book the tickets - which is why he needed to tell his mum as he was a bit short of cash.

Ryan couldn't wait to see his mum's face. This was something they had dreamed about for most of Ryan's life. He had decided to tell her on Saturday morning, as he was certain Dwayne would be out the house. Then the two of them could catch the bus into Chatham and go and book the tickets. Now all he had to do was try and keep his mind focused on anything other the trip to South Africa.

Saturday morning.

"Mum, can we talk for a minute, I've got something to tell you."

Betty was busy cleaning the house - her usual Saturday morning chore, and was quite relieved to have a break. She had been worried about Ryan for the past few days, he really hadn't been himself and her stomach suddenly tightened, "Is something wrong?"

Ryan gave Betty a big toothy grin, wrapped his arms around her and chuckled, "Not at all, Mum, I have some good news – let's sit down in the kitchen, I'll make some tea and then we can talk - we have a lot to go through."

Betty was absolute intrigued now, so she followed him into the kitchen and sat down. She tried her best to get Ryan to talk, but he refused until the tea was made.

Finally he sat down next to her, clasped her hand in his and revealed his plan. Ryan had been dreaming about this day for so long, that he actually felt giddy, it was going to happen, they were going to get their life back.

Only, Betty didn't quite respond the way he expected, her eyes filled with tears, and her face creased over with worry. "Oh Ryan, what have I done to you."

"Mum, please don't cry, we can do this, I have it all planned. We've got a place to stay, and some work, it will be a bit tight for a while, but we can make it work, I promise Mum, we don't have to live like this anymore - you know he will eventually kill you if we don't get out."

Betty sighed, and looked over at Ryan with sad eyes. "Ryan, I can't leave him. He is my husband, and I know it is not the life I hoped for but, Ryan, we married under the eyes of God for better or worse. My son, I can't just walk away from him. I believe that God has a plan for all of us, and this is obviously what he planned for me. Your dad will find his way, I am sure of that, and I will be there to guide him back. This is God's plan my love, and I have to respect that."

Betty leaned over and tried to hug Ryan, who

instantly shrugged her away. He couldn't believe what he was hearing. He felt like his whole world had just been ripped out from beneath him. His dad had hurt him over the years, but never before had he felt so let down and disappointed in his life. The one woman who he loved and respected more than anyone else had let him down. How could she really believe that it was right to stay with him? Ryan could feel the anger building up inside, and for the first time ever his anger was directed at his mother. He knew he had to get out of the house before he did something he would regret.

Ryan stood up and forcefully pushed back the kitchen chair, for the first time ever he was seeing his mum through fresh eyes, and he didn't like what he was seeing - a pathetic woman who would rather live in this shit hole with an animal for a husband, simply because she believed it was God's will. Well if God was so fucking great, then why did he make her suffer so? Ryan was fuming, he grabbed his jacket and headed out of the door, slamming it so hard the house shook.

Betty just sat in the kitchen clutching her tea and crying, what had she just done?

Ryan ran all the way to the mosque. The only person he wanted to see was Mr Ahmed, who he knew would help him release his anger. Ryan waited for over an hour before he finally caught up with Mr Ahmed by then he had calmed down slightly.

"Aah, Ryan, you have come back for more, if I didn't know any better I would think you were stalking me." He laughed gently until Ryan raised his head, and he saw the tear streaked face, "Ryan, come, let's find somewhere quiet, we need to talk."

For the first time all morning Ryan finally felt some sort of calm. He nodded his head, whilst wiping his nose with the back of his hand. He followed Mr Ahmed into the mosque, automatically took off his shoes, and then allowed Mr Ahmed to usher him into a side room.

"Now before you say anything let me put the kettle on and make us something warm to drink, you just sit down and try to relax." Mr Ahmed gently put his arm on Ryan's shoulder and settled him into a chair.

"I noticed a few days ago that something was bothering you, and hoped that you would turn to me for guidance, now you start at the beginning and tell me what has upset you so much."

Mr Ahmed voice was so soft and soothing and his tone was kind of magical. Ryan suddenly knew that this man was special, this was a man he could trust, Mr Ahmed would not let him down.

Ryan told Mr Ahmed everything, he spoke about his father and the beatings, his love for his mum, and his plans to take her away. He talked and talked, only stopping to sip his hot chocolate, which was filled up time and time again. Mr Ahmed didn't interrupt, he just sat quite still and nodded now and again. When Ryan finally finished he felt absolutely drained, but it felt like a huge weight had been lifted off his shoulders.

"Ryan, you may never understand how you got to this point, but I believe that you have been chosen. It is no coincidence that our paths have crossed. You have been chosen by Allah. The life you have led, the decision you have had to make, and the sacrifice you were willing to make for your mother just confirms my thoughts - I knew from the moment I met you that you were destined for great things, but didn't quite know what. But now I understand. Come Ryan, it is time to meet the Iman."

Ryan followed Mr Ahmed into the main section of the mosque. Evening prayers would be starting shortly and the mosque was starting to fill up with men. Mr Ahmed whispered a few words to the Imam, who nodded his head, whilst taking in the boy standing in front of him. Ryan wasn't quite sure how best to describe the Imam, but friendly did not come to mind. His face was old and wrinkled and he stooped slightly at the shoulders, but there was nothing old or stooped about his voice, which when he spoke seemed to silence everyone. Ryan seemed to get the impression that the Imam was not overly happy at having Ryan present, but Mr Ahmed didn't seem to mind. And once the brief conversation was over, the Imam nodded towards Mr Ahmed, and forced out a toothy smile at Ryan. He then ushered both Ryan and Mr Ahmed on their way, the only word Ryan had caught was Wudu, which Ryan recognised as the ritual of washing prior to prayers. It was then that Ryan realised that they would be staying for evening prayers and needed to wash.

Ryan sat on his hunches at the back of the mosque next to Mr Ahmed. The Imam began to chant the prayers, his voice bellowed out and seemed to reach all the corners of the room. Ryan had no clue what was being said, but he liked the sound of it. The lilting voice and strange words filled him with a sense of calm and peace. Ryan had listened intently to Mr Ahmed that afternoon, and now hearing the prayers being chanted rhythmically out, everything seemed to slip into place. Ryan finally realised that Mr Ahmed was right, and he was always intended to find the Islamic faith - sitting there in that mosque he finally felt like he had come home.

Ryan walked home with Mr Ahmed that evening, and had a billion and one questions. Firstly he asked Mr Ahmed about what the prayers had been about.

"Aah, Ryan, I was wondering if you would ask, well, I realise that you didn't understand the prayers, but they were chosen tonight specifically for you, and are hoped to provide you with some sort of understanding for what you have had to endure all these years. But, Ryan, I am not going to translate them for you - that is something that you are expected to do yourself, if you choose." Mr Ahmed handed Ryan a piece of paper, with a list of numbers scrawled across the page. "Each number represents a prayer that was said today - go home and find the prayers in your Koran."

Ryan eagerly grabbed the piece of paper and stuffed it into his pockets just as they were turning into White Road. Ryan stopped in his tracks, and thanked Mr Ahmed for all he had done, he then proceeded to explain to Mr Ahmed how he had been engulfed with a sense of belonging whilst sitting in the mosque with the other Islamic brothers.

"Ryan, that by boy, I believe is another sign of what you are destined for. The Islamic faith believes that we are all born Muslims, just not everyone realises that, and so when the time is right, you revert to Islam, rather than convert. It seems to me that you are slowly recognising your true faith. Now, you go home and get some sleep, we will speak more later in the week."

Ryan thanked Mr Ahmed again and wandered off towards his house, feeling one hundred times better than when he left earlier that day.

CHAPTER 26

June 2006.

The weekend that Ryan and Betty were going to be leaving for South Africa had arrived, and so rather than packing his bags for the last time, Ryan packed for the rugby tour. Betty had decided not to join him, she realised that Ryan was still very angry with her, and so thought it best to give him some space. She had discussed the situation at length with Nassir, and asked her to please keep a close eye on Ryan over the weekend, as she was concerned. He seemed to be drifting away from her into a world of his own, and she blamed herself for his distance.

Nassir naturally relayed the conversation to Abdul, who was relieved to finally get to the bottom of Ryan's strange behaviour. He loved that childlike one of his own, and it was hard to see him hurting so. Abdul made a silent promise to himself that he would make a concerted effort to spend some quality time with Ryan during the weekend - give the boy a chance to just talk.

Ryan threw his rugby boots in the bag, grabbed his jacket and then shouted goodbye to his mum. She leaned over and tried to hug him, but Ryan just shrugged her away. It was just four in the afternoon and he could already smell whiskey on her breath and this just made him hate her even more. She sadly pulled away, but managed to stuff a £20 note into his hand.

"Buy something nice for yourself my son, and have a good weekend. Ryan, I love you, please don't forget that." Betty tried once again to reach her child, but the look that he shot her was icy cold, with not an ounce of love. What had she done? Betty was struggling to cope with the realisation that she had caused this drift between the two of them, unfortunately she found that she was only able to rid her heart of this dreadful pain by drinking. She realised that she was starting earlier and earlier, and also recognised that this made her no better than Dwayne, but she really didn't know what else to do.

Ryan slammed the front door, and took a deep breath, how he needed to get away from this shit place! Ryan had been so distracted with Mr Ahmed and the mosque of late that he really hadn't given the rugby tour much thought, but now that the day had arrived he was actually kind looking forward to it. And more than anything else it gave him an excuse to get out the house for the weekend, and the opportunity to spend some time with his real family. Yes, these days he felt that the Khan's were his true family, he had always felt comfortable with them, and they had always made him feel like he belonged.

Ryan walked up the drive of the Khan's house, with his bag slung over his shoulder. Abdul saw him arrive and felt a pull at his heart. How he loved this boy. Abdul smiled gently to himself as he watched the young man strolling up the drive. Abdul had watched Ryan grow up into a strong and handsome young man. He had such respect for the tall, blonde, boy who had suffered so much over the years but had managed to keep his own life on track.

"Give me a minute Ryan, I'll just grab the car keys and then you can stick that bag in the boot. And then best you get into that kitchen as Nassir has cooked up a storm for you two boys. We can't be travelling on an empty stomach now can we?"

Ryan smiled warmly at Abdul, and at the mention of Nassir and food his belly started to rumble. Aaah, yes, this is where I belong, he thought.

The rugby tour was in Devon - they were staying in a holiday complex called Ladram Bay, which was just outside Exmouth. This meant about a four hour drive - depending on how lucky they were with the M25. Unfortunately they were leaving at rush hour on Friday evening!

As it so happened they were lucky with the traffic and arrived just after nine. Fareem gave the coach a call just as they were entering the complex, and he met them at reception then led them to their accommodation for the weekend.

Steve, the coach, had managed to get Friday off work, so had arrived early on in the day to ensure he was there when his team arrived. It also meant that he could make the most of the weekend - and in true rugby tour style he had found the bar just after four in the afternoon, so by the time the Khan's arrived it was clear that Steve was well on his way to getting rather drunk. Steve was a rather charismatic bloke, who got more and more entertaining with the more beer he drank!

Ryan and the Khans were staying in a three bedroom chalet, which was small but cosy. Steve explained that due to his excellent planning skills he was able to ensure that all the rugby families were in the surrounding chalets - they had taken up ten in total.

Steve laughed and joked with the boys as he helped unload the car, then gave the family twenty minutes to get settled and then make their way to the bar for a team meeting for the boys and a drink for the parents!

Ryan and Fareem were eager to go to the pub and meet up with the rest of the team, stating that they really didn't need to freshen up and so would walk back with Steve. Nassir and Abdul agreed, and were quite relieved actually - sitting in a pub with a bunch of drunk men was not really how they enjoyed spending their time. However they did promise to join everyone within the hour.

Fareem did quickly head to the bathroom and spray on some deodorant, splash some after shave on and give his hair a quick comb - his girlfriend, Megan would be waiting at the pub. Her brother Mick played rugby with Ryan and Fareem.

For a while Ryan had been slightly jealous of Fareem's relationship with Megan, but since he had met Mr Ahmed and the "brothers" at the mosque, he really couldn't be bothered about Fareem and his girl!

He personally was not interested in girls. Actually, no, that was not quite true. Ryan liked girls and everything, he was definitely not gay, but he just didn't feel the need to get involved with anyone. Ryan truly believed that he was just waiting for the right girl, unlike Fareem, who was more than happy to play the field shall we say! This did mean that slowly but surely Fareem and Ryan were drifting apart. Neither of them would admit it if asked, but it was clear for the outsider to see.

Abdul and Nassir finally decided that they could not delay their walk to the pub any longer, so headed out the door. Whilst walking along they could hear the waves crashing onto the rocks, but couldn't really see much - other than a full moon and a sky full of stars. Abdul had a feeling that the place would look spectacular when they woke in the morning.

They arrived at the pub a short time later, just in time to see the boys and Steve all huddled in a corner discussing team tactics. Megan was planted firmly next to Fareem, and didn't seem at all fazed about being the only girl included in the team talk. It was clear that Fareem wasn't concentrating too much on Steve's talk either. He could feel Megan's leg next to his, and could smell her perfume. His heart was pumping excitedly, his mind was focused solely on Megan and what she was wearing under her jeans and tight t-shirt! He was brought back down to earth rapidly by his team mates patting him on the shoulder, and Megan leaning over to plant a kiss on his cheek – "well done" she whispered.

What the hell had Steve just said? Fareem did his best to hide the fact that he had no clue what had been said, but noticeably was not doing a very good job. Fortunately Ryan came to his rescue - he grabbed hold of Fareem and got him into a head lock and ruffled his hair,

"So captain, what is your plan for tomorrow games?"

Wow, Fareem couldn't believe his luck, not only was his girl going to be watching him play rugby all weekend, but he had also been named as captain. Things were just going from strength to strength for him at the moment.

"Well, buddy, the first thing I'm going to need is a vice captain - so do you think you are up for the task?" Fareem managed to wrangle his way out of the head lock, and punched Ryan on the arm.

Nassir and Abdul watched on with pride, the boys were both doing so well. Abdul turned to Nassir and commented on how the rugby tour would do them all good. Ryan had seemed so distracted of late, and so it was good to see the two of them together again, mucking around just like the old days.

"Come on lads, it's time to hit the sack, we have a few big games tomorrow, and I want you all to be feeling your best," bellowed Steve as his downed the last of his pint of beer.

It was close to eleven o'clock, and all the boys were starting to look a little weary. The parents were also looking a little worse for wear - some of them at been in the pub for quite a few hours!

Everyone gathered their belongings and headed for the door. Fareem and Megan were engrossed in conversation, and Nassir was catching up with one of the other rugby mums. Ryan was walking along on his own, so Abdul decided to join him.

"Ryan, wait up." Abdul jogged over to Ryan, and

the two of them headed back to the chalet. They chatted for a while about the rugby, but the conversation eventually ended up with the Islamic faith - just like it usually did with Ryan and Abdul.

Ryan told Abdul that he had been reading the Qur'an, and asked specifically about one of the Surah that Mr Ahmed had given him - 4:84 'So fight (O Muhammad) in the way of Allah - You are not taxed (with the responsibility for anyone) except for yourself - and urge on the believers. Maybe Allah will restrain the might of those who disbelieve. Allah is stronger in might and stronger in inflicting punishment.'

- 4:85 'Who intervenes in a good cause will have the reward of it, and who intervenes in an evil cause will bear the consequences of it. Allah oversees all things.'

The hairs on the back of Abdul's neck started to rise. There had been talk amongst the Muslim community about the young boy that Aarif Ahmed had seemingly taken under his wing. It was the quote from the Qur'an that was the final piece of the puzzle. Abdul's old friend, Shafiq, had commented to Abdul the other day about the prayers that the Imam at the Chatham Hill Mosque had chanted, specifically on request of Aarif Ahmed, for the "new brother" as Ryan was now being called. The prayer was the one that Ryan had just asked Abdul about.

Abdul didn't know much about Aarif, but what he did know he wasn't too keen on. However it wasn't quite anything Abdul could put his finger on. The young man was just a bit too radical in his thinking for Abdul's liking, but saying that, he definitely had a way about him. The mosques in Medway had been battling for some time now to engage with the Muslim youngsters.

Many of the youngsters were second generation British, and didn't speak Urdu, let alone Arabic. And as all the Imams in Medway delivered the prayers in Arabic, this didn't hold much interest for the younger generation - that is until Aarif Abdul arrived on the scene. He was charismatic, handsome, and well versed in the Qur'an. He had been welcomed into the Chatham Hill mosque with open arms, when they realised that he was bringing the younger generation back to the mosques. Abdul had discussed Aarif at length with Shafiq and others from the mosques, and all of them seemed to be willing to turn a blind eye to his "radical" views because they all liked seeing the children and grandchildren back in the mosques.

In fact just last week Abdul had got into a rather heated argument with one of the elders when he questioned Aarif's motives. Abdul realised that they were not willing to listen to an educated university lecturer, who was quietly spoken and never really noticed. It had been made clear to Abdul that if he continued to express his dislike for Aarif then perhaps he would need to find another mosque!

Abdul had stewed over the argument for days, and had eventually decided that he was obviously the one in the wrong. Abdul put it down to the fact that he was overly paranoid about such things - and yes, he had to agree, it was great to see the youth of today taking a greater interest in the Islamic faith.

But now, realising that Ryan was the boy that Aarif had taken in, brought his fears and reservations back. Saying that, Abdul was also sensible and intelligent enough to understand that he would need to tread carefully with this, otherwise he would more than likely push Ryan further away! So Abdul spend the rest of the walk back to the chalet discussing the quote with Ryan, hoping that his voice didn't portray his concerns.

Ryan didn't pick up on any of Abdul's concerns, and while Abdul spent the night tossing and turning, Ryan slept soundly for the first time in ages - even in the small bed, with his feet dangling off the edge! The chalet beds were not built for boys his size!

Ryan was away from his folks, with the family he loved, and looking forward to a couple of hard games of rugby the following day. He had also enjoyed chatting to Abdul about the few quotes that Mr Ahmed had given him. Since he had been speaking to Mr Ahmed he had at times found Abdul's views and opinions slightly outdated and old fashioned as Mr Ahmed said, but it was still good to talk.

CHAPTER 27

The rugby weekend had been a great success. Ryan had played some exceptional rugby. He seemed to move into a different level. Steve commented more than once to Nassir and Abdul that he had never seen Ryan play with such passion and vigour. Nassir was alarmed at the aggressiveness that seemed to erupt out of Ryan whilst on the pitch. The quietly spoken gentleman who she knew so well was nowhere on site once the whistle blew and the match began.

As for Ryan, he found the rugby matches invigorating, it gave him the excuse he needed to release all of his pent up anger and frustration. He couldn't quite explain what happened to himself that weekend, but whilst on the pitch he was able to block out all his troubles and simply focus on the game, and for some strange reason this seemed to bring out the best in Ryan's rugby. He scored three tries in the first game, which meant that the team took an early lead in the competition.

After the first game Steve pulled both Ryan and Fareem to the side. He gave Fareem a bit of a bollocking, as it was clear that Fareem was not as focused as he should be, and had missed several opportunities that would have pushed their lead even higher. Steve realised that Fareem's lack of concentration was down to Megan being present, and so told Fareem in no uncertain terms that if he did not sort himself out he would ask Megan to leave! This did the trick and Fareem quickly changed his attitude.

The second game was against their all-time rival – Canterbury. Out of the last six games against Canterbury they had only managed to win two. Today's game turned out to be quite something to watch. It was hard to remember that the boys on the field were only sixteen, as the level of rugby was outstanding. And when on form Ryan and Fareem made one hell of a combination. With Ryan's strength and Fareem's speed, there were not many players that could get in their way. And that is exactly the way it went during the second match. They ended up thrashing Canterbury, and went on to winning the tournament.

Saturday night was spent celebrating on the beach with a BBQ. The weather was glorious, and the atmosphere was euphoric. Ryan was on top of the world. Considering it was only a few weeks ago when he thought his whole world had come crashing to an end, it was amazing how now things were working out so well. Ryan was starting to really believe what Mr Ahmed had been saying to him - it all seemed to make so much sense. If his mum had agreed with his plan then they would have left for South Africa yesterday and he would spend the next few years battling to make ends meet. He knew that if they had left a further education would have been right out of the question, and there was no way that rugby would have been an option - it would have been doing as much work as possible to try and get some savings together. Whilst planning his escape it had never really bothered Ryan that he would be sacrificing his life for his mum's, it was just the way it was going to be.

But now, things were different. His mum had made her choice, and for the first time ever Ryan realised that his future looked good. He had a promising rugby career ahead of him - he knew that everyone at the tournament had been talking about the tall blonde lad with the dynamite tackle and awesome skills! But putting the rugby aside for a minute, he also now had this new calling in life, the one that Mr Ahmed said was all part of Allah's (may peace be upon him) plan. Well Ryan wasn't too sure about the plan part yet, but what he did know is that he felt more at home when with his Muslim brothers as they referred to each other, than anywhere else. Finding the Islamic faith just felt like the missing piece of the jigsaw puzzle.

As Ryan sat on the beach watching the waves crash down contemplating his life he felt happy for the first time in a long time - perhaps ever. He was suddenly whisked out of his day dreaming by someone planting a kiss gently on his cheek! He turned towards the direction of the kiss to be confronted with the most beautiful image he had ever seen. A girl with long, black, flowing hair, a gorgeous body, and skin the colour of toffee was standing next to him looking down at him with her hand on her hips, head tilted to the side and a big smile spread across her face.

"Well, Mr Rugby Star aren't you going to introduce yourself, I've been cheering you on all day and feel that I deserve at least an introduction. I'm Shakela by the way, and my brother plays for Canterbury!"

Ryan quickly came to his senses and ended up spending the rest of the evening talking to this most amazing girl - could his life get any better?!

Sunday arrived all too soon, and it was time for them all to head back home. Whilst packing up the car Ryan was a little alarmed when he saw Abdul deep in conversation with Shakela's dad. His heart went cascading to the ground. He realised that last night was too good to be true - he was certain that Shakela's dad must have seen them together and was now complaining to Abdul about the unacceptable "friendship" that had developed between Ryan and Shakela. He became even more nervous when Shakela's dad started walking towards Ryan.

Ryan quickly wiped his hands on the front of his jeans, trying to remove the nervous sweat and put out his left hand to greet Shakela's dad. "Sir, pleased to meet you."

"Aah, Ryan, I know who you are, Shakela hasn't stopped talking about you all morning, and Fwaad my son is in awe of your rugby skills, I was just inviting Abdul and the family over for lunch next Sunday and thought you might like to join us."

Shakela's dad could see the confused expression on Ryan's face, who was by this stage at a loss for words.

Abdul joined them and patted Shakela's dad on the back, "Ryan, this is my old friend Sadad. We met at the Canterbury Street mosque years ago, but then Sadad and his family moved to Canterbury and we haven't seen much of each other since then. And then this weekend we meet up again after all the years, only to find that the two boys play rugby, and Shakela has taken a shine to you! So, Ryan, are you going to join us all for lunch next Sunday?"

Ryan was beaming from ear to ear, his heart was pumping second to nothing, his whole body seemed to be on fire - he was convinced his face must be the colour of beetroot! "Er, yes, Sir, that would be lovely." Ryan then quickly looked towards Abdul, seeking confirmation that he was doing the right thing.

Abdul wrapped his arm around Ryan's shoulder and gave him a squeeze. "Well, then, that is settled, we'll see you next week Sadad, best we just exchange mobile numbers, then we can sort out times etc. during the week?"

"Oh, I've got Shakila's number, so I'll get the details Abdul," blurted Ryan, who then suddenly regretted what he had said. Sadad might not approve of Shakela handing out her mobile number! He sheepishly looked towards Sadad and began apologising, he knew how protective Dads could be of their daughters - oh hell, he hoped he hadn't blown it and gotten Shakela into trouble. He tried very quickly to back track saying that they hadn't exactly exchanged numbers just yet but he was hoping to.

Sadad's eyes crinkled up at the sides as he held back a chuckle, he was quite enjoying watching this very nervous young man doing his best to impress him.

"Aah Ryan, I realised a long time ago that Shakela

had a mind of her own - a rather strong one at that. She is quite a strong headed young lady, saying that, she is a good judge of character and so if she has decided to pass on her number to you then that is fine by me."

Abdul decided to put Ryan out of his misery, so sent him inside to get the bags. He then turned to Sadad and said seriously, "Are you sure you are okay with Shakela and Ryan? He is a good boy, but they did look pretty cosy last night!"

"Well, Abdul, ummm, how can I explain, Shakela is quite a 'handful' should we say, and it looks to me like Ryan might be just the type of boyfriend she needs - and to be honest, it has to be better than the last one! Saying that, I am not quite sure Ryan is fully aware of what he is getting himself involved in! Like I said, she is quite a determined and strong headed, intelligent young lady! He is going to have his hands full!"

"Sadad, I think that is just what Ryan needs at the moment! Long may it last! But now, my old friend, I must get moving, I am not looking forward to that long drive home, and would like to be back before dark. So, till next Sunday."

The two men shook hands warmly and then went on their separate ways.

Abdul contemplated the events during the last 72 hours and was so pleased with the way things had turned out. His initial fears about Ryan and Arif had subsided with Ryan's recent clear besottedness with Shakela. Like he said to Sadad, long may it last!

CHAPTER 28

December 2006.

The last six months seemed to fly by in a daze for Ryan. His life finally seemed to be moving in a positive direction. He was spending more and more time in Canterbury with Shakela, which meant less and less time at home and this suited Ryan just fine.

Meeting Shakela had played a big part in Ryan ultimately deciding what to do with himself on completing school. He was absolutely besotted with her, and had been since that day in June many months ago. He would willingly spend every spare minute with her, which is why he decided to go to a college in Canterbury.

Ryan really had no clue about what he wanted to do with his life, so when it came time to choosing a course he turned to Arif for advice. Over the past few months Ryan seemed to be turning to Arif more and more often for help and advice. As far as Ryan was concerned Arif was the only person who really knew him, and so it seemed natural to go to him once again for his views on a college course.

Arif laughed his big hearty laugh and ruffled Ryan's hair when Ryan explained that he didn't really care what he studied so long as it was in Canterbury.

"Aaah, it seems like this lady friend of yours has really captured your heart! That my friend is good, we

309

all need a good woman behind us, just don't sacrifice your own dreams and goals for women!"

And so with the assistance of Arif, Ryan decided on religious studies. This was a three day a week course, and Arif had agreed to let Ryan work for him the other two days of the week. Arif was determined to make sure that Ryan recognised his full potential, so was encouraging him to see college as a stepping stone for university, which he was certain Ryan was capable to getting into. Arif told Ryan that they would both be helping each other out, as Arif was desperate to have someone assist him with his research - teaching full time and doing a Master's degree was taking its toll on him. So employing Ryan to help with the research would assist Ryan in reaching his full potential as well as help Arif with his studies. Ryan couldn't thank Arif enough, he was expecting to have to go out and find some dead end job at McDonalds or something - could his life get any better?

As for Shakela - oh she was definitely head strong and at times she frustrated Ryan beyond belief. Every now and again Ryan would question her devotion to Islam. She clearly did not dress with modesty which was something the Koran emphasised. Her attire was something that really wound Ryan up, but rather than make an issue out of it he was certain that once she eventually became his wife he would then be able to set down some ground rules. Until then he just did his best to turn a blind eye, and it really didn't seem to bother Sadad that much. And to be fair, Ryan knew that he couldn't really complain. Yes, her clothing was not quite what Ryan would want her to wear, however it was still a damn sight better than her friends. Ryan frequently wondered why they even bothered to wear anything at all!

Shakela often complained that Ryan was too intense, and that he needed to lighten up and have more fun. However, even since Ryan had come on the scene her dad seemed to have taken the pressure off her slightly. And this suited Shakela just fine! All she had to do was manage Ryan effectively, and her dad would stay off her back. As for Ryan, as long as she declared her undying love for him, and gave him a kiss and a cuddle now and again, he seemed happy. Ryan did concern her at times, his obsession with the Islamic faith, and his friend Arif were kinda creepy. And although she came from a Muslim family, she was not a practising Muslim and had no intention of going down that route! But for the time being, Ryan suited her needs just perfectly, so she was more than willing to put up with his "odd obsessions" now and again!

It was the last day of term before Christmas break, and Ryan was looking forward to spending the evening with Shakela before heading back to Chatham. They had agreed to meet at p.m. in town, and catch an early movie -'Night at the Museum' was showing, and then get a bite to eat. Ryan loved his time with Shakela on his own and he was especially looking forward to tonight. He wasn't going to be seeing her over Christmas so was planning on giving her a present tonight - a gold charm bracelet with one charm in the shape of the world. Shakela always went on about how she wanted to travel, so this was Ryan's way of saying he respected this wish, and looked forward to joining her on her travels. He planned to buy her a charm in every country they went to. Yes, he was certain she would love it, and also understand how much she meant to him - she was his world!

It was ten to five so he started to save his work and log off of the computer - the library was normally quiet on a Friday evening, but tonight it was completely deserted. Most students were out celebrating the end of term.

Ryan's phone started buzzing next to him. He glanced down and realised that Shakela was texting him. He smiled to himself as he realised that she was probably running late - she was always running late! Ryan unlocked the phone and read the message, "Hey Ryan, soooooooo sorrrry but gonna have to cancel 2nite - long story, will call 2morrow. luv ya - Shak xxxxx"

Ryan's heart sank, so much for a night on his own with Shakela. He glanced down at this watch and realised that if he hurried he could catch the 17:15 train to Chatham - but then what was he going to do? The last thing he wanted to do was go home, and Arif had an important meeting today with his university tutor this evening, so he too would be out.

Ryan plonked himself heavily back into the chair and powered up the computer - he may as well continue to work on his assignment. If he caught the 20:00 train he could get back to Chatham in time for evening prayers. Yes, that's what he would do. Arif was having a meeting after evening prayers tonight with the select few, and he would now be able to make that - something at least to look forward to.

Ryan worked for another two hours, and by that stage his stomach was grumbling and the computer screen was starting to blur. That quick bowl of cornflakes was not enough to last the rest of the day, so he finally shut down the computer, gathered his books and headed out the door. The library assistant breathed a sigh of relief as he left, she had been hoping to close early tonight - I mean, who would want to do any work on the last Friday evening before Christmas?!

Ryan pulled his zip up on his jacket and put on his gloves and scarf before heading out into the cold winter's night. He chuckled to himself as the sub-zero air hit his face with full force - last year this time he had been out in South Africa with the Khan family. Gee how time flew. Ryan's thoughts drifted towards the warm sunny days from last December hoping that it might help keep the icy wind away from his bones!

Ryan headed towards the train station with his head buried deep into his jacket. His mind was miles away, so he didn't notice the group of girls heading his way. They were dressed in not much, and were full of the joy of Christmas, clearly out on the town for the night. They were also in a world of their own and so didn't notice Ryan until they walked straight into him.

"Oh, sorry mate, didn't see you there." Ryan felt the soft weight of another collide with his shoulder and

313

heard the apology, but this was not what turned his blood cold. It was the familiar scent of perfume, and the long soft hair that brushed his face. He looked up straight into those big brown eyes that he had come to love so much over the last few months, only these eyes were not "his", they were caked in thick makeup. He grabbed hold of her wrists but had to step back, the alcoholic fumes wafting out of her breath were suffocating. Ryan stood back and took in the image in front of him.

Shakela was dressed like a whore. She had on a pair of shiny red "fuck me" boots, and a skimpy skin tight red dress, which was so low cut that her small perfectly shaped boobs were near enough on display for everyone to see.

"Shakela, are you okay, I thought you were busy tonight?" Ryan questioned her in confusion, his brain was battling to comprehend what was going on.

"Oh Ryan, why don't you just bug off, I'm out with me mates tonight." Shakela wriggled out of Ryan's grip and stumbled backwards. She flicked her hair out of her face and laughed out loud, "Hey girls, what do ya think? Should I head on home with my boring boyfriend, or should I hit the town with you and look for a bit of COCK!" Shakela and her friends collapsed on the floor with laughter.

Her girlfriends than grabbed hold of her and led her off giggling away. One of the girls looked back at Ryan's stunned face and laughed. "She's moved on mate, best you do too! Wow Shakela, you weren't joking when you said he is sooooo boring."

314

Ryan was frozen to the spot for a full ten minutes. He was stunned. What the hell had just happened?! It was his phone buzzing that brought him out of the trance. He slipped his glove off his hand which he sank into his jeans pocket and grabbed the phone. It was Shakela.

"Hello."

"Aaah Ryan, sorry mate, but I think we should call it quits, it's just kinda not working you know, so I guess this is kinda like a break-up call."

Ryan could hear someone shrieking in the background, "Give me the phone Shakela, I'll tell him like it really is. Hi, mate, Shakela needs someone to party with, and someone who can give her a good time, ya know what I'm saying."

Ryan then heard another voice shouting into the phone, "She wants a big dick, and a man that knows how to use it!"

More giggling and laughter before the phone eventually went dead.

Ryan put the phone back into his pocket and put his glove back on, then slowly made his way to the train station. Ryan couldn't' recall much of the train trip to Chatham, however by the time he arrived the shock of seeing Shakela looking like a whore, and worse acting like one, was rapidly turning to anger. He barged off the train with his teeth clenched and fists tightly scrunched up in his jacket. He didn't notice the young girl that had to grab onto the hand rail to avoid falling over after he stormed passed or, nor did he notice the security guard backing away from him. Ryan was a big lad and the anger and aggression was pouring out of his body, no one in their right mind was going to get in his way tonight.

As soon as Ryan got out of the train station and out into the open air his legs automatically started to run. It seemed like his body had reverted back to the young boy who time and time again had left his house at speed in an attempt to rid his body of the pain and anger that his father had caused. In the old days the anger and adrenaline would force its way from his soul into every muscle in his body, and finally escape through his pores in a mixture of sweat and exhaustion. In the past this feeling would be replaced by dreams of his future - the future where he rescued his mum from the hell that her life had become.

But Ryan was no longer a child, and that dream had been shattered long ago. And it didn't matter how hard and fast he pushed his body: the anger and pain were not planning on leaving his body anytime soon. His head was spinning, images of Shakela the whore and Shakela his angel kept flashing before his eyes, these were interwoven with memories of his mother as she had been in the old days, not the drunk she had turned into.

Ryan reached the bottom of Chatham Hill and stopped to catch his breath. The sweat was pouring down his face and his clothes were drenched. But rather than releasing the anger it seemed to have dug deeper into the core of Ryan's body.

Earlier on when Shakela had bumped into him her

hand had brushed past his chest. Ryan could still feel the heat from her fingers on his heart, only now that heat felt like a stabbing pain, which got worse with every step. Ryan clutched his heart as tremors seemed to rip through his body. He lent his head back and let out the most almighty roar. All his heartache and pain seemed to engulf the retched sound that emitted from his lips. The screech was similar to that of a wounded lion.

Ryan so badly wanted to cause pain to himself and anyone else who happened to cross his path. He knew that if he didn't get a grip of himself soon the wild animal that was always lurking just beneath the surface would return, and Ryan knew better than most that nor he or anyone else could control the monster once released. He was about a ten minute walk away from the mosque. Ryan was certain that if he could make it to the mosque without causing any pain then he would be alright - Arif would see to that.

Ryan started walking up Chatham Hill, but his legs were itching to go faster, perhaps, he thought, one last surge of power up the hill and maybe, just maybe the anger would leave his body, like it had in the past. So Ryan quickly picked up the pace. His legs powered up the hill, he pumped his arms and pushed himself harder than he had ever before. By the time he reached the mosque he was struggling to breathe. The icy cold air seemed to have replaced all the oxygen in his lungs, causing him to take deep raspy breaths. So much for the steep hills assistance in depleting the anger. No such luck. All it had done was cause his lungs to scream out in pain and his legs to turn to jelly. He tried to take a few deep breaths in an attempt to appease his lungs, and then slowly pushed open the door to the mosque. The evening prayers had already started, so he quietly bent over to remove his shoes. He untied his laces with great difficulty, the sweat was flowing freely down his face and stinging his eyes, and his breathing had still not returned to normal. Ryan realised that there was no way he could walk into the mosque looking the way he did and join his brothers in payer. So instead he tried to calm himself down whilst waiting for the Imam to finish chanting the last surah. Ryan tried to block the flashing images of Shakela out of his mind by doing his best to focus solely on regulating his breathing and think good pure thoughts, but it was not working. Arif found Ryan five minutes later pacing around like a caged lion. Arif tapped him gently on the shoulder, Ryan spun around with such force that the feral glint in his eyes and taunt facial muscles startled Arif who rapidly stepped back before the stranger in front of him lashed out at him.

The sight of Arif stepping away from Ryan in fear caused Ryan such sadness, that he finally sank to the floor and began to sob. What had become of him? The fury that had overwhelmed his body had caused him such anger that even Arif was afraid of him.

Arif slowly took a step towards Ryan and tentatively placed a hand lightly on his shoulder, "Come my son, come with me and we will talk."

Ryan wiped his big hand across his eyes in an attempt to stop the flowing sobs. He then looked up at

318

Arif and pleaded to him to take the pain away. Arif then realising that Ryan was not going to lash out at him, bent down to his level, grabbed his arm by the elbow and then ushered him up and out of the room.

"Come Ryan, we will walk and you will talk, then we will make things right."

Ryan relayed the evening's events to Arif, who listened without interrupting. Ryan finally finished his story by describing the pain in his chest and the anger that was threatening to buddle over, he described how all he wanted to do was cause pain and hurt to Shakela just like she had done to him.

They had been walking for well over half an hour when Arif finally came to a stop and tapped gently at someone's front door. Ryan had no clue where he was, and didn't quite understand what Arif was doing - surely he could see that Ryan was in no fit state to see anyone at the moment.

A short while later the door was opened by the biggest most muscular Asian man Ryan had ever seen. Arif whispered something to the big man, who then nodded his head and opened the door wider, allowing them both into the house. He led Arif and Ryan through the house and down the stairs into the basement, which had been converted into a gym. The big man then left the room and headed back upstairs.

"That my friend, is Anwar Mohammad, my old friend and now a rather successful boxer, he has agreed to allow you to use his gym for the next hour, so now Ryan, I am going to help you rid that body of your anger, but first I want you to hit that punch bag over there until your arms are aching so much you can't lift them up."

Ryan obediently walked over to the punch bag and started pummelling the bag with such force and speed that Arif doubted he would last ten minutes. However twenty minutes later Ryan's speed and strength seemed to have increased. He had finally been able to block the images from his mind and focus solely on transferring all his pain and frustration into the bag. After an hour Arif began to wonder if the boy would ever tire, it was now evident that Ryan's arms were aching, as his swings were getting slower and slower, but still he refused to stop. Yes, Arif thought, this boy has what it takes to go far, now more than ever before I am convinced that he is the chosen one, and it is up to me to direct him towards Allah's will.

Arif smiled gently to himself. The little incident with the girlfriend was just the type of drama Arif needed to focus Ryan. Yes, things were going to work out just fine.

Finally Arif dragged Ryan off the punch bag and told him to stop - it was now time to talk. Ryan argued, saying that the anger was still inside him, and he needed to keep pushing himself harder so that he could expel the wicked thoughts that were threatening to take over.

Arif spun Ryan around and forced him to look directly into his eyes, as he grabbed him roughly on each shoulder, "Ryan, that anger I believe is there to stay. What we will do now it make that anger work for you and not against you, so stop punching the bag, grab your jacket and come with me, we are now going to talk, we are going to explore your feelings together and Ryan, I can assure you that by the time we have finished talking you will be feeling a sense of power and understanding that you had not dreamed possible. Today is the day your fate is decided, now come with me boy."

Once again Ryan obediently did as he was told, he was already comforted by Arif's words - he knew that Arif would make it all better. Ryan and Arif finally headed back upstairs, Arif thanked Anwar and said they would let themselves out. Anwar raised his hand in acknowledgement, and continued to sip on his cup of tea.

The cold air hit Ryan like a ten ton truck. He pulled the zip up on his jacket and dug his hands deeper into his pockets. His body was aching all over, and although he was still mad about Shakela, he no longer had the energy to do anything about it. He suspected that that was Arif's reasoning for taking him to the big man's punch room.

Twenty minutes later Arif let a shivering Ryan into his house. He ordered Ryan to sit next to the heater, and then disappeared into the kitchen to make them both something warm to drink, but before he left he told Ryan to start thinking about exactly who he was so mad with. Ryan gave Arif a perplexed look. It was obvious - he was mad with Shakela and her behaviour. Arif just smiled back at Ryan, and told him to think deeper than just Shakela.

A few minutes later Arif reappeared with two hot cups of tomato soup, and a couple of big junks of bread.

"Now Ryan, tell me why you are so mad?"

Once again Ryan looked oddly at Arif. He lifted the cup and took a sip of the soup before responding in a condescending tone, "Arif, you know why I'm so angry - I told you all about it earlier, must I tell you the story again?"

"No Ryan, that won't be necessary, but tell me, I thought you said Shakela came from a good Muslim family - that is not the behaviour of a good Muslim girl, now is it? Perhaps you should be blaming her father, I mean, Ryan, she is just a woman after all, and we all know what weak creatures they are - look what your dad has done to your mum. She too was once a good Christian woman, so surely you can't blame Shakela or your mum for losing their way."

For the first time that evening Ryan's head began to clear, and he was able to appreciate what Arif was saying. "Yes, Arif, I understand now, but no, I can't blame Shakela's father, he, like me would be devastated if he knew how she was behaving. No, it's this new crowd that she's hanging around with, they are the ones who have made her this way."

"Aaah," exclaimed Arif, "so now we are getting to the heart of the matter. Tell me more about these so called friends of Shakela's?"

Ryan snarled back at Arif, "They're all sluts, disgusting white trash, who have brainwashed my beautiful Shakela."

"Whoa, Ryan, calm down, let's talk about this more. What else can you tell me about these aaa, 'white trash sluts'?"

"They have no respect for men, in fact they have no respect for anyone, just like my dad and the whores who he would rather be with than my poor mum. They all have no idea how much pain, hurt and humiliation they cause by their random remarks and complete disregard for true love, they should be saving their bodies for their husbands, and not displaying their parts with such disregard."

And so the conversation continued long into the night. Finally Arif yawned, stood up and stretched. He was exhausted, but most importantly Ryan could now see that his anger was not to be directed at Shakela, this was just the catalyst - it was the Western world who he was angry with. Those ignorant individuals like his dad who made Muslims around the world suffer.

"Arif, I'm sick to death of sitting around and watching men like my dad continue to humiliate and harm the good, peaceful Muslim people. It is the Muslim people who had only ever shown me love and respect - something I never got from my own father."

"Yes, yes, Ryan, you are right, the time has come for us to finally show the rest of the world that we are not going to sit back and allow the Western world to treat us this way. But Ryan, now we need some rest, tomorrow is the start of the rest of your life, tomorrow you revert back to the Islamic faith, tomorrow you will become a true Muslim brother, and then we will begin to make our plans for the future."

CHAPTER 29

Ryan reverted to the Islamic faith on Saturday 23 December 2006.

For Ryan it was a special day, one that he would remember for years to come. He woke early, and automatically switched on the radio next to his bed. The sound of Leona Lewis's silky, sully voice was pouring out of the speakers - "A moment like this." Ryan truly believed that his moment had come, he had finally found "his love, his chosen path." Just as Leona sang, "Some people wait a life time, some people wait for ever," Ryan thought, my wait is finally over. Just like Arif said last night, today is the day that the rest of my life begins. My path has been chosen, it is time for me to start walking that path.

Ryan made his way to the mosque where he met Arif and some of the other brothers. Ryan had been planning on reverting for a while now, in fact he had all intention of telling Shakela on that fateful Friday evening, but this way was better. Yes he could have completed the ritual alone, but that was not what Ryan wanted - he wanted to share the glorious occasion with his fellow brothers.

Ryan knew what was expected of him - to become Muslim he needed to have full conviction and a strong belief that Islam is the true religion of God. Of this he was certain. So all that was left was for him to pronounce the "Shahada" - the most important of the five pillars of Islam.

A short while later Ryan stood in front of the brothers and recited, "La ilah illa Allah, Muhammad rasoolu Allah."

He had spent most of the evening before working on the Arabic pronunciation - he wanted to get it just right, prove to the brothers that he not only believed and understood the meaning, but also that he could say it correctly. And that was all he needed to do to revert to the Islamic faith - of yes, and of course change his name! He had decided on Karim Malik.

Ryan, or should we say Karim, had considered the name change long and hard. He wanted a strong, powerful name that would be a constant reminder to him of the importance of making the Western world appreciate and accept the Islamic faith for what it was - the only true religion. And at the same time he wanted a name that would instil in him all the good that he had experienced from the Islamic people who he had come to know and love more than his own flesh and blood. It was for this reason that he chose Karim which meant generous and giving, and Malik which represented the king!

Karim spend the rest of the day at the mosque with the brothers and was a little disappointed when Arif finally stood and indicated that it was time for everyone to wind their way home. He felt a kinship to these men like nothing he had ever experienced before, and the thought of leaving them to return to the excuse for a home left him feeling rather empty.

However as they walked out Arif turned to Karim, ruffled his hair, gave him a big broad toothy smile and agreed to meet the following day to begin his teachings of the Arabic language. "Oh yes, Karim, I am certain now more than ever that you are the chosen one, and so you need to learn to read, write and speak Arabic - tomorrow I will begin to teach you, now, my brother, go and get some sleep. It has been a long day."

The two men hugged briefly and then went their separate ways.

Karim returned to a house full of darkness, however the lounge light in the Khan household was still on so he decided to go and see them instead. He was desperate to tell someone about his new found happiness.

Abdul opened the door and smiled warmly at 'Ryan'.

"Come in Ryan, Nassir was just complaining that we hadn't seen you in a while. She has a fresh batch of her homemade bread just waiting for you."

"Well, Abdul, that sounds too good to resist, but I also have something very special to tell you all."

"Aaah, you now have me curious, Nassir is in the kitchen, but Fareem, as you may well have guessed is out with his girlfriend - again."

Abdul helped Ryan out of his jacket and then whilst Ryan was pulling off his shoes, Abdul called out to Nassir to put the kettle on. They both then joined Nassir in the kitchen, Nassir wrapped her arms around Ryan.

"Ryan, my son, it is good to see you, you need to come around more often, you know you are always welcome."

Ryan soaked up the warm smell of Nassir, and enjoyed the feeling of her small arms doing their best to envelope him. He knew that she meant every word she said.

The three of them settled down around the worn kitchen table, Nassir and Abdul turned towards Ryan.

"Well come on son, what news have you got for us?" asked Nassir expectantly.

Ryan clasped his tea cup tightly, raised his head and looked at the two of them through his big blue eyes. A smile was beginning to form at the corners of his mouth. "My name is now Karim Malik, I am Muslim."

Nassir smiled proudly at Karim, "Oh my son, this is such wonderful news."

"Hmmm, that Shakela is obviously a good influence on you," laughed Abdul, who then stood up, walked over to Karim and gave him a big hug. "Well, Karim, tomorrow we will celebrate."

Nassir gently nudged Abdul, "My love, tomorrow is Christmas day, and Ryan, sorry, Karim may well be spending the day with his mum."

Both Karim and Abdul looked up in surprise, both having completely forgotten about Christmas.

"Aah, yes, so it is, well, then we will celebrate on the 27th December, when everything is open again. Yes, that's what we'll do. I will take us all out to dinner, just like we did in the old days, how does that sound?"

As it so happened, Karim and his mum had not made any plans for Christmas day, in fact Ryan/Karim was not expecting much to be happening at home on the one day that was supposed to be special for all Christians. In the past Betty had made an attempt to try and get the family around the table. She would spend hours in the kitchen cooking a traditional Christmas meal, but on too many occasions Dwayne had returned home from the pub drunk and abusive, and so the day never turned out as planned. Betty had finally given up trying. In fact just last week she had commented to Ryan that she guessed he would be spending the day with his girlfriend and her family anyway. Ryan knew that was just her way of letting him know that she really didn't expect him to have to endure another disappointing Christmas day at home.

So, he would not be spending the day at home with his mum, and he had absolutely no intention of visiting Shakela and her family, however he was more than happy for the Khan family and his mum to think that he had plans - as it was he would be spending the day with Arif. Karim had promised to do some more research for Arif, who was in return was going to help with him with his Arabic.

CHAPTER 30

Over the next few months Karim spent more and more time with Arif and the brothers. Both Betty and the Khan family thought that he was spending his time with Shakela. Karim had still not been able to tell them about their break-up, and to be honest, it was now working in his favour. He realised that Abdul had his reservations about Arif - he had expressed his views to Karim on more than one occasion, and as for Betty, well, she just wouldn't understand. Karim still had not told her that he had reverted to Muslim, once again, she just would not understand. And so, Karim just continued to let them all believe that he was in Canterbury with Shakela.

It didn't take long for Karim to realise that the research that he was doing for Arif had nothing to do with Arif's Master's degree, and was to do with something much much bigger than that. Karim was pleased when the brothers finally confided in him, as he was continually voicing his opinion on how it was time that they did something to make the Western world take them seriously. For a while he thought that Arif was all air and no action, however, now he realised that this was not the case, and in fact a plan was slowly developing, which he was now a part of it.

Karim soon realised that as far as "Western" experiences were concerned he was the expert amongst the brothers. Karim was the only revert, and obviously lived in a Western home all his life. Karim also had first-hand experience of exactly how "infidels" ticked - Dwayne, his father, was a prime example. And so when the brothers met to discuss ways to let the world know that they counted, it was generally Karim who ended up directing them down the right route.

For the first time in his life Karim felt important and needed. People were slowly starting to look towards him for advice and assistance. Karim soaked up the attention, and the more attention he received the more he seemed to grow in statue. He knew these men respected him and it felt great.

Little did he know that it was Arif that had actually orchestrated the whole thing - he had recognised his talents and abilities long before Karim had. And slowly Arif had moulded Ryan into Karim. Arif was now taking a step back and guiding Karim from behind. Karim may have believed that he knew just what made the infidels tick, however Arif was the one making Karim tick. Arif knew that the brothers needed a young, strong man, who could bring fresh insight into their world to lead them. It was Arif's role to identify this person, and slowly change him into the leader they needed. Once completed Arif would then move on, and start the whole process again in another part of the country.

Karim became more and more caught up in the world of Islam and taking the brothers forward, and bit by bit all other parts of his life began to disappear. Arif had stressed that he had to do his best to continue as normal for as long as possible otherwise people would start asking questions, and both Arif and Karim knew that this was the last thing they needed.

And so Karim continued to attend Rugby practice, but his heart was no longer in it. The passion with which he had played with the last session was no longer evident. He was frequently late for practice or left early. The coach naturally had spotted the lack of enthusiasm, and was surprised and disappointed. He really believed that Ryan was one of those special, talented boys that would go far, perhaps even play for England one day.

The coach had seen it many times over the years - some lucky people were born with talent, but it was the truly exceptional people that took that talent and made it work for them. Unfortunately as young men became aware of women their interest often turned away from the rugby pitch and towards other "delights." It seemed like Ryan was no different.

Although he had noticed that not only had Ryan's interest in rugby faded, but his whole attitude in general had changed, in fact it was just last week that he overheard some of Ryan's team mates commenting on his strange views about Sharia law.

Anyway, the coach was not going to lose any sleep over Ryan and his odd behaviour, he would just start focusing on a new up and coming talent, and hope that the next one would actually appreciate the talent that God had given him and work hard to exploit it to its full extent!

Incidentally Karim had only told the Khan family and his brothers about his name change - once again Arif had advised him that the less people who knew the better. In fact Arif was not too impressed with Karim re telling the Khan family!

The other area of Karim's life that began to drift towards insignificance was college. Karim popped in now and again and made a point of showing his face at the odd lecture or two, but as far as the assignments were concerned he was way behind. His class tutor had tried time and time again to make an appointment with Karim to discuss the sudden change in his work ethics, however Karim always managed to cancel at the last minute.

What did confuse the tutor was that Ryan seemed to spend all his spare time in the library - they had bumped into each other on more than one occasion, and the library assistant had also commented to him about the strange boy that seemed to spend most of his day working on the internet with his face hidden away in the most absurd books. She realised that he was studying religious studies, but his interest appeared to be centred on the persecution of others, death, torture and anything else inhumane. The library assistant had said this much to Ryan's tutor, who just brushed the statement away and replied that at least one of his students was taking his course work seriously!

As for the use of the internet, Arif had warned Karim about not using his own computer to research the finite details of their plan.

"Best to use computers that the public have access to as there is less opportunity to trace your internet history," Arif explained.

However it wasn't just Karim's behaviour that

people were starting to notice. Arif's neighbour, an elderly lady who prided herself on belonging to the neighbourhood watch, and was always keen to pass on a snippet or two of information to the local police, commented to the local bobby one afternoon how she was certain that something odd was taking place in the small basement flat next to her. On this particular occasion she invited the local police man to come and check it out. He was a mature man who was looking forward to his retirement in two months and his days of chasing criminals down dark alleys were over. He would be more than content with spending his last two months plodding the beat and stopping every hour or so at the numerous tea stops he had acquired over the years.

Mrs Miggans always had excellent homemade cakes up for offer, so PC Brent was more than happy to listen to her prattle away. This is exactly what she was doing on this particular afternoon - she kept going on and on about her neighbour who she was convinced had links to Al Qaeda. She explained she frequently saw men coming and going at strange times of the day and they were, well you know, 'dark', with big bushy beards, and some would wear those robe things.

"Really, is that so, well, thanks so much for that vital bit of intelligence, yes, yes, thanks," said old PC Brent whilst stuffing his face with another piece of chocolate cake, and slurping away on the mug of tea. PC Brent finally lifted his large frame out of the sunken in sofa, wiped his hands on the back of his trousers, and assured Mrs Miggans that he would go directly to the police station and report this interesting bit of intelligence to the superintendent.

As he was leaving dear old Mrs Miggans he actually came face to face with the so called Al-Qaida operative.

"Afternoon officer, and how are you today?"

"Er, fine, thank you, you must be Mrs Miggans' neighbour."

"Yes, yes, that I am, however I have to say I don't really get to see her much. I am a school teacher you see, and most of my time is spent at school, or assessing papers, in fact I am heading back to the school now, I have a meeting with the head as I am looking to take the year 8s on a tour of Wembley stadium. Sometimes I think it is not worth the effort - the trip needs to be risk assessed, and that entails tons and tons of paperwork!" Arif rolled his eyes, then put out his hand to shake PC Brent's. "Sorry, you probably have much more important things to do than to listen to me complain about paperwork, I'll let you get on your way." With that Arif made his way down the road to his car which he had parked around the corner.

Well, thought PC Brent, once again Mrs Miggans has got carried away. Last week she was complaining about the drug dealing on the corner, this week Al-Qaida; he just couldn't wait to hear what she would come up with next week.

As far as PC Brent was concerned the neighbour seemed more British than most, had no trace of an accent, wore Western clothing, and he even shook hands with PC Brent. Way back in the recess of his mind he could remember vaguely receiving "diversity" training. He remembered that they were taught not to offer to shake hands with a Muslim as this was offensive, no, no, he thought, was that Hindu people? No, or was it only female Muslims that would not shake your hand? PC Brent really couldn't remember, but either way, as far as he was concerned if the person he had just spoken to was an Al-Qaida operative, then he was a girl.

He had been around long enough and had what they called that copper's nose. He could smell out a dodgy character for miles and that polite young man was not a dodgy character, in fact he came across as more British than some of the new police probationers. Just last week PC Brent had been complaining to Mrs Brent about the new 'probis' that he had taken out on patrol with him. Well one of them was not only black, but was wearing a turban as well, and his accent was so strong that PC Brent eventually had to ask one of the others to translate! How times had changed since he had joined, it was all about equal opportunities and positive discrimination. PC Brent didn't class himself as racist or anything, it was just that, well, it just didn't seem right. Roll on the next 58 days, this new world of policing was no longer for PC Brent. Hell, these days is wasn't even politically correct to get the probi to make the tea!

And so without giving the little bit of intelligence from Mrs Miggans another thought he headed on back to the station, thinking of the fine meal his wife would be preparing for him for when he finally got home, only two more early shifts and then two days off - and only another 58 days to go - not that he was counting of course.

And then there was Fareem. He was under no illusions about what his old friend was up to. Everyone just presumed that all he could think about these days was his girlfriend, which to be fair, was true most of the time. However Ryan/Karim was like a brother to him, in some ways he thought they were even closer than brothers. The experiences they had shared over the years had created a bond between the two of them that not even a girl could break. And so, when Ryan reverted to Islam and became Karim, and started spending more and more time away from home Fareem got in touch with Shakela. On discovering that they had broken up before Christmas and Shakela had not seen him since Christmas, alarm bells started ringing for Fareem. It didn't take him long to find out that Karim had got himself heavily involved with a new group of young Muslim men, whose ideals were not quite favourable. Fareem could not believe that Ryan could be so stupid as to get involved with the likes of Arif and his band of merry men. He did try a couple of times to talk to Ryan as in the past they had been able to talk about anything. But these days Fareem found Ryan to be rather distant and illusive. He made it quite clear to Fareem that he appreciated his concern, but really, there was nothing to be concerned about. In fact on the last occasion that Fareem had tried to speak to Ryan, Ryan had made him feel rather foolish, and laughed at the absurdity of

Fareem's concerns.

After that final conversation Fareem gave a big sigh of relief. Ryan, or Karim may well be acting a little strangely at the present time, but Fareem knew deep down that Ryan was a good person, and the people he might be hanging around with might well have undesirable intentions, but Ryan would naturally steer clear of that.

Ryan had also always been there for Fareem - Fareem had lost count of how many times Ryan had stuck up for him over the years, especially after 9/11 when it seemed like the whole of the school was against Fareem. Yes, Fareem remembered those dark days well, and if it hadn't been for Ryan, he didn't quite know how he would have made it to school and back each day. And it was for this reason that Fareem kept his concerns to himself - he felt honour bound to support and 'protect' Ryan for a change.

PART 4

Shattered: Sallie Baisley

CHAPTER 31

May 2007.

The Khan family returned to their old house on the White Road Estate a month after that early morning phone call that had turned their lives upside down. Nothing seemed to have come out of the police activity on that fateful day. Karim Malik had still not been found, and once again the residents of the White Road Estate were blaming the police for acting on a whim rather than solid evidence. Saying that, they still didn't quite like the idea of a terrorist living amongst them, but they knew better than most that the police had a way of, shall we say, 'exaggerating the truth' when it suited them.

It was Abdul's old friend Dirk who had tested the waters for the Khan family, and eventually gave them the heads up that it would be safe to return.

Dirk had gone into the good old Bell Inn a couple of nights in a row. To start with he just sat quietly listening to the locals, and then once he felt like he was staring to be accepted he asked the odd question now and then. It was quite clear that the locals had moved on to more interesting topics - Dwayne Arnold and his Muslim son were old news. The talk had turned from terrorism to drugs to the latest bit of stolen goods that were doing the rounds - this week it seemed like you could pick up a flat screen TV for next to nothing as long as you were in the know! Dirk quickly realised that the Khan family returning was not going to cause any issues.

Betty was pleased to see them return. In a strange way the events that had caused both her and the Khan family's lives such turmoil and heartache had actually done her a favour. After being kicked out of her house for a good week or two whilst the police tore it apart she took refuge in the church, and for the first time in a long time she began to take stock of her life and what it had become. Those first few days were dark and depressing, she did not like or approve of what she had become, but with the help of a counsellor, Betty was able to say goodbye to alcohol. She realised she had taken refuge in a bottle rather than facing up to her problems. But the biggest step she took in those dark days was to actually file for a divorce. The realisation that it had taken the loss of her son - who she doubted she would ever see again as the police were still keeping tabs on the address - to get her to finally sort herself out saddened her terribly. But she truly believed that God had a path for everyone, and she, along with Ryan (wherever he might be) was simply walking this path.

Dwayne took the divorce better than she expected - in a strange sort of way that saddened her too. She had always just presumed that he would never let her leave him. That was not quite the case - his latest bit on the side was pregnant, and he admitted to Betty that he was deeply in love with her, and keen to make an honest women of her! Betty smiled bitterly to herself - she recognised that look in Dwayne's eyes, and could only pray for the young pregnant women that Dwayne had perhaps changed his ways, and was now also walking down a path that God had planned for him.

But, Betty didn't dwell on Dwayne and his lack of love towards her for too long, as she had her own admirer - Dirk, Abdul's old friend. They had bumped into each other one evening when Betty was returning from the corner shop with a pint of milk, the weekly Kent Messenger newspaper and bar of chocolate (her after dinner treat), Dirk was just leaving the Old Bell. He ended up coming back to her house for a cup of tea, but that turned into a couple of hours, which turned into dinner - Dirk offered to get a takeaway, but Betty wouldn't have it. If the truth was known she was thrilled to have someone to cook for.

Dirk was just so different to Dwayne. They seemed to be able to chat about everything and anything, and most importantly he made her laugh, and feel good about herself. At one point the subject even turned to football and Betty surprised herself by having the confidence to converse about the up and coming big FA Cup final - Chelsea vs. Manchester United - without her stomach turning into a tight knot. Chelsea was Dwayne's team, and a loss would mean a beating for Betty. A loss at the FA cup final, well, Betty didn't even want to think about those horrific times.

Her stomach did actually do a couple of turns that night, but that seemed to have more to do with that wonderful feeling of cheeky butterflies, that seemed to dance and summersault every time Dirk smiled at her - could she actually be in love? Fortunately football was not one of Dirk's favourite topics either, and he had noticed how Betty had ever so slightly cringed at the mention of Chelsea, so he rapidly changed the topic to the very next thing that came into his head and that happened to be the newspaper article that was lying in front of him.

"Hey Betty, look at that, Ryan's old school have finally got a teacher who recognises that sometimes you just have to get kids out of the classroom and provide them with real live experiences - a tour of Wembley stadium. Not only is it known as the 'cathedral of football' but it is also the place when dreams will be made. Wow, that place has only just opened. That teacher must have called in a favour or two to arrange something like that - good on him."

Dirk watched Betty visibly relax as the topic veered off football. He made a mental note to himself to tread carefully, this lady was damaged goods.

As for Betty's friendship with Nassir, well, the two of them got things back on track. In a strange way it was just like the old days, except without the stress of children and abusive men - well it was really one man for Betty had never known Abdul to even raise his voice let alone his hands.

The two ladies resumed their bus trips to Chatham town centre, and then the walk to Rochester with a cup of tea and a cake as a treat in Rochester High Street. Those outings had been unceremoniously brought to a halt after the horrific racist incident of the hamburger being thrown at Nassir. But those days all seemed to be a thing of the past, people in general seemed more tolerable and accepting than before.

CHAPTER 32

May 20 2007. 20:00. BBC World News.

"Britain is still trying to come to terms with the events of yesterday that have left the nation in shock. For those of you that have not heard, Wembley stadium is no more. More than 89,000 people packed the stands yesterday for the FA Cup final - Chelsea vs. Manchester United. But two minutes before the final whistle the country was brought to a standstill by the live images of a tremendous explosion which ripped its way through the belly of the stands causing untold numbers of death and casualties."

A fundamentalist Islamic group which is believed to have Al-Qaida links have claimed responsibility for the attack. Scotland Yard are expected to release a statement at noon today.

The casualty contact number is 08007903432

Once again the world has been given a stark reminder that terrorism has no boundaries.

This is Greg Burrows, BBC world news."

Thousands of miles away a smile gently caressed Karim's face as he listened to the BBC world news on the old radio that he had managed to acquire. He slowly rose and switched off the radio. He was engulfed with a sense of victory, and a feeling of anticipation, for this was only the beginning.

THE END